Praise for Mandy M. Roth's **Loup Garou**

5 Angels! Fallen Angels Recommended Read! *"Mandy M Roth is an imaginative and brilliant author that readers will line up to read each and every story by her. This story has definitely earned its place in my permanent bookcase. For Mandy M Roth and Loup Garou, I am giving the best rating that I can: this story and author have truly earned 5 Angels and a Recommended Read!"* ~ Jessica, Fallen Angels Reviews

"Loup Garou had me captivated from the first page. It is action packed and full of emotion. The story is clever, witty, hip and sexy...My fingers are crossed in the hopes that Ms. Roth will be sharing more of this story. I would love to read about the surrounding characters as well. It's a great book, I was thoroughly entertained!" ~ Nannette, Joyfully Reviewed

By Mandy M. Roth

A SAMHAIN PUBLISHING, LTD .publication

Loup Garou
Copyright © 2006 by Mandy M. Roth
Cover by Scott Carpenter
Print ISBN: 1-59998-043-6
Digital ISBN: 1-59998-003-7
www.samhainpublishing.com

Samhain Publishing, Ltd.
PO Box 2206
Stow OH 44224

First Samhain Publishing, Ltd. electronic publication: January 2006
First Samhain Publishing, Ltd. print publication: April 2006

Loup Garou

By Mandy M. Roth

Dedication

To Angie for seeing the potential in Exavier and Lindsay. Okay, and in me too. With your nudge they stopped hiding in my hard drive and came to life.

To Crissy for spreading your wings and allowing us to soar with you.

To the women who meet me for coffee each morning and support me through my "that zapping."

And to every man who has turned me on by playing his guitar and singing in front of millions. I'd list them all but then there would be no room for the actual story.

ᴘʀoʟoɢᴜᴇ

The smell of my fear was intoxicating to them. I couldn't seem to stop my pulse from racing or the light sheen of sweat wanting to develop on my palms. Both had started the moment I'd sensed the threat.

I'd foolishly been preoccupied with thoughts of attending a birthday celebration for a three-year-old boy and had allowed the group of were-panthers to get the jump on me. I knew better than to believe I could have a night without violence. A night without being stalked by creatures of the dark who wanted nothing more than to see me dead. After I helped them find their dark prince.

As if I even know who the dark prince is.

Three years was a long time to live in fear. I'd pulled back from the public eye, hoping to avoid incidents such as this but it hadn't helped. No. They were attacking at an alarming rate. Where once it had been random, yet violent, it was now bordering on nightly.

Low growls sounded from the shadows, the places the security lights didn't reach, reminding me I wasn't alone. I'd counted four of them but I'd been fooled before. Two lay in bloody heaps less than ten feet from me and two more stalked me. Their supernatural senses no doubt heightened to the point they could hear even the slightest intake of breath on my part. I lacked the ability to shape shift. Part of me was glad, less shaving and all, but another part was envious. I was tired of them having the advantage. While I wasn't weak, I wasn't exactly a die-hard killing machine. I knew enough to get by but "getting by" seemed to be harder as of late.

I stared down at the blood-covered, colorfully wrapped birthday present. The tiny train pattern was perfect for a little boy turning three, or had been prior to me bleeding all over it. I'd found Rickie a group of engines for the wooden set he'd be opening at his party—a party I'd sworn I'd be at but would not make. Even if I somehow managed to survive, I couldn't show up in my condition. I wasn't sure of the extent of my injuries, being immortal tended to skew my judgment when it came to what one would consider mortal wounds, but I knew I was in bad shape.

Already, I'd lost feeling in one arm but I was thankful. Before I'd managed to kill two of them, they'd slammed me off the hood of seven different vehicles. The white-hot pain in my shoulder had now eased to a dull ache. I did my best to stay upright but went to one knee all the same. I could feel them moving in on me. They were close but still put off by my display of power. I hadn't intended to use as much magik as I did but was grateful I had.

My gaze flickered to the dead men. I should have felt remorse for taking lives. If I lived through the night I just might have guilt. Though, with the rate they'd been attacking and what they'd stolen from me in the past, I doubted I'd have too many issues with it all. My vision blurred at the same moment I felt a familiar presence closing in on me. It radiated safety. It was also the only solace I had as I gave in and collapsed completely to the hard surface of the parking lot. I blinked and forced my gaze upwards. I didn't want the last thing I saw in this world to be a dead were-panther. The moon would work nicely as a substitute.

Chapter One

"Tell me again who I'm meeting today," I said, holding onto one of my closest friend's shoulders, while I stretched my leg high in the air. The need to work the kinks out of my sore muscles before daring to go on with a day filled with exercise seemed wise when I started. Now, as I stood there with visions of caffeine dancing through my head, I began to second guess myself. Coffee was up next to sex on my list of things I'd rather be doing. So far, my caffeine intake was lower than it should be. I thought about wearing a button warning others to exercise extreme caution when dealing with me but with the skimpy outfits I wore to workout in, there really wasn't a lot of places I could pin it to.

"Exavier Kedmen, he's the front man for the rock band Loup Garou," Myra said, never missing a beat. She was a machine when it came to her quest to keep me on track and I loved her for it. At least one of us knew what the hell I was supposed to be doing. I was happy when I remembered what day of the week it was. I'd say it was an exaggeration but I'd already thought it was the wrong day twice and had only been awake a little over an hour.

"I love the name Exavier. I once knew a boy with that name." Slight understatement if I'd ever heard myself voice one. I'd more than known that Exavier. He'd been my best friend, first love and greatest let down. Too many years had passed to bother thinking hard about it now. I missed him and most likely always would. Since I hadn't seen him since I was seven and he was ten, it was safe to say he'd had an impact on me. Sighing, I dipped my head down and pressed my forehead to Myra's shoulder. Thankfully she was tall too. She made a wonderful mobile "post" for me to hang on to. I'm sure she'd rather I not do it but since she hadn't verbalized a concern, I went with it.

I stared at the dark grey Berber carpeting in Myra's office as I continued to stretch. I'd rather be staring at a latte. The carpet would do nothing to chase away my bitchiness or help me stay awake. Though it did have a rather odd and nearly impossible pattern in it.

I shook my head. If I was to the point I was willing to stare at carpet, the day was going to be a long one. At least I was in Myra's office and not at the station in my friend Jay's office. He was a detective and seemed to be able to locate everything but his desk with the mess he had in his office. I spent more time wondering if I saw a stack of papers move with the help of rodents and trying to figure out what the mystery odor was than I did visiting Jay. Probably why I stopped visiting him there.

Myra's neat freak tendencies never left me concerned about things crawling up my leg. Her office was done in shades of grey with black and white accents. To me, it was depressing. To Myra, it was perfect. Whatever made her happy worked for me. She'd given up a life in corporate America to help me with the center and had never once complained.

"Why exactly is a front man of a rock band meeting with me? I'm not in the business of choreographing anymore. I'm sure the word's out by now. If not, I'm happy to spread it."

Myra held her day planner up behind my head and ignored me. The planner was her version of a bible. I learned very quickly that touching it was begging for the death penalty. I was also informed, in the event of a fire I was to save the day planner first, small puppies and endangered species second.

That involved touching the book so I was a bit confused on what Myra wanted. "You have a ten o'clock appointment with the Ferris family. They want us to protect their great-grandfather who is convinced the reaper, I kid you not, is coming for him."

"How old is he?"

"One hundred and two," she said, somehow managing to keep a straight face.

Grinning, I switched legs. "Would it be wrong for me to confirm his suspicions?"

"Lindsay, pretend to have a heart. It makes us all feel better about being near you."

"Fine." I rolled my eyes and let out a soft laugh. The man was one hundred and two. Of course the reaper was on his heels. Unless he was immortal. Somehow, I doubted it. "I still don't know why word keeps spreading about us. It's not like we've got a mystery machine parked out front with our own talking dog. Why come to us for the paranormal?"

She snorted but didn't give me an answer.

"Anything else I need to know about? There aren't any more surprises this week are there? I've had no coffee yet today and have already taken an abnormal interest in your carpeting. Please tell me my week's looking up."

She murmured something I couldn't quite catch. Never a good sign. "Umm, try that again, this time in English."

Myra rolled eyes and gave me a wry grin. "You are supposed to have dinner with your parents tomorrow night."

"Sun sets around eight lately so I have a while to come up with a good excuse as to why I'm not going to be able to make it."

"Lindsay!"

Grinning, I kissed her cheek quickly. "You know you love me."

Myra snickered as she thumped her hip to mine. "God help me, I do."

"The idea of my mother trying to set me up with someone else makes my stomach tight. You go in my place. She always picks men who are right up your alley." It was true. Myra's idea of the perfect man was my idea of a boring one. She seemed drawn to the executives. My idea of the perfect guy generally swayed more towards bad boys with big toys. Basically, everything she hated in a man. It made for a great friendship. It wasn't like we ever had to worry the other would try to steal our boyfriend.

"Thanks, but I'll pass."

"Suit yourself." I dropped my leg down and walked towards Myra's black desk. The oversized unit had a raised glass top with silver feet. A matching wall unit sat against the wall behind her and went to the ceiling. Every tiny paperclip had a home in Myra's office. I moved things around once and she spent a week complaining. The temptation to do it again was great. I held back. It was hard.

"Want to fill me in on this Loup Garou guy?"

She arched a well-defined brow and gave me a questioning look. "I thought you weren't entertaining going back into the business again."

"I'm not." I didn't want to admit the second she told me the band's name I had actually considered taking the job. "I'm curious as to why they'd name themselves after the French word for were-wolves. That's all. Are they supernaturals?"

So many supernaturals gravitated towards careers in the entertainment industry. What better way to hide from humans than right under their noses. Plus, I'm fairly sure god complexes came into play but since I too had worked in the field, I thought it best not to dwell on the topic.

"You could always just ask the front man personally." Myra glanced out of her office window. I did my best to follow her gaze but the light grey slotted curtains blocked my view. It wasn't an exterior window. More for decoration than anything, it gave her a decent view of the front lobby and the reception desk.

"Right. I'm supposed to believe the guy showed up an hour early? It's eight in the morning. Next thing you'll be telling me is Gina is going to be on time for once today."

Myra laughed.

Gina, another close friend of mine, who also happened to be a demon slayer, seemed to run on her own time. I stopped questioning it and started telling her that her classes were earlier than they really were. It seemed to do the trick.

I winked. "Band members do not rise before lunch. It's like an unspoken rule. I tried to get my hands on the manual once but they keep it hidden and protect it with their lives. It's almost as sacred to them as their guitars and groupie black books."

The smug look Myra gave me was an all too familiar one. "Enjoy your class, Lindsay."

"Will do. Page me *if* this guy happens to show. Should the Ferris family call, give them my condolences. The reaper just showed up for dear old great-granddad." I pushed the office door open, staring at Myra the entire time I walked backwards into the lobby.

"Please tell me you're kidding, Lindsay. I hate it when you do the mumbo-jumbo get a vibe and spit it out thing. It's creepy." Myra's face paled. She ran a hand through her long, wavy hair and shook her head as she hurried out behind me. "If I find out he's gone I'm going to pay the voodoo guy on the corner of Fifth and Pearl Street to put a hex on you."

"Take some of my hair. He'll need it." I winked at her. "Oh, and be sure to tell him that I'll pretend not to notice his power while he's doing it. It'll keep his ego up. He always hates it when I sense him. See if he can do anything about how sensitive my eyes are to sunlight. I'm fine with everything about myself except the fact I need sunglasses for more than a few short minutes in direct light. Try not to freak him out by telling him my dad is half-vampire though. Ooo, and give him triple if he can find a man I don't creep out. Tell him I'll double that too if the guy is hot and well equipped."

Oh, yeah. Supernatural and hung like a horse. Who wouldn't want it?

"No amount of money is going to solve the problem of you keeping a man. Stop being weird and you'll increase your chances by about four percent, maybe."

"Bite me." I grinned. Egging on a female cat shifter wasn't the smartest thing I'd ever done but it sure was fun.

Myra wagged her brows and gave me a daring smile. "Don't tempt me."

"Here kitty, kitty, kitty," I said, puckering my lips and making cat noises at her.

"Ms. Willows. Ms. Willows!"

Sighing, I forced a smile onto my face as a tall blond guy with a body to die for but little more going for him rushed towards me. He was the single reason I never implemented a dress code for my employees. His love for running around without a shirt on was the highlight of my day. Since we worked at a recreation center, we could get away with next to nothing on. As I stared at his bare chest and let my gaze run down to his jogging pants, I suddenly wished I'd made him sign a paper promising to walk around in the buff. "Blair, what can I do for you?"

"It's Brook," he said, grinning from ear to ear, looking as though he was about to pose for a toothpaste commercial.

"Pardon?" I asked, concentrating on the way his pelvic muscles formed a V.

"My name is Brook."

And I care about this why?

Forcing my gaze to return to his face, I patted his arm. "Yeah, right. Sorry. I'll pay more attention to it next time. It takes me a bit to get everyone's name down."

"Ms. Willows, I've been here for two years now. You're the one who hired me. Remember?"

Nope.

Myra snorted. I wanted to strangle her. It would be my luck to have her bear witness to yet another humiliating moment in my life. Not that I had a shortage or anything.

Deciding to rectify the situation, I pulled my sweatshirt off slowly, knowing exactly how I looked in the camouflage bikini-like, exercise top I had on. I also knew it would provide a nice little distraction. Brook was human, and they were always easier for me to seduce, not that I wanted to bed him. I just wanted him to lose track of the fact I never bothered to get to know him or his name.

As I stared at his rippling abs, I reconsidered the idea of sleeping with him. He could prove to be interesting for about fifteen minutes or so. Humans never lasted long in the stamina department with me. My magik tended to drain them long before I was sated.

Brook's gaze dropped rapidly. As he stared at my breasts like they were breakfast, I tapped my foot. "So, Blair...umm...Brook. What was it you needed?"

"You," he answered softly, his gaze never moving from my breasts.

Myra and I both laughed. I followed it with a cough. He didn't seem to notice so I didn't worry too much about laughing at him. "Come again?"

"Umm...err...youth basketball. The attendance has plummeted."

I nodded. "Makes sense. The weather is breaking so the kids are hanging around outside more."

Myra leaned against the reception area's counter. "We need a creative way to get them in here. It's hard to compete with the guys with fancy jewelry and flashy clothes. We were doing great. Not one of our kids had been in trouble over the winter."

Covering my eyes, I thought about the situation. "Okay, we'll do this. Blair," Myra nudged me, "umm, Brook, you spread the word we're planning a big bash before school starts back in session. Let them know that every day they show up and participate in the program fully, they're entered into the contest."

"What contest is that?"

"The one where the winner gets to select what concert the rest of the group goes to." I glanced at Myra. "You need to go through and find out who is hot for their age group. Get me a list of four bands—artists in alternative, hip-hop and pop genres. Make sure they're age appropriate. Have permission slips drawn up, listing the potential groups and the type of music they play. Keep it simple so the parents don't have to use the force to decipher what the hell we're talking about. The bands and their music confuse *me* and I know a lot of them. Every kid who signs up for the program needs a guardian's signature. I'll talk to Lynette down at children services for the handful who aren't going to be able to track their parents down."

Brook looked a little lost. I rolled my eyes and did my best to remember to keep it simple for him. "Brook, get their sizes for jerseys. Get the list to Myra and she'll see to it they're ordered. When the night comes for the concert, I'll have them picked up in limos, taken for pizza and then the show. That's the best I can come up with. Do you think it will work?"

"That's going to cost a fortune," Brook said.

"You can't put a price on their safety, Brook. If I can keep them here and off the streets then it's worth every penny. I'll set up similar contests for the other things we offer. We'll call it a Summer Bash and hopefully draw more kids into the program."

"Okay, sounds good." He turned and jogged toward the back of the facility. Myra and I tipped our heads, sighing as we watched his tight ass move. It was a sight worthy of late-night-pleasure-myself moments.

I waited for Brook to be out of earshot and laughed. "He kills me."

"Why can't you ever remember his name? I'm going to make him start wearing a name tag again."

It was more of a name sticker because pinning something to his perfect chest hadn't seemed right. I didn't correct her. "Because when he told me it, I was staring at his abs. I really think my biggest weakness with the opposite sex is oblique muscles. I want to lick the indent all the way down and then lick whatever else," I wagged my brows, "I find there. If he was fine with me calling him six-pack, I'd get it right every time. Well, it wouldn't hurt if I actually cared what his name was. I bet I still screw it up two years from now. Too bad he's human. I bet he'd be fun to take for a test drive."

Myra hit my arm and snorted. "Honey, you'd eat the poor man alive."

She was right. I would. Men like Brook never held up well under my pressure. "Gina told me she walked in on him changing and was very impressed with what he had to bring to the table."

"I bet you'd remember the name he calls his dick," Myra said, nudging me softly. I rolled my eyes and she laughed. "Come on, you know they all name it. When I was with Chad I had to listen to him talk about *The Shark* all the time."

I arched a brow. "The Shark?"

"Yeah." She nodded. "Don't you remember when I found him at the club with the blonde with fake boobs?"

My mouth dropped. "Ohmygod, that's why you kept calling him guppy instead of his name the rest of the night."

She nodded, looking proud of herself. "Yep. Okay, I shared a naming of the penis story. What do you have?" Myra closed her day planner and stared at me. It was a momentous occasion if I'd ever seen one. "You, of all people, should have at least a thousand stories, Lindsay."

"A thousand? Hey, that's a bit harsh." I smiled wide and rocked my hips to a beat I heard in my head. "And before you bother pushing the issue more, I'm sure I've run across men who name everything—penis, car, blow up dolls—but I really don't bother remembering them. It's not like I want anything more than a night of fun from them. Too much information leads to second dates. They spiral into thirds. Shaking them after that becomes all but impossible."

She cast a worried look at me. "You think like a man—find them, fuck them, forget about them."

"Thanks."

"That's not a good thing." Myra sighed. "How are you going to find that perfect someone if you don't bother with anything intimate—I'm not talking sex. You need to open up to a guy. Any guy. Hell, call Brook back here and tell him something personal about yourself. Call Jay. He knows more about you than most men. Tell him some big thing. Anything, Lindsay."

Putting my arms up, I shrugged. "I'm sorry but I'm not understanding what you're talking about. You can't be telling me there is anything above and beyond sex with a man." I winked, knowing Myra would yell. I knew all too well there was more to it. I just wasn't willing to share myself with anyone. There was a time when I would have but it had passed. Myra was also painfully aware I had been more than intimate with a man in my life. It had ended badly for all involved. I didn't care to let anyone else in.

"You can't keep men at arm's length forever, Lindsay. You will have to let one back in at some point." She gave me a stern look and I could have sworn she was reading my mind. "That heart of yours will shrivel up and turn black at the rate you're going."

"So, Dr. Myra, how much is this session going to cost me?"

"Bitch," she whispered.

Leaning over, I kissed her cheek. "I lubs you too, honey."

She growled. The cat shifter in her made it sound very real.

"What? I'm only young for like, eternity, so let me have a little fun. I'll settle down...umm... I can't even get that out without getting sick to my stomach." Shaking my head, I snickered. "I need to go before my buddy, Stalker Stan, shows up."

"Put your sweatshirt on, a T-shirt, anything or you'll never shake him. The man will follow you around the center like a lost puppy. A very scary puppy." Myra turned me to face her. "Seriously though, Lindsay, he's crossed the line. Showing up on your front doorstep is too much. I read the note he left on your car the other day and I find it hard to believe you were destined to be with him."

I shuddered at the thought of being Stalker Stan's soul mate as I put my sweatshirt back on. The man, while not bad looking, had an air about him that had always left me on edge. "Eww, or that *anyone* would be. Yuck."

Myra nodded, agreeing with me. "Besides, he lets off a vibe. It's scary as hell. And if I find him scary, we've got issues. Let me start reporting the things he pulls or let me deal with him behind the scenes. The last thing I want is to show up at your house and find out something's happened to you."

"I can handle Stan."

"Like you handled Victor?"

I swallowed hard and covered my throat with my hand automatically. "That's not fair, Myra. He waylaid me after hours and you know it. Besides, he wasn't your average guy." I didn't come right out and shout about him being a vampire but I wanted to. Any humans around us would think I was crazier than they already believed me to be.

"What's to say Stan won't waylay you too, Lindsay? And what's to say there isn't more to him than meets the eye. We've been fooled before. Never forget that."

"Point taken." I motioned towards the back of the facility. The last thing I wanted to do was continue to be chastised by Myra who never seemed to have a stopping point. "Erotic striptease awaits."

"I still can't believe how many people are dying to get in that class. The waiting list for it is absurd."

"Hey, who wouldn't want to see me gyrate on a pole?" I asked, sarcastically. "Doesn't everyone sit around waiting to see me make a fool of myself?"

Backing up fast, I slammed into something solid. A warmth laced with soothing power wrapped around me. My breath caught and for a moment, I could do little more than stare at Myra with wide eyes.

"We never have to wait long for you to make a fool of yourself." A slow smile spread over her cocoa-colored face. She winked and my brow furrowed.

Turning slowly, I found myself staring up into the blue eyes of one of the sexiest men I'd ever seen. He had to look down at me and that alone was enough to do it for me because at five-nine, I had trouble finding a man I could wear pumps with and not be taller than them. This stud was about six-five so there was no way I'd end up taller than him. His tousled black hair hung to his strong chin, putting emphasis on the tiny dimple there.

I had difficulty tearing my gaze from his thick, corded neck and found my willpower only worsened as I dropped my eyes lower, tracing his broad chest displayed nicely in a snug navy T-shirt with a faint outline of a dragon on it. The thing looked like it had been worn several hundred times but I knew it was a designer piece instantly. The inner shopper in me applauded.

"Umm, sorry." As I went to move away from him, he took hold of my arm and sent fire shooting up it. My breath hitched as my inner thighs tightened.

What?

I stared at him, confused, horny, mesmerized.

He raked his blue gaze over me slowly, heating various portions of my already aroused body. "Lindsay?"

"Do I know you?"

Please say yes. Please say yes.

"Linds?"

I drew a blank and offered up a soft smile. "Again with the 'do I know you' because I really don't think I'd forget a body...err...face like yours."

A black brow went up as a sexy grin moved over his face. I got the feeling he was hiding something. If I wasn't so shocked and horny from his sheer presence, I'd have thought to question him more. As it stood, I was a little more concerned with begging him to have his way with me than anything else.

"I believe we have an appointment."

It took me a minute to register what he was saying. "Oh, you must be the guy from Loup Garou. Umm...?"

Myra leaned into me and whispered, "Exavier Kedmen." The way she said it made me think I was supposed to just know him by his name. As much as I wished that was the case, I didn't.

My eyes lingered on his sexy lips as I nodded. He tilted my chin upwards a bit, leaving me envisioning how it would be to kiss him. The very idea of sliding my tongue over his lush lips made my heart beat faster.

"Did you catch what she said? My name is Exavier. Not Blair."

Instantly, heat flared through my cheeks. "You heard that, huh?"

He nodded.

"Well, in my defense, I wasn't staring at your abs when you told me your name. I was fixated on your mouth, Xavs." The second I realized a shortened versioned of his name had popped out of my mouth, I shook my head. "Exavier, sorry."

There was something so familiar about him. I kept staring, studying him for anything that would trigger a memory. Nothing came to me.

His lush lips curved upwards. I bit back a sigh.

He smiled. "I know I'm early but I was in the neighborhood and thought I'd stop in. I brought coffee."

I perked up. "Coffee?"

Turning, he glanced towards one of the two circular tables in the lobby. A travel carrier full of large cups of what I prayed was French vanilla flavored coffee sat there. I bit my lower lip and whimpered. The man was a dream come true. Sexy and bearing caffeine.

"Lindsay?" Myra nudged me. "I think I smell vanilla."

"Vanilla?" It took all I had not to moan.

Exavier nodded.

I stared up at him and did the only thing I could think of doing to a man who brought me coffee, I threw my arms around his neck and hugged him tight. Lifting me up and off the ground, he took me by surprise. I expected him to act stunned, not to play along.

Never one to want to lose the edge, I wrapped my legs around his waist and planted a kiss on his forehead. "Trust me when I say I won't be calling you Blair any time soon."

"Lindsay Marie Willows, what are you doing?" Myra asked, an edge to her voice said she was doing her best not to laugh even though she didn't agree with my choice for displaying gratitude.

"Thanking the nice man for bringing me coffee." I wagged my brows. "You know, I was just thinking about how coffee was right up there next to sex with things I'd rather be doing."

Myra smiled. "You certainly are well on your way to fulfilling both things then, aren't you?"

I glanced back at the coffee and then down at the man who held me as if I weighed nothing. Visions of licking coffee off his smooth, tawny skin came to mind. I sighed.

Myra laughed. "Oh, sweetie, I can see it in your eyes. No. It will burn him. That would be bad. Now, get down off the nice man before he presses charges."

"Hey, I hugged him. He's the one who picked me up." I tapped his shoulder. "He's also the one who is putting me down now."

Exavier set me down but kept his hands on my hips. I did my best to appear anything but happy. I think I failed.

"Okay, where was I before he went and distracted me with his lips, dimpled chin, blue eyes, broad shoulders..."

Snorting, Myra shook her head. "Gee, anything else?"

"Yes, coffee." I gave her the evil eye. "That was just low. I think you tipped him off I'd be less than receptive about meeting with him. You told him to come bearing something I can't turn down."

"What's that? A great chin? Ask to see his obliques. I'm guessing they're as perfect as the rest of him." She winked at me and wiggled her hips in a sassy motion.

"Bite me," I said, blowing kisses at her.

Snarling, Myra made fake scratching motions at me.

Exavier ran a hand through his hair. "I can come back if this is a bad time."

"Nonsense," Myra said, pushing past me. I could almost smell her enthusiasm as she took hold of his upper arm. The woman never stopped her endless attempts to find me Mr. Right. She was almost as bad as my mother. Though no one was quite that bad. "Why don't you head back with Lindsay? She's got a short class to instruct and then she's free until ten. She'll be free for the entire day after two." She patted his muscular arm. "Just in case you need her for something longer than a talk."

Take him with me? What? There was no way in hell I was dragging this hella hunk with me while I danced on a pole.

"What class is she instructing?" he asked, staring at me and licking his bottom lip. I silently prayed the moan I was holding back didn't escape.

Myra nudged me again. "Erotic stripping and pole dancing. You'll love it. The music is right up your alley. I've heard your stuff. You've got a great blend."

Exavier bit the corner of his lower lip and I could easily imagine those lips on me, sampling my body as I sampled his. "Hmm, I guess this will give me a taste of what you have to offer."

"Excuse me?"

He chuckled. "I was told you're the best when dealing with music that crosses genres. This will let me see what you can do. A sample so to speak."

Do not beg this man to throw you against the wall and make mad monkey sex with you. Do not do it.

I did my best to listen to my inner voice. It seemed to lack the conviction I'd hoped it would have in a case like this. Though, Exavier wasn't something you planned on.

"I'm sorry, Mr. Kedmen but I stopped working in the industry three years ago. Now I just teach dance here and deal with the recreation center. It's not glamorous but I'm happy."

He nodded. "I know you left the field. Though, I can't say I know why. Come to think of it, no one I've spoken with in regards to you seems to know why it is you left, only that you did."

The topic wasn't one I wanted to discuss. It didn't matter how cute his chin was. "I know. I didn't advertise my departure for a reason. One I will not be giving you, coffee or not."

He didn't seem phased by my frankness. "The label said they wanted dancers on the tour. They sent us too many to count but I refuse to accept them unless you come on board and advise. I'm in a pinch and needed you two weeks ago. Sorry I took so long to get to you, Lindsay." The way he said the last part left me tipping my head and giving him a questioning look.

Sorry I took so long to get to you?

Puzzled, I shook my head. "Why me? I can recommend some people who are excellent with cross-genre music and still very active in the business."

"I want you," he said, leveling his blue gaze on me. "No one else."

My entire body reacted to his statement, leaving me biting back an "I want you too" declaration. At a loss for words, I shrugged. "You are obviously a bigger pain in the ass than me. Come on. We'll discuss this after my class is done. If you'd rather play basketball, or *anything* that will keep you out from under my feet that would be great. I can meet you in my office when I'm finished."

"Oh, I wouldn't miss this for the world."

"Yippee," I said, walking away from him before I could make a fool of myself by kissing him.

"Are you always this sweet to someone trying to hire you?" He grabbed the coffee and followed me. I could really get used to him.

Snorting, I kept walking. "This is as sweet as I get when it comes to men in the music industry." Myra laughed and I rolled my eyes. "Fine, men in general. Take it or leave it. And I'd like to point out that *if* I should decide to help you, I don't get any nicer. In fact, I normally get worse. Trying to teach men who aren't born with the ability to follow a beat to dance tends to make my PMS come out and play when it has no reason to be there. Again, take it or leave it. I'm not the one who needs help, Mr. Kedmen."

He chuckled. The sound moved over me slowly. "At least you're honest. The last choreographer they sent couldn't stop kissing my ass."

"Mr. Kedmen, if you should be lucky enough to find me kissing your ass it will have nothing to do with my job and I can guarantee it will be an experience you'll not soon forget."

Did I just proposition him?

I replayed my words in my head.

Yep, I did. Good for me.

ChapteR Two

Stopping outside of a multi-colored door, I smiled. "Umm, my class is down and around the corner. I'll be there in a minute if you'd like to wait."

Arching a brow, he eyed the door. "Is this your office?"

"No, but I am stopping in and saying good morning to them whether or not it interrupts your schedule." I knocked and then opened the door to the center's daycare room to find the room full of children. They ranged in age from about two to five and were already beginning the activities planned for them.

They took one look at me and their faces lit up. Mine did too. "Lindsay!"

"Linds."

"Windsay!"

"Zay-zay."

The variations of my name and anything close to my name poured out of the children as they scurried towards me. Bending down, I put my arms out and they cuddled in close to me. "Good morning, how's everyone doing today?"

Mrs. Fenton, a retired school teacher and now full-time children's activity coordinator for the rec center waved at me. "Morning, Lindsay. I was just going to come and find you." She glanced at Jenny, a full-time daycare provider. "Will you take over here for me?"

"Sure." Jenny nodded. "Morning, Lindsay." She eyed Exavier. It was clear she thought he was handsome. I couldn't agree more. "Morning, Lindsay's friend."

Aisha, one of the children, tugged on my sweatshirt. "That man is very big."

Glancing back at Exavier, I licked my lower lip. "Yes, he is."

Rickie ran up to me and wrapped his hand in my hair. "He's hug-bage."

Snickering, I nodded. "Huge. Yes." I eyed Mrs. Fenton. "Has the speech pathologist been in this week to work with him?"

She shook her head and put her hands up. "Now, don't go calling her and making trouble, Lindsay. She's a busy woman. I think she covers two districts."

"I know. I want you to touch base with Myra. Tell her to dig through that rolodex thing she makes me keep and find the number to the children's hospital. She'll know what to do. It's spooky how well that woman knows me."

Mrs. Fenton gave me a knowing look. "You cannot go forcing big time doctors to come down here twice a week for Rickie. It doesn't matter how cute he is."

"I kuut," Rickie said, grinning from ear to ear.

I ruffled his hair. "You are adorable." I glanced up at Mrs. Fenton. "He will be paid to come. Trust me, Myra will handle it and I'd really appreciate it if we not talk about it in front of..." I motioned my head towards Rickie who took it as a sign to kiss me.

He planted a big, wet kiss on my cheek and hugged my neck tight. "Wuv, Windsay."

Pinching his chubby little cheeks, I laughed. "Listen to you, big boy. You're three now, huh? Did you have a birthday yesterday?"

Mrs. Fenton came and stood before me. She put her hand on her hip and gave me a pointed stare. "I think you know he did. In fact, from what his mother told me this morning when she dropped him off, the entire block now knows it was his birthday."

I cringed. "I'm afraid I don't know what you're hinting at."

"Oh, really." She tapped her foot. The woman had school teacher written all over her. She had a way of making me feel as though I had to be on my best behavior. "So, you have no idea why a mini circus showed up on his street with a permit, lunch, presents and a cake?"

I batted my eyes and did my best to appear innocent. Somehow, I don't think it worked.

Mrs. Fenton pursed her lips. "Right, just like you have no idea how a group of ballerinas showed up for Aisha's birthday and took her and her family to dinner and their show. Just like you have no idea how the—"

I shrugged. "Uncle. Maybe I did hear something about it all."

"You do it for every one of the children here, Lindsay." She shook her head. "You spoil them."

"No. I don't. It never comes from me. It comes from…"

She nodded and waved her hand in the air. "I know. I know. Rickie's mother said the man in charge of it all told Rickie it was from her, not you."

"It *was* from her."

"Lindsay," she said, scolding me with just a look. It worked.

I bit my lower lip. "How mad was she?"

"She wasn't mad. She was in tears. All of the parents appreciate it more than you'll ever know, Lindsay."

Rickie kissed my cheek and smiled. "I wike k doo-keys."

Chuckling, I hugged him to me. "You liked the donkeys? Oh, I bet they were great. I'm sorry I didn't make it to the party, sweetie. Something came up and I couldn't get away." I didn't tell him the truth. No one needed to hear I spent my night being attacked by crazed were-panthers only to wake with no clear memory of how I got home. "I wanted to be there. More than you'll ever know, sweetie. Show me how old you are now. Hold up your fingers. Can you do it?"

He grinned from ear to ear as he put three, and an almost fourth finger that seemed to want to follow, up in the air. "Free."

"Yes, Rickie, three." I gave him a tight squeeze and went to stand. All of the children climbed on me at one time, taking me to the floor with ease. An eruption of laughs broke out and I couldn't help but join them. I did my best to get up without success.

A strong hand took hold of mine and tugged me to my feet. Looking up, I found Exavier staring at me with an odd expression. It looked like a happy one but beyond that I wasn't sure. He held the coffee out with his other hand, far from the children. "I thought I might never see you again for a minute there."

"Thanks," I said, unable to stop myself from smiling. "I've got to go teach a class now. You guys promise to be good?"

A chorus of yeses followed.

Exavier kept hold of my hand and winked at the kids. They giggled as we headed for the door. Once we were in the hallway I tried to take my hand out of his only to find him giving it a squeeze. "They really like you."

"I really like them too."

"So, do you have any kids of your own?"

My gut clenched and I instantly felt nauseated. I ran my hand over my lower abdomen and fought hard to keep memories from the past away. It was hard but I managed. "No." I pulled my hand free from his and drew in a deep, calming breath. "Okay, the natives await."

"Ah, the dancing on the pole. Can you believe I almost forgot?" he asked, a sly grin spread over his handsome face. He handed me the coffee.

I took it and savored the smell of it. "No fair using bribery to get on my good side."

"Wait, you have a good side?" he asked, just as I took a sip. Instantly, I found myself laughing and choking at the same time. He patted my back gently and gave me a rather cocksure grin.

Death by way of coffee with a hot guy as a witness. Yep. A very "me" kind of moment.

Rolling my eyes, I entered the room and waited for Exavier to join me before shutting and locking the door. Turning, I smiled at the class, doing my best to ignore the hunk at my heels. They all smiled back and then looked at Exavier like he was fresh meat. In truth, with this crowd, he was.

"Mmm, do we have a new participant?" Betty, a class member asked, her eyes on Exavier.

Turning, I glanced at Exavier. He cast me a worried look. I wagged my brows. "Maybe. Everyone, this is Mr…"

He leaned forward. "Exavier is fine."

I shrugged. "Fine then. Class, Exavier. Exavier, the class."

They all smiled and waved. Exavier nodded.

"Hey, Lindsay, we've been working on the belly dancing portion. I think we've almost got it."

Susan, a woman who'd been taking classes at the center since I opened it, smiled. "Pfft, I think I'll never be able to move again. I tried to have sex after doing it and my husband had to take over, my muscles were too sore to do any sort of riding. I just lay there, letting him take me. I was too tired to care if I played too or not."

Exavier coughed, clearly taken aback by the woman's comments. If he thought that was bad he'd never make it through the session. Susan had the ability to make even me blush. That was hard to do.

"The offer to meet me in my office still stands." Before I realized it, I had hold of his large, warm hand. Some piece of me wanted to comfort him. While I was amused by his discomfort, I was also slightly bothered by it. I couldn't explain the feeling. And yanking my hand away now would only draw attention to it. "Do you want to meet me in a little bit?"

"I'm…umm…good," he stammered, looking a bit pale. Exavier cupped my hand gently and caressed my wrist with his thumb. It was something that generally occurred between two people who felt comfortable around one another.

I didn't know him, so why did I enjoy the tiny caresses and feel so at ease with it—with him? "Stay close and I'll do my best to protect you from the horny housewives."

He took a large step towards me, pushing his muscular body against me. I sucked in a sharp breath and went to put distance between us. I needed air. I needed him. Exavier slid his arm around my waist and held me close. Effectively trapped, I stilled.

One of my class members cleared her throat. "My inner arms were sore for like two days. I'm thinking this class is working. I'm waiting to be able to move my breasts without touching them. I have no clue how you manage to do it, Lindsay."

"Onto any subject but making your breasts move." I clapped my hands. "What mix would you like to listen to?"

Exavier caressed my hip gently and chuckled softly. "I'd like to see that trick."

I ignored him. "Which routine, ladies?"

They all cast me a "guess" look. Dorothy, another woman who had been coming since I opened the place, smiled wide. "Go with the belly dancing one. Gina was on to something when she made you that mix."

Susan laughed. "Do you remember when we all went out to the strip club and the one guy pulled Lindsay on stage? She did her best to weasel out of it until you told them to play that song. The one she seems to zone out on."

They all snickered while she continued talking. "I thought we were going to have to pull her down and beat the living hell out of those eight sexy men in G-strings who came rushing out to dance with her."

Hanging my head, I sighed. "Anyone have any naked pictures of me we can share with the group? They might embarrass me too. Better yet, naked baby pictures. Embarrassing childhood moments? Come on? I once walked into a tree because I was too busy staring at a boy I had a crush on when I was like five. I split my lip open and ended up crying. He was kind enough to hold a cold compress to it but I really wanted a kiss. I've got at least a hundred equally as mortifying memories. Want to hear them?"

Exavier grunted and rubbed his body against me. I should have been offended or taken aback. I wasn't. I was horny. "I, for one," he whispered, "am all ears."

I turned to face Exavier, ending up wrapped even tighter in his arms. Our gazes locked and for a moment everything around me faded away. I knew him. Somehow, I knew in my heart we'd crossed paths at some point in my life. I just wasn't sure when or where. Reaching up, I touched his face. The urge to be near him was so great I couldn't deny it. What was wrong with me?

I didn't make a habit out of rubbing against men I'd only just met and I certainly didn't keep telling myself I knew them when it was clear I didn't.

His warm breath moved over my cheek and for a minute, I could do little more than stare up at him. His blue eyes seemed to call to me, demand that I look into them. If I didn't know better, I'd have sworn Exavier had mesmerized me. Whatever he'd done, he'd made it so that I instantly liked and trusted him. Not many people could make that claim.

"Hey," he whispered. My body responded to the very sound of his voice. *This isn't right. Snap out of it, Lindsay.*

Coming to my senses, I took hold of Exavier's muscular arm and grabbed a handful of CDs from the shelf near his head. I handed them to him. "Here, make yourself useful and do something other than make me think of you naked." I froze. Had that really just come out of my mouth?

He arched a black brow as a cunning grin crept over his handsome face. "Naked, huh?"

Yep. I'd said it.

Deciding it was best to just avoid discussing the topic of him being naked, I shoved the CDs at him. "One of those is marked LG mix. It's the one we're looking for. Just push play and we'll be set."

"Just push play," he said softly. "Mmm, I think I can handle that. I have to admit, I'd rather play the part of the pole or hear more about you picturing me naked. Maybe we could even swap embarrassing childhood stories."

"The part of the pole, really?" Grinning, I glanced back at the room full of women. The class was full, meaning I had over thirty students. Thankfully, the room was large and accommodating. "So, which one would you like hanging on you? They all seem interested. I'm sure all you have to do is make your intentions known and you'd have at least ten volunteers."

"Very funny."

"Thanks." I winked. "I do try."

"No," he leaned into me, "you come by it naturally."

Walking away, I left him standing there, the entire time praying it was my ass he was fixated on. I knew if positions were reversed, I'd be staring at his, I can guarantee my thoughts would be anything but pure.

Putting my arms above my head to stretch, I winced as pain shot through my body. My shoulder especially hurt. My run-in with a group of bad guys the night before had left me broken and battered. With supernatural blood pumping through my veins, I healed quicker than others. It didn't mean I didn't hurt like hell though. "Ready to warm up?"

"Rough night, Lindsay?" Betty asked.

"She was probably giving the stud by the stereo a private showing," Susan said, laughing softly.

My eyes widened. All I wanted to do was pretend the "stud by the stereo" wasn't in the room with us. "Susan, you have to be the most sexually charged woman I know. You've got me beat. That's for sure. And no, I was not giving Exavier a private show. I didn't sleep right. Once we get going here, I'll be fine."

"Mmmhmm," she murmured.

"Places everyone," I said, the second the music began. It was a hip-hop blend with a dark metal vibe to it. The group it came from was one of my favorites. Too bad I didn't bother to catch their name. Thankfully, I had Gina to keep track of musical details for me. She was a walking book of useless song information.

"We'll start with some side-stepping. Okay?"

They nodded and stepped back and forth, touching one foot to the other. We kept going, speeding the process. "Let's move up to tap-step add a clap and increase with the beat. All right, ladies, let's go into it."

I rocked my hips before stepping to the side and running my hand over my breast and down my side. Watching the class in the mirror, I made sure they were keeping up. We moved seductively as we covered our fake stage area. Reaching down, I began to work my sweatshirt off slowly, only slightly mindful Exavier was still present.

"Whoohoo," Dorothy called out. "You can't tell me that isn't empowering."

Laughing, I began to weave my arms carefully, making sure the motions were sexy, fitting to the beat. "Rib cage rolls." I leaned back slowly and worked my stomach muscles, causing them to ripple. Some of the class grunted. Some moaned and some just laughed as we did it. "Come on, ladies. Move it. Own your body. Use it as the sexual weapon it is."

"Lindsay darling, if we're talking bodies as weapons than yours is a nuclear warhead and mine's a fly swatter," Diane yelled out.

Shaking my head, I did a full body roll. "Diane, you are beautiful. I see the way Mike watches you when he comes in to workout. You've been married how long?"

"Seventeen years next month."

I whistled. "Well damn, find me a fly like that. I'll swat the hell out of it. I can't get a guy to stick with me longer than a few months, tops. Apparently, the word's out. I really am nuclear."

They all laughed. They didn't realize how very much I'd craved being a wife and mother at one point in my life. Now, I simply craved a quiet, uneventful life. Somehow, I doubted I'd get it.

"Okay, I'll do one twist on the pole today. Next week, you'll all be up here doing it. Roger is supposed to install a row of these for us in the next couple of days."

"Honey, we'll break our necks. Roger may be a hell of a handyman but even he can't rig up something safe enough for all of us. We've got two left feet so we're likely to hurt ourselves."

Laughing, I shook my head as I continued to belly dance with the rest of them. "No way. I'm way more accident prone than any of you. I was in a hurry the other day. Gina and I were running through routines in here. I turned and walked right into the pole. My head hurt for the rest of the morning. If I can survive the pole, anyone can." My gaze flickered to Exavier and I found him biting back a smile.

Susan's eyes widened as the mix CD played on, the first portion winding down. "Here comes the spot we lose her in!"

"You don't lose me. I just like the guy's voice. No harm in that."

Diane tipped her head. "Mr. Hunky at the door should invest in this then because if you move like that when you like someone's voice, he'll want it on twenty-four hours a day."

I laughed. "He has his own music. And I'm sure his voice is amazing as well." Glancing at Exavier, I offered a small smile. He seemed to have a way about him. One that let him fade into the background and helped me feel comfortable. "Now, we are focusing on the second half of the routine. Not Mr. Hunky at the door. Don't forget to keep your elbows in a bit when we get to the head thrashing portion. If you keep them even with your body you look like you're throwing your breasts out into everyone's faces. As great as that sounds, it looks better, sexier, if you don't."

I took my spot. "Okay, prepare to strip."

The song morphed into another, this one had a metal, gritty edge with a fantastic beat that not only lent itself to dancing, but seemed to demand it. Not only that, but the singer's voice seemed to move through me. It was a sound I never tired of.

Bending down, I seized hold of my breakaway running pants and yanked them off, leaving me in boy-cut camouflage shorts. Tossing them aside I took hold of the pole nearest me and let myself get lost in the song. Swinging around it once, I held tight, put my legs out wide and thumped against it several times.

Wrapping my right leg around the pole, I slid around it slowly, sinking lower and lower until I touched the floor. I rolled seductively onto my stomach. I quickly went to all fours only to begin to crawl across the floor, dropping my shoulders down low and moving my head in an animalistic manner. My shoulder decided to pick then to act up as a spasm moved through it. Considering the injuries I'd sustained in it, I was damn happy to be able to move it at all so I didn't complain. I simply bit my lower lip and went on with the show.

I went to my knees, closed my eyes and thrust my head back and forth, careful to keep my elbows in a bit. The music ran through me and the deep voice that accompanied it pulled at me, seemingly drawing me to it. It was something that always happened when I heard anything by the group. The man's voice seemed to command me, order me to submit and I, unable to resist, did. I gave it my all, moving, dancing, thumping my body. The beat consumed me. It was as thought he sang to me and no one else. Like he was sending a summons out over millions of people but meant it for me and me alone. It was a foolish thought but one I couldn't shake. I didn't even want to shake it. No. I loved my version of reality.

Before moving quickly to my feet again, I pretended to strip my bikini top off and continued on with the routine. The belly dancing portion returned and I glanced up to find all the women moving along with me, some slower than others and some completely off beat but all having fun. Since that was all that mattered, I kept going.

Grinning, I made my way through them, helping to straighten everyone out. Taking hold of Susan's hips, I led her on the hip rotating portion she kept beating herself up over. "Mmmhmm, that's it, push, push, swing, circle."

"I can't get this."

Rubbing her shoulders, I shook her slightly. "This is easy. Come on horny lil' bunny, move like you do while riding your hubby." Taking hold of her hips again, I helped to guide her. "Are you a left, right or head on gal?"

"Huh?"

Moving up next to her, I smiled wide and winked. "Okay, picture him pinned under you. He's there, ready, deep in you. What do you do?"

"I don't know. I never thought about it before. What do you do?"

"I have a tendency to start most of what I do with my left side. That's odd considering I'm right-handed. Still, it happens. Of course, I hop up there for a ride and depending on the guy, I may stay upright or lean down."

"Huh?" Dorothy asked.

Susan grinned. "If she likes the guy, she'll lean down to be closer to him. If she's just taking the scenic route or screwing for something to do, she stays sitting up. It keeps it less personal. I bet Lindsay avoids kissing men like the plague. That's something a commitment-phobic person tends to do."

My jaw dropped. "Mention riding a guy in front of a sex therapist and she instantly pegs you. That'll teach me."

"So, are you a kisser, Lindsay?"

I wagged my brows. "Come here, I'll show you."

The room laughed.

Snickering, Susan shook her upper body fast, in a teasing manner. "Show me the riding thing. Inquiring minds want to know."

Rolling my eyes, I shrugged. "Okay, but I'm not that exciting. Once I'm there, I make tiny figure eights, leading with my left side, like this," moving my body, I did exactly that, "then if I'm bent down, I'll thrust up and down on him a couple of times. I vary that up a bit, fine tune what's working for the both of us and end up brushing my entire body over his while I'm on him."

I did the entire routine for them without stopping and grinned as Louise wiped her forehead. "Sweetie, I'm not sure who told you that you're not that exciting but we've got a porn collection at home that would beg to differ."

"Umm, I'm not sure if I should feel honored or concerned. I've been known to allow a camera in the bedroom before," I said with a wink.

"Unless you're one of those women who grabs a few guys and uses them until they drop, you should feel safe because those types of pornos make up the majority of our collection. My husband has a thing for one woman with multiple guys. Let me just say that if he even thinks for a minute that I'll do that he'll be pulling my foot out of his ass."

Not wanting to answer Louise's subtle question, I clapped my hands and smiled. "Are you guys good to run through it once on your own?"

"Ohmygod, Lindsay has been in bed with more than one man at a time," Dorothy screamed out.

My eyes widened. "Dorothy?"

"We have known you long enough to catch the change-of-subject-instead-of-answer routine, babes. Spill it."

"About that run through," I said, trying desperately to get off the current subject. It could lead to nowhere good.

Susan smiled. "You're doing it again, Lindsay. Changing the topic."

Louise looked shocked. "Holy shit, you were linked with that rocker guy. That one who had a string of women in his life. What was his name?"

I cringed. "And you all wonder why it is I refuse to date men in the music industry anymore. See, nothing is private with them. Nothing." I smiled, doing my best to joke away the pain of it all. "Next thing you know you'll be telling me you downloaded a taped session of us from the internet."

Susan touched my arm. My power flared, racing through her and showing her my memories. I jerked back, shaking my head, doing my best to lasso it and make her think it was something she'd read in a tabloid, not really a memory she'd picked up from me.

She covered her mouth. "Oh, Lindsay. Sweetheart. Didn't I read somewhere you'd lost someone close to you? Was he a boyfriend? Oh, my, wasn't it that rocker guy?"

"Umm." I glanced down at the floor, not wanting to talk about it. "I've lost a lot of people in my life. Some boyfriends, some not." My gaze flickered to Exavier quickly and I had to force it away.

Louise smiled. "Care to share more about your latest? He's been staring at you like he can't wait to get you home and get that private showing." She motioned to Exavier.

I snickered. "Uh, he's not my anything."

"Oh, really?" Exavier asked, catching me off guard and making the women all sigh. "You sure about that?"

I nodded. "Really."

Susan laughed. "Do you think he'll be like all the others? Unable to keep up with you?"

I snorted. "Yeah, that's it. I haven't been lucky enough to run across a supernatural, ever-lasting guy with a stamina that rivals my own. Jot that down. We could put that on my Christmas list. No blonds. Oh, and they have to be taller than me. I get sick of the Sonny and Cher jokes. And their butt needs to be wider than mine. That's a given. What else sounds good? Great obliques. Always a plus."

"Supernatural?" Louise asked. "Great, this makes my husband right. He keeps spouting off that you're a witch or at the very least a temptress."

I bit my lower lip and tried not to laugh. "That beats the rumor that I'm a vampire. At least I still get to eat ice cream if I'm a witch. That type O-neg diet would have really put a cramp in my junk food addiction. Speaking of which, am I the only one who is hungry for a cheeseburger?"

Susan reached out and ran her finger over my arm. "Honey, you're something all right. You haven't broken a sweat and we're all dying here." She laughed. "You're a nympho, aren't you?"

"Yes. I am. Too bad I swore off men for awhile. I hope withdrawal doesn't set in. I might end up tackling that Blair guy. I really love his abs."

"Brook," they all said, laughing. Even Exavier shook his head, obviously getting in on the joke.

"Yeah, him too."

Chapter Three

I waited until the class had cleared out before smiling at Exavier. "Sorry about Dorothy pinching your ass."

He rubbed his left cheek and wagged his brows. "She's got a hell of a grip."

I bent to shut the CD player off and winced as pain shot through my upper back. I'd thought I'd worked all the kinks out but my run-in the night before had done more damage than I thought. Closing my eyes, I leaned down to try it again only to find Exavier beating me to it.

"You okay?"

"No, I'm old. You don't want to hire me. Go home now."

Chuckling, he held my elbow as I stood tall. "Nice try. What's up? Sleeping wrong doesn't leave someone this sore. I noticed you favoring your left shoulder earlier. What happened?"

How the hell did he pick up on all of that? "Nothing, I'm fine. Just stiff."

"Lindsay?"

Exhaling, I decided truth was the best policy. That and it would make him run away. "Okay then, on my way to my car last night, four big guys jumped out, partially shifted into panthers and managed to bounce me off six, no seven vehicles before I even knew what hit me. They then accused me of being some prince's mate and tried to put me in a big van. Apparently, princes' mates are in high demand and there is a market for them or something. Don't know. Don't care. I unloaded an assload of power on them." I winked. "Because I'm magikal. Killed two, I think, and managed to injure the other two." I grinned. "There ya go. Feel better knowing?"

Something moved over his face that wasn't friendly. "Lindsay?"

"I'm crazy. Run while you can before I start talking about vampires too. Any minute now someone from the neighborhood is liable to show up and ask me to cleanse their house of evil spirits. I'm a regular spook fest."

Exavier moved in closer to me. "So, do things like that happen often or was it a one shot deal?"

I *would* find the one man that was good at taking me in stride when I'd officially sworn men off.

"Let's see. Up until three years ago, things like that would happen every now and then. A vampire here, a lycan there, a whatever-the-hell-else-exists sprinkled in for effect. It was rare and they never demanded I give up some prince guy, they just attacked because they said they could sense my power."

"What happened three years ago?" he asked, his face never switching to an amused look. The fact he seemed to be buying the truth worried me.

"I was on tour, with a client. We were in England and he'd taken sick. That was weird in itself." I left out the part about Tim being a supernatural who shouldn't have ever fallen ill. "Needless to say, the show didn't go on. I didn't think anything of it until I knocked on his tour bus door and he didn't answer. We were friends to start with and I knew he'd never ignore me and I could sense him in there. I used my oh-so-spooky gifts and opened the door. I found his mutilated body spread all over the bus. After I pulled myself together, I ran to get help only to find the friendly gang of spookables on my heels." I waited for Exavier to run the other way. He didn't.

The events surrounding the attack three years ago weren't something I'd ever talked about outside my immediate circle of friends. My parents weren't even aware of what had truly gone on. They knew I'd been attacked. They also knew Tim died. I didn't offer any details beyond those. I'd already told Exavier more than I'd confessed to my father and I was a daddy's girl.

"They ruled Tim's death an accident," he said, his voice low.

"Yeah," I whispered, staring into his blue eyes, surprised he knew Tim. It did make sense. They were both in the entertainment industry. "It's not like they could label it for what it was. Besides, other than you, humans don't believe this shit when people start spouting it off."

"Humans, huh?"

"Yeah, I'm not human. Run. Hurry up before I drop a house on you or something. Click your heels. Quick."

Exavier didn't budge. "Tim was a good guy, Linds."

"No, he was a great guy. He was special too, like me—like others that hide among people." I stared up at him. "Please know, I might be crazy but I don't generally talk about our kind in front of yours. I don't talk about the attack if I can help it. Myra and Gina know the details because they had a hand in making it all better." I didn't tell him my ex also had a major hand in saving me. It wasn't Exavier's business and even with my sharing mood, I didn't want to discuss Eion with him.

Exavier did a rather long blink. I continued, "They should have never been able to sneak up on Tim. But they did. He should have sensed them. Certain things emit a negative energy. A sort of signal others like me can pick up on. The amount of evil they came packing and the numbers they arrived in should have warned him…pfft…all of us way before we even got to England. Somehow, they masked themselves from us. It's damn hard to hide evil from me. Everyone I know who is different says I'm way more sensitive to evil than they've ever seen anyone be. The fact they got past says just how powerful they were."

Exavier leaned into me. "How did you manage to escape them that night?"

"I didn't."

He drew in a sharp breath. "What do you mean, you didn't?"

"I mean what I said, Mr. Kedmen. I did not get away from them that night. I was taken as leverage. A pawn in their game to play with some man I don't know and don't care to meet." It was hard to hold my emotions in check. The attack had been brutal, well thought out and had forever changed my life. It robbed me of my happiness and left me to have to learn to live on despite my loss.

"Did they hurt you?"

I expected him to tell me I was crazy or not funny. I didn't expect genuine concern.

I nodded as I bit back tears. "Yes."

He hugged me and I welcomed it, feeling compelled to go on. "I spent four days in what can only be called hell at their mercy before two of my closest friends and a man I was closer than close to found me and got me out of there because I couldn't walk to do it myself. This ends the discussion. Feel free to think I'm crazy. I'm used to it. It was nice to meet you. If you need those names or referrals, let me know. They're normal so you don't have to be concerned about ending up with nutcases."

I went to walk out of the room only to find Exavier moving to block it. "I want you, Lindsay. I already told you that. I haven't changed my mind."

"I forgot to mention the aliens."

Folding his arms over his chest, he leaned back against the wall. He looked so smug, so cocksure that I wanted to smack him right before I begged him to fuck me. "There were aliens?"

Blowing the raspberries, I rolled my eyes. "I almost wish there was. Would it have chased you off?"

"No."

"Are you insane?" I asked, wanting desperately to throw myself into his strong arms but not daring to do so.

A wry smile covered his handsome face. "Would it matter?"

"Probably not. Would you like to discuss details of me *possibly* helping you out in my office?"

Exavier chuckled and the deep sound moved over me, settling in the apex of my thighs, making moisture pool there. His smile widened as he shook his head, sending his unruly hair in every direction. "Yes, but I'd rather discuss it over lunch. Can you get time away today?"

The door to the room opened fast, startling me. I jumped slightly and Exavier pulled me to the side, putting his body in front of mine before I could blink. He reached back and put his hand on my hip. It only made the horny state he'd put me in worsen. I pulled back enough to maintain contact with him and get a peek at his ass. I knew I could get lost in this man and I knew he'd be more than willing to let me. My head said run. My body said stay with him.

"Lindsay, are you in…?"

The sound of Stalker Stan's voice made me cringe, as it always did. Instinctively, I went into Exavier's body more, pressing myself to his back and resting my palms on his muscular body.

"Who are you and why are you in Lindsay's room?" Stan asked.

"I could ask you the very same thing," Exavier said, caressing my hip slightly and doing a remarkably fine job of making me feel safe—something I rarely felt.

"I'm Lindsay's boyfriend."

My jaw dropped when Stan's words sank in. It took me a second to realize that I'd begun to claw lightly at Exavier's back. I stopped and planted a tiny kiss on the spot I'd marred him.

Oh shit, I kissed him.

I wanted to back away then. It was too much, my need to touch him, to be touched by him. I didn't kiss men I just met. Not even on the back.

Exavier chuckled, sounding anything but amused. "Hmm, that's funny because at last check, I was her boyfriend. In fact, we're a little bit closer than boyfriend, girlfriend but that's between us, not you. Stop fucking showing up places you shouldn't. Stop obsessing about a woman who doesn't love you and doesn't want you. And if you come near her again I will personally hunt you down. I can guarantee that you do not want me on your bad side."

What?

Stan didn't respond. The sound of the door closing told me he'd left. Exhaling, I did my best to calm my nerves. Exavier twisted around and I found my face dangerously close to his cheek and neck. "Sorry, if I was out of line, just tell me. I got the sense that you didn't want to deal with him. I also overheard your friend Myra talking about him. I'll hunt him down and apologize if you want me to."

The thick cords in his neck moved as he spoke, driving my body crazy, making me want to see them moving above me while he pumped the full length of himself into me. I stepped into him more. I wanted to kiss him and could only hope he wanted it too.

"Linds?"

Snapping out of my stupor, I stared up at him. "Thank you. Claiming the local witch is quite a move. People will no doubt arrive with medals to pin to your chest."

"You're not mad?" Exavier smiled and my entire body reacted to the sight. My breath hitched as a shiver ran over me. He reached for me and I backed up quickly, scared that I'd beg him to take me if I let him too close. "Are you okay?"

Nodding, I ran towards the center of the room and grabbed my clothes, grunting softly as I bent over. "I'm getting too old for this shit."

Strong hands slid over my back. I froze and choked back a scream as I shook instantly.

"It's just me." Exavier wrapped his arms around me and eased me up. "You're shaking."

Letting out a nervous laugh, I tried my best to play off just how much he'd scared me. He was fast. Faster than he should have been. He didn't seem like a supernatural to me. I couldn't sense any sort of power in him. No. Exavier seemed all too human. Every ounce of me wished he wasn't. I could easily see myself falling for him. The only problem was, a human would never last with me. "Guess I'm jumpy. Normally, when something gets that close, that fast, bad things happen."

He gave me a comforting hug and I closed my eyes, letting myself relax for the first time in a long time. "I'm sorry, Lindsay."

Unsure what Exavier was sorry about, I glanced up and looked into the mirror before us. His gaze met mine and my hands moved over his as he rocked me gently. It was something lovers did, not strangers. Why were we doing it?

"I'm sorry it took so long for me to get here, Linds. I would have come sooner but I thought you had someone in your life. I thought you'd push me away."

I went to question him about his comment when the door burst open. Gina poked her head in, spilling waves of auburn hair all about her shoulders. Her large green eyes locked on me and her jaw dropped. "Right then." She went to leave.

"Gina, wait! What's up?"

"Myra wanted me to tell you that you were right about the Ferris family and that you have no doubt paved a wonderful path to hell for yourself." Gina smiled wide. "She also wanted to know when you were going to just leap head first into the pits of hell and begin dating the devil to save time. She's still convinced you were made to be his mate. No one but you could tame him."

Laughing softly, I shrugged, doing my best to ignore the fact Exavier was hearing all of this. "I can hardly be blamed for the reaper showing up for Great-Grandpa Ferris. Like it was a surprise to anyone. Hell, the reaper has been nipping at my heels for over a decade. I'm close to seeing if he wants to start hanging out for drinks on Friday nights."

"Be careful," Gina offered, licking her lower lip. "The reaper is exactly the kind of man you attract."

"Well, I do like to screen men to weed out the nice sane ones. It's only fun if you're running for your life with them, from them, in the vicinity of them." I watched Gina's face fall as anger took her over. She was never one to enjoy me joking about the attempts on my life.

"That's not funny, Lindsay. Not in the least. If the man holding you now steps out of line one bit I will personally kill him. Understood?"

I laughed nervously and patted Exavier's arm. "We're all eccentric here. Pay no attention to Gina. She clearly missed her meds and coffee this morning."

Gina entered the room and stood tall. At five-foot-six, she was shorter than Myra and I but that didn't stop her from verbally coming at us whenever possible. Her temper seemed symbolic of her hair—flaming—if allowed to go unchecked. She had an iron-will and the ability to kick almost anything's ass. The slayer in her tended to rule her temper as well. "Like hell. I don't care if the man thinks we're all nuts. If he steps out of line with you I will chop his head off and feed it to a pack of wolves. You've got enough of them trying to kill you that it shouldn't be hard to find a group of them."

"Gina, stop."

Gina gave me a hard look. "They're coming faster, harder and in bigger numbers than ever before, Lindsay. It's never been this bad. Call your dad and ask him flat out what he knows about the man currently known as Prince."

A soft laugh tore free from me.

She didn't share my amused state. "Let this prince guy deal with them, Lindsay. There have been too many close calls lately. You weren't born a slayer and you aren't like Myra. You don't get nine lives. You get one. One that they are more than willing to end."

"Gina, darling, you're going to scare people away because of your need to feed into my delusions. I'm fine. *Really*."

With no outside interference, I knew it was about to get ugly. "Lindsay, I don't care if the man behind you runs to every tabloid in the country blabbing about shit he can't possibly understand. You will listen to me. We've been friends way too long for you to think I'll back down on this. You find out who this fucking prince guy is or I will. Trust me, honey, with as many times as

I've seen you go through hell on account of him, I will not be kind to him when I do find him."

Giving in just to get her to go away, I nodded. "I'm going to dinner with my parents tomorrow night. I'll ask then. And for the record, I'm fine."

She crossed her arms and tapped her foot. "So, how is Detective Gonzales doing?"

"I guess Jay's good. He's supposed to be getting back today from Chicago. I'll let you know. I'm sure he'll give me a call. We may not be dating anymore but Jay still can't go too long without checking in. In fact, he calls three times a day normally. You know how overprotective he is."

Something passed over her face and her nostrils flared. "He already did call about twenty minutes ago. Your class had started so Myra took a message."

I tossed my hands up. "Well, there ya go. See, he's fine. Why the hell are you asking me about him then?"

"Yeah, he wanted to check on you. He was worried sick because he stepped out long enough to grab breakfast for the two of you this morning, came back to your place and you were gone."

That got me.

"Breakfast? What the hell are you talking about? I think I'd have noticed if Jay was sleeping over. He snores so loud that I've thought about barricading the extra room's door with pillows in hopes they'll soak it in before it reaches me. I'm going to sight that as reason number one hundred on the list of why we didn't work out."

"Lindsay."

"Yeah?" I asked, wryly.

"Jay was terrified because you hadn't stirred from your sleep since he found you in the center's parking lot late last night, unconscious and barely breathing. He said you had a birthday present wrapped in children's wrap, addressed to Rickie, lying next to you, just out of reach. Makes sense since you told me you were heading to Rickie's party and then home. Jay also said that he found two dead were-panthers near you and that a trail of fresh blood led away from you."

I cringed.

Gina glared at me. "Jay also mentioned that you'd lost so much blood he ended up giving you some of his own—something he swore he'd never do. Apparently, you made him promise not to ever mix blood with you— something about making him a target too. Anyway, he went against your wishes to save your life. Then he spent the entire night watching over you, convinced you might die. You're fucking immortal. We all are. Dying shouldn't be something mentioned when it comes to us, Lindsay. Yet it's all that comes up anymore when talking about you."

This wasn't what I wanted to talk about. Not in front of Exavier anyway. Gina didn't care. "I can't blame Jay for being terrified that whoever the hell wanted you dead this time came back while he was grabbing you something to eat and finished the job, Lindsay. My guess is that you don't even know how you got home last night. Only that you woke up there, battered, bruised and with the knowledge that you almost died. I bet you're sore as hell too. Bet it just about killed you, knowing you missed that little boy's party, because you love him like you do all the kids."

I looked away, strong, safe arms holding me tight.

"Look at me, Lindsay. Tell me the truth. Jay said it was horrible. He said that one of them bit your upper thigh open, striking an artery and your shoulder was not only out of socket but your arm was damn near ripped off. I gotta say that I've seen you fucked up. I've seen your body almost ripped in half. I'm not like Myra. I can't sense others' emotions, their pain, but I don't need to be like her to know that you've gone past the point of pain and entered whole new territories."

Instinctively, my hand went to the shoulder that had been hurting all day. I met Gina's gaze and her nostrils flared as she pointed at me. "Lindsay Marie Willows, your body has a limit. These things are damn close to pushing you past it! Do you know that Myra only just hung up with Jay? He was that upset. Hell, he damned near called your father to help him with you last night. He said it was that bad."

I tried to take a step back only to find Exavier's large frame blocking me.

Gina glared at me, not giving an inch. "Were you going to tell Myra and I or were you going to sweep this one under the rug like the two attacks before that? Don't think we don't know about the vampire ones, Lindsay."

My eyes widened. "No, there weren't any—"

She cut me off. "Bullshit! When you dozed off in your office the other day you started screaming out in your sleep, terrified that they'd found you again. Myra rushed in and I followed right behind her. She flat out asked you if you'd been attacked again recently. You said *yes*. You even told us that they'd come twice. One was waiting in your car and the other tried and failed to get into your house." She tossed her hands in the air. "We have to interrogate you when you're in a sleep-like state to get the truth out of you. We were created to help keep you safe. We can't do our job if you lie to us."

I tried to come up with an explanation. I got nothing. "Gina, don't do this. We'll talk about it later."

"No. We will talk about it now!" She put her hand on her hip. "They come after you and are shocked when you put up a fight. I get the sense that they assume you're defenseless. I honestly think they're only expecting a pretty showpiece. A prince's play thing—his toy. Yes, you give them more than that to deal with but you were not born with a violent streak. You may be a bitch when it comes to the men in your life but you are the most nurturing woman I know when it comes to these kids—these people."

"Gina, please." I'd do anything to get her to stop discussing this in front of Exavier. Hell, to stop talking about it at all.

She shook her head. "No. This prince of darkness guy is supposedly some big bad ass. If what they say is true, that you're his other half, then it makes sense that you wouldn't be aggressive. You'd just buck heads the entire time. The bad guys operate under this assumption. My gut tells me it's true—that you aren't supposed to have to fight for your own life, that he's supposed to be the one doing it. I also think that's why we were all drawn to you, Lindsay. Each of us is a warrior by some right. Each of us has a burning need to see you safe."

"Gina."

"No. I think the Fates brought us all together to keep you alive. I think they realized that Prince Fuck-Up was going to be a no-show and tried to cover their asses. I think they underestimated you big time, too. They didn't just get a pretty showpiece, a sexy toy, they got a woman who could and would give all she had to keep herself and those she loves safe. And the bad guys underestimate you too but they're coming in numbers we can't control."

I cringed. None of this was new information. She'd been very vocal all along about her feelings towards my said mate. Having her express her opinion and get her feelings off her chest was never an issue. It was getting Gina to stop expressing them that was tricky.

She pointed at me. "You need to start meeting me for lessons on how to protect yourself again. I know how much you hate having to hurt someone and that makes it even worse but someone has to show you how to take care of yourself in the event one of us isn't there to protect you."

I sighed. She continued, "Jay doesn't just freak out for no reason. He doesn't call around in tears, frantically looking for anyone, Lindsay. Jay doesn't cry! He's an alpha lycan. They don't show emotions like that. When the man does it, it's fucking serious! I can only imagine what kind of shape he found you in that made him not call us. He knows that Myra won't survive finding you like we did before. He knows that she'd snap. She damn near didn't mentally come back from the first time. It would turn her into a killing machine you couldn't possibly imagine. She loves you like a sister. I love you like a sister."

"I didn't...err...there wasn't...umm."

"Lie to me about it, Lindsay, and I swear I'll kill you myself and save the rest of the underworld the trouble. Everyday I worry that it's the day those fucks will win. I worry you'll disappear for days again—only this time when we find you there will be no bringing you back to life, that your heart won't restart, your body won't mend."

Desperate for her to stop, I did the only thing I could think to do. I begged. "*Please*, Gina."

She froze and I wasn't sure if it was the please or the desperation on my face. I didn't care. A puzzled look came over her. "Why aren't you yelling at me and making me dive out of the way of lightning strikes that you swear you can't create yet always seem to happen when you're pissed?" As she stared at me, I watched it hit her. Her eyes widened and she looked from me to Exavier and back again several times before blushing. Since Gina wasn't one who was prone to being embarrassed, I was at a loss as to how to help. If worse came to worse, I'd plead insanity. With the talk that had been going on directly in front of Exavier, I doubted he'd question me on it. Hell, he'd probably have me committed himself.

Gina ran a hand through her auburn hair and nodded, doing her best to look calm and collected. It didn't work. "Oh, right. Yes. Umm, you have someone new here. Someone, umm… I'm sorry. You didn't get a chance to tell your *friend* that I moonlight as an actress on a paranormal soap and you help me with my lines, did you?"

I choked back a sob as a tear fell down my cheek. "No. I didn't mention that."

"Right, so he probably thinks we're in a cult and worship the devil or something." She smiled wide at Exavier. "Sorry about using you as an extra. You did surprisingly well by, umm, doing nothing to interfere. Way to fade into the background. Thanks."

"No problem," he said in a low tone.

"Thanks for clearing that up for me, Gina." I wanted to run to her and hug her but leaving the safety of Exavier's arms wasn't an option for me just yet. "He already thinks I'm odd enough. We need to quit watching scary movies and get lives."

Gina nodded slowly. "Yeah, no movies. Lay off those movies, mmmhmm." She pointed behind her. "I've got a self-defense class to instruct. I really think you should stop in. We can practice for the heck of it. Run more lines. I could even show your friend some stuff if you want. I do think you should stop in, though. Okay?"

I nodded.

"Take care. I should probably warn you that Jay's headed over here. The second Myra said you were here I guess he freaked out. Umm, you know how much he hates to miss out on me running my lines and all." A nervous chuckle escaped her. She went to leave and paused. "You know, your friend looks really familiar."

"I will. I promise. And I agree, Exavier looks *very* familiar."

On her way out, she stopped. Her eyes widened as she stared at Exavier. "Ohmygod, you're...umm...holy shit."

"Huh? Oh, yeah. I forgot to tell you that he's with a band, Loup Garou, I think Myra said, and that he started off here with the idea I'd be able to help out but I'm guessing he's seen the light by now."

Gina's green eyes stayed locked on Exavier as she spoke to me. "Honey, you really need to stop using that two-hundred disc player or start putting the artist's names in the memory bank so it displays something other than the disc number."

"Why? I have you, the walking book of useless facts on every artist out there. And I can't forget, the master of my mix CDs. How you dig through and find what you need out of that mess is beyond me."

She smiled. "Stop throwing away the cases and inserts, Lindsay. You'd be able to see photos of the bands then. Better yet, turn on a music video channel or attend the damn concerts we try to take you to all the time."

Sighing, I did my best to work the kink out of my neck without knocking Exavier out. "I can't stand the clutter. I'm a freak. You tell me so all the time. I didn't throw them all away. I kept the ones from that one group. Yeah."

"Be more specific."

Grunting, I shook my head. "Gina, you are doing your best to point out the fact that I'm not only terrible with names, I also suck shit at pairing up band names to their songs. And I have yet to know the actual song title of anything. In my defense, once I hear it, I instantly know what feels right dance-wise with it."

"At least he'll know you're not an obsessed fan that's out to bear his love child."

Pulling out of Exavier's arms, I slipped my sweatshirt on and laughed. "I think he's safe from either of those things occurring. For one, obsessed people are scary. I'd never put someone on the other side of that and play stalk them when I know what it's like. And secondly…well, you know."

Gina's face fell. "Oh honey, I didn't mean to bring up having children. I just was using it as an example…umm…shit. I didn't mean to drag that up, Lindsay. I swear."

"No biggie."

Liar.

The attack three years ago had robbed something precious from me and left me unable to ever have children. I no longer dreamt of a house full of children, a husband who loved me and a white picket fence. No, my dreams nowadays ran more towards nightmares than anything else.

Gina rushed towards me and began helping me re-snap the buttons on the legs of my pants. "Lindsay, I am so sorry. I wasn't thinking. It was a typical me being me moment. I'd like to yank my foot out of my mouth. The…umm…accident in Europe was hard enough to go through, but me tossing something you want so bad but can't ever…shit, shutting up now. Sorry."

I dropped my voice low enough that I hoped Exavier couldn't hear me. "I'm fine, Gina. I've had three years to get used to the idea that I'll never be someone's mommy. Don't keep apologizing. I'm good. Really. Besides, I could be wrong but I think I need to find the right guy before I even dredge up the fact that I can't have his children. Don't you?"

She kissed my cheek and winked at me. "Umm, what routine did the ladies do today?"

"What do they always do?"

She beamed. "Did you do it too?"

"Yes," I said, slowly. "Why?"

"No reason. Meet me for self-defense today or else!" She took off running towards the door, laughing all the way.

"Yeah, you're a *real* riot. I'll do my best to contain my laughter."

Exavier turned me to face him. "So, how's acting working out for her?"

I glanced at the floor, not wanting to meet his eyes. "Umm, good. I think. I don't know. I just run lines with her."

"That's really nice of you."

I stepped out of his grasp and forced a smile to my face. "Since my ten o'clock apparently kicked the bucket, I'm free for a couple of hours. I need to grab a shower and change into something other than workout clothes but if you want to…umm…still want to get something to eat? Some friends of mine own a place down the street. The food is good and—"

"Sounds perfect."

I smiled as I headed off towards the showers.

Chapter Four

"Did that guy just shake his ass on his way to the kitchen?" Exavier asked, folding his arms over his chest.

"You do that a lot."

"Do what? Notice guys shaking their asses? Umm, no."

I smiled and glanced at the menu, which I knew by heart. "You take a very manly stance by crossing your arms that way."

Arching a brow, he smiled slightly. "A manly stance? Hmm, is that so wrong?"

"No, Xavs, it's not bad at all." Wrinkling my nose, I did my best to look sweet and innocent. "I have no clue why I continue to butcher your name. I'm sorry. I swear I'm doing my best not to but…"

Nodding a bit, he gave me a sexy, mysterious grin that sent heat rushing through my cheeks. "It's more than fine by me."

"Do I know you from somewhere?"

Licking his lower lip, he drew it in slightly. "What makes you ask?"

"Never mind." I was too embarrassed to tell him why.

"Hmm, you strike me as a rather gutsy gal. I'm surprised you'd back down so fast when I asked you a simple question."

I baulked. I was not backing down. "If you must know, you remind me of someone I used to know. A little boy I used to play with, Exavier Kondrashchenko." I rolled my eyes, knowing my cheeks were flaming red now. "It's the name and the dark hair. I called him Xavs. I'm sure that's why I keep butchering your name. Sorry."

Exavier nodded. "Hmm, Kondrashchenko. That's a hell of a last name."

I thought back to when I was little and a soft laugh came from me. Exavier tapped the table. "Tell me what you're thinking about."

Doing my best to appear innocent, I wrinkled my nose. As I glanced at him, my cheeks flushed. "I'm fairly sure I technically proposed to him. But, I'm not positive. I might have just informed him I was going to marry him someday. Does that count as a proposal or a threat?"

The deep laugh that came from Exavier warmed my heart. "Hmm, tell me more."

Covering my face with one hand, I did my best to hide my mortification as I continued, "His last name was too hard for me to spell so I also informed him he'd have to change it." I shook my head. "I can't believe I actually said that to him. Granted, I was like five-years-old when I told him this, but still."

"I bet that boy is kicking himself now."

I gave him a puzzled look. "What makes you say that?"

He leaned back in his booth and shrugged. "I'm just imagining what I'd do if a little girl said that to me when I was younger...uhh...I'd have probably done something stupid like leap away from her like she had *cooties* or something."

A half snort, half cough tore free from me. "Ohmygod, that's exactly what he did. Must be a boy thing. He couldn't have gotten away from me faster if he tried. Great, now I'll surely continue to call you Xavs. On a bright note, I won't beg you to play dolls with me."

His lips twitched. "Dolls. Hmm, you made him play with dolls?"

"Not exactly." I winked. "I asked, he said no. I cried. He gave in and did a rather bad job of playing along. The point is that he did it."

"Ah, so you used tears as a weapon." Exavier ran his fingers over the edge of the menu absently. "No guy can resist tears."

I let out a soft laugh. "I wish I was that good at getting my way. No. I'd found out we were moving away that morning and I was so upset about leaving him that the second he said no I couldn't hold it in anymore. He thought it was the doll thing. It was really an 'I didn't want to say goodbye to him' thing. I had the biggest crush on him."

"Really?" He licked his lower lip again, a habit I was beginning to really like. "So, you're saying I've got some stiff competition."

I just laughed.

"Oh my word, do my eyes deceive me or has my angel brought a man with her?"

Looking up, I smiled as I found a six foot tall man with short brown hair standing in front of us. He had on his double-knit polyester pants and oh-so-sexy disco days shirt as did every other person working at the diner. He rubbed his chin and stared at Exavier harder than I had. Winking, Harly smiled. "Oh, he's a looker, Lindsay. Does he have a name or will he answer to Dark and Dangerous?"

Exavier shifted uncomfortably and cleared his throat.

"We certainly have a straight one here. Have no fear, Dark and Dangerous. I'm happily married."

"That's right!" Charles called from behind the counter. He waved at me. "Hey, hon. How are you feeling? Any better? Jay mentioned you were sick or something last night."

"I feel wonderful, Charlie. Thanks." Glancing up at Harly, I winked. "I'm liking the Dark and Dangerous name, though I sort of like Hella Hunk too. It's a shame someone already got to him and named him Exavier."

"Well, what would the two of you like today?" Harly rolled his eyes and tossed his hand in the air. "I don't know why I'm bothering to ask you, Lindsay. You get the same thing every time you come in here. We're still trying to figure out where you put all the food you eat."

Grinning, I tried to push my stomach out. I lifted my red-ribbed t-shirt and patted the almost non-existent mound. "Here." I held it out until I was forced to exhale or burst. I chose the first option.

"She's a nervous ball of energy. That's how she burns all that food off. It's in her aura, Harly. I told you that already." Charles poured several cups of coffee, talking over the other patrons as he went. "I'm telling you, she doesn't leave her lights on for any old reason. The girl can't sleep and when she does, it's fitful at best."

Smiling, I shook my head. "Charlie, they have stalking laws you know."

Harly tapped my arm. "Speaking of stalkers, that Stan guy you've been having trouble with showed up again this morning. Jay went crazy on him. He even threatened to shoot him if he dared get near you again. No offense to Dark and Dangerous but why is it you never meet Jay here for lunch anymore? Half the time you barely miss each other. Are you two on the outs again?"

Great, just great. Jay was already gunning for me about the attack. Couple in Stan the Stalker showing up after I left and Jay was sure to be pleasant.

I shuddered and did my best not to dwell on that. "I don't know. Make up an answer and I'll smile prettily and agree with it."

Charles leaned over the counter. "Sweetie, never give Harly permission to make something up. You know that."

Harly laughed. "Oh, I don't need to make things up where Lindsay and Jay are concerned." I went to object and he arched a brow. "I know. I know. You two are not a couple anymore. I understand that but it still didn't diminish the drama and I'm all about the drama."

"Drama?" Exavier asked, taking more of an interest in the conversation than I liked.

Harly grinned. "Our Lindsay has a bit of a temper."

"Really, I hadn't noticed." Exavier winked at me and I almost melted. "Tell me about some of this drama between her and Jay."

My eyes widened and I cleared my throat. "Umm, Yes, I'm ready to order. I'll take the usual. Exavier?"

"I'll have what she's having. Thanks."

Harly walked away giving me a rather funny expression as he went. Glancing at Exavier, I found him biting back a smile. "You have some interesting friends."

"Yeah, they're great."

"So, are you going to tell me any more about your first crush?" He ran his finger over his spoon as he looked out from under thick black eyelashes. "I'm curious as to what I'm up against."

I couldn't help but laugh. "Sorry, but no guy wins over him."

"Really?"

"Yep." I took a sip of my diet soda and nodded. "Filling his shoes is a big task. I cried myself to sleep for an entire year after we moved. It's pathetic, I know, but I did. I can assure you that has not happened with anyone other than him so don't fear me stalking you."

He looked so sexy sitting there that I wanted to crawl into the booth beside him. I held back. "That's good to know. Do the two of you still talk?"

"No." I forced a smile to my face even though the subject wasn't one of my favorites. "For a while, right after I moved away, we wrote letters back and forth and talked on the phone every now and then. He's almost three years older than me and I think he got to the dating stage before me. Plus, he sort of lost interest in our friendship."

Exavier's brow furrowed. "Why do you say that?"

"For a variety of reasons. I have a childhood lumped full of let downs. I was ten and my parents told me I could spend a month with my grandparents back west. I called his house, so excited that I'd get to see him again—keep in mind that we moved when I was seven and I hadn't seen him in all that time. His mother answered. I left her a long message for him and when I got to my grandparents' and tried to get ahold of him, his mother told me that he'd decided to go away to some boy's camp and must have forgotten it was the same time I was coming home. I get that he was thirteen then and had better things to do. It just hurt a little that he'd forgotten. No biggie."

Liar.

Exavier's jaw tightened. He cleared his throat and took a sip of his soda before looking at me. "Hmm, if you two were as close as it sounds like you were, I'm surprised he'd forget something as important as you coming home. Did you try to reach him again after that? He might not have gotten the message."

I nodded. "I did. I left so many messages for him that it hit me just how pathetic I was being so I stopped. We were friends when we were little but that's it."

"You don't sound very convinced." Exavier tipped his head slightly. "Is that all there is to the story?"

"Pretty much."

"You never tried to contact him again?"

I rolled my eyes and let him have another pathetic snippet of my obsession with a childhood friend. "I sent him a gift for his eighteenth birthday." I tapped my fingers on the table, doing my best to stay removed from it all. Why I even felt the need to tell Exavier all of this was beyond me. "I was hanging out with my girlfriends. You met them, Gina and Myra. Anyway, we walked past this shop that had the coolest looking black guitar in it. It had the eye and part of the nose of a wolf airbrushed on it. I saw it and immediately thought of him. Please don't ask why. I have no clue but I did. I bought it, had it packaged up and Myra actually mailed it for me. It was only after it was long gone that I found the card I'd gotten to go with it lying half under Myra's bed."

Exavier snickered. "So the guy got a guitar in the mail with no card attached?"

"Yep. It gets better." I rubbed between my eyes and laughed. "Myra put her return address on it. She's, umm, different at times—she can sense things and was adamant that he would not get the gift if my name was anywhere on the packaging. She seemed to think someone would keep it from him or something. I don't really know. That's why she took it and mailed it. I don't argue with her. She's scary."

"Ah, so he got a guitar with no card and some girl's name on the packaging that he didn't know."

"Yep. And I'm guessing he never in a million years suspected it was from me. He hadn't seen or talked to me for almost ten years at the time. I did try to reach him the summer after that. I was headed in to spend the entire summer with my grandparents and was hoping to at least see him for a couple of minutes. Didn't happen."

"Why's that?"

Shrugging, I took another sip of my drink. "I drove over to his place and got to visit with his mother but that was all. She informed me that he'd met a really nice girl at college and decided to spend the summer there with her. She was fairly sure that he was planning on proposing to the girl. I left a note with her letting him know that I was happy that he was happy—sounds lame. I know. But I was, am, happy for him." I traced the edge of my glass, collecting condensation as I went. "I left, ran into the ass end of some guy's car with mine. He got out. I fell for him. We hit it off and dated the entire summer. The day before I left we watched the sunset and talked about things that we'd sort of forgotten to talk about over the three months we were together. He brought up one of his close friends, Xavs, and I couldn't breathe."

"Why is that?" Exavier asked, his face a mask of nothing.

"Because as much as Xavs didn't want to see me, I still wanted to see him. But the idea of seeing him, knowing I'd just lost my virginity to one of his best friends, didn't seem as appealing any more. I never tried to contact him after that and he's *never* tried to contact me so that was that. Now, it's your turn. Tell me about your first crush."

He just sat there, staring at me but not saying a word. Harly came out carrying our food and easing the awkward moment between us. He set a platter full of thick cut fries and a cheeseburger in front of Exavier and a matching one in front of me.

"There you go, you two. Behave yourselves."

"Thanks, Harly."

"You can thank me by making us uncles, darling."

My appetite instantly dissipated. I nodded at him and let out a soft laugh.

"We are dying to get to shop for a little one. And we want permission to take the baby for long walks. You're our only hope of getting to be uncles."

"Harly, go pester Myra about settling down." I wanted to be off the subject of having a family and Harly seemed dead set on it.

He shook his head. "No honey, it's not Myra I see down at the park laughing and hanging around with the children. I know how you are, Lindsay. Those mothers down there are not your type of people. You go down to be by the little ones. It's not Myra who drags me to the hospital once a month to hold premature babies who need the stimulation and whose parents need a little break. It's you. It's not Myra who opened a rec center to keep kids out of trouble and to provide daycare for women who couldn't normally afford it."

Glancing down at the table, I tried to will myself away. It didn't work. "Umm…"

"I like your place here, Harly. It's like a step back in time." Exavier held up a fry and tipped his head a bit. "And the food is delicious."

Harly looked at me and beamed. "Oh, he's a keeper, Lindsay. Don't toss this one back, honey."

"I'll do my best."

"Do better than your best, Lindsay."

I waited for Harly to go into the kitchen before I sighed. My cell phone rang. Digging in my handbag, I pulled it out. "Hello?"

"Ah, there you are. I have been trying to reach you at home all morning."

I smacked my forehead as punishment for not checking the caller ID on my phone before answering. "Hi, Dad. I was at work all morning."

"Lindsay, the recreational center is far from work. Stop dumping money into a section of the city that will never get better."

"Dad, I made more money than I could ever dream of spending in my first year of choreographing alone. You invested it for me and I kept earning beyond that. Am I in danger of going broke anytime in my lifetime?"

He snorted. "No."

"Am I spending your money?"

"No, but that is not the point."

I couldn't help but laugh. "I'm sorry. There's a point to this lecture? Continue on." I knew he was seething mad and it only made me smile more.

"Lindsay, there are better ways you could be…"

I put my hand up then realized he couldn't see me. "Hold on. If you're going to launch into the spiel about me dumping money into other programs and freeing myself of the 'burden' of the center again then I'm going to hang up and change my number. Those kids and those people mean the world to me. And, to be honest, I can't see how it's any of your business what I do with my time or my money."

"You studied dance, not how to swing around a pole, Lindsay."

"I know I studied dance, not how to swing on a pole." I wanted to strangle him. I held back doing it over the phone. "Daddy, it's not nice to have hired eyes everywhere. We've talked about this."

"Someone needs to watch over you. You are reckless and—"

"Oh, hey, you called just in time for the lunchtime toss-myself-in-front-of-a-bus meeting. Thank gawd you got your digs in before I leapt in front of the mother load of horseshit."

He snarled. I guess he didn't like me offering to toss myself in front of a moving vehicle just to avoid taking anymore shit about my life. I smiled. "Lindsay, we will be meeting at eight tomorrow evening."

I hissed. "Darn it. Eight tomorrow just won't work for me, Dad. I'll have to take a raincheck. See that's the time I do table dances and give men four times my age lap dances. I make a hell of a killing in tips. Granted, I have to pull the money out of my thong, but still."

He didn't find it as amusing as I did. "You are attending. There is someone special in town that I wish for you to see. I will discuss the matter no more with you."

"Psst, you aren't sounding as young as you should. Use contractions, Dad, they're all the rage. Ooo, better yet, start using one of the like hundred languages you speak. How many of them are obsolete now? Your French accent is all but gone, Daddy. Come on, pull out the big guns."

He chuckled slightly. "So, I will see you tomorrow evening?"

"I don't know. This isn't another one of Mom's attempts to fix me up with one of her friends' sons is it?"

His silence spoke volumes.

"Uhh, Dad, I thought you agreed with me that the men she picks are about as lively as a brick wall. Half of them are as thick as one too. Please mesmerize her and make her think I came, it was great and we all went home happy."

"I do not mesmerize anyone. I 'push' with my voice, Lindsay. And I would never do it to you or your mother."

"There's a difference?" I put my hand up again. "Don't answer that. Just please get me out of this, Dad. Do the daddy-mind-trick. And you're wrong. I remember you using it on mom when you broke her favorite, one of a kind, little angel statue thingie. You so made her think the wind knocked it off the table. So, don't tell me you don't use it on Mom. Please help me get out of this."

"*Non.* Not this time, Lindsay. I think you will be most pleased when you arrive."

"Most pleased? Ugg. Get a cape. Run around town telling people you want to suck their blood. Do it, Dad. Skip to the chase. Bela Lugosi them. Do it."

The sound of him laughing made me laugh too. "*À demain*—see you tomorrow. And, Lindsay, it is a formal dinner."

"Ooo, formal? Am I dining with the President? Does this mean I have to shower? I bet I can't wear shorts. Damn."

"Lindsay."

"*Allez, salut!*" Hanging up, I found Exavier giving me a lopsided grin that he somehow managed to make look sexy. "What?" I popped a fry into my mouth.

"Nothing. I just forgot how funny the two of you are together."

"Huh?"

"So, you do know that you're hired? Can you leave with me tomorrow night? After you're finished having dinner with your parents, of course. I can make sure you have the manpower at the center to keep it running smoothly if I can have your undivided attention. I want you all to myself. I'll even see to it that every birthday for the little ones at the center is covered, Lindsay."

Choking on the fry, I just stared at him.

He took a bite of his burger and wagged his brows. The tiniest bit of ketchup oozed out and onto the corner of his mouth. My first instinct was to lick it off. It would assure my tongue was close to his mouth. I held back and motioned to it with my hand.

Exavier's tongue darted out and over his bottom lip. He slid it over and cleaned the ketchup away with such erotic ease that I whimpered. He looked as though he were trying not to laugh. "Are you going to yell at me for not using a napkin?"

"No, I'm going to fantasize about what else you can do with that…oh…yeah, you should use a napkin." I dropped my gaze, mortified by what had come out of my mouth. The fact I was embarrassed spoke volumes. I normally didn't care what I said around anyone.

Harly came back with a refill for Exavier and nodded towards the parking lot. "Let the drama begin."

I glanced out the window and instantly felt as though I'd been kicked in the gut. The first thing I spotted was the black motorcycle pulling in. The second was the man riding it—Detective Jay Gonzalez. His jean shirt was unbuttoned a bit, leaving his caramel-colored chest showing. The way he'd rolled his sleeves to just under his elbow left his muscular arms in plain view. His stubble-covered jaw line never ceased to make me want to kiss it. The color matched his close cut hair. I already knew how brown his eyes were even though they were obstructed by sunglasses.

Harly began fanning himself with his hand. "Oh, honey, he doesn't look too happy. What did you do this time?"

"Me? Why do you assume I did something to piss him off?"

Charles laughed so loud from behind the counter that I wanted to crawl under the table and hide. Harly shrugged. "Gee, Lindsay, let me think. You're the one who got mad at him for insisting you lock your doors at night so you locked him out while he was in nothing but a pair of," he winked, "banana huggers. Whew, that was quite a banana they were hugging too. The ordeal started because *you* did something stupid and upset Jay."

Charles leaned over the counter. "Then there was the time Lindsay brought home that homeless guy and he turned out to be some vagrant wanted on attempted murder charges. Jay was so mad he actually spent the night teaching her to cross the street at the corner, stop, drop and roll and anything else he could think of. I thought it was cute since he was trying to prove a point. If she hadn't figured out that bringing home strangers wasn't a good idea, she might not have gotten other fundamentals that children in kindergarten do."

Harly laughed. "If memory serves, didn't Jay end up spending weeks begging for her forgiveness? He finally showed up on her front lawn with the children from the center and flowers. He knew she'd open the door for them. Well, that or he planned on using them as a buffer. With Jay, one never really knows." He nudged me. "So, what did you do this time, Lindsay?"

Staring at Jay as he pulled his bike to a stop in the center of the parking lot and dismounted, I shook my head. "Honestly, it wasn't my fault this time. I don't remember anything past one of them leaping at me and me letting my power out. I can't stop them from coming after me."

"Can't stop who from what?" Harly asked. "What power, honey?"

Realizing my slip, I forced a smile to my face and glanced at Exavier. "Excuse me for a minute."

He looked less than pleased. I touched Harly's shoulder on my way out of the booth. "If I'm not back in here in like five minutes, call Gina to come calm Jay down."

"You mean kick his ass back around the corner to the center?"

"That too."

Harly nodded and I headed towards the exit. The minute I walked out, the afternoon began to burn my sensitive eyes. Jay stared down at me from his six-foot-three-inch height and chewed his gum. It was something he did when he was annoyed. Since he'd given up smoking it seemed to be a constant. Come to think of it, once he and I began dating, it was even worse. Thankfully, we weren't an item anymore and hadn't been for a while.

Hmm, me cause someone stress? No.

Reaching into his front breast pocket, he pulled an extra pair of my sunglasses out and slid them on me. "You forgot these this morning." His voice sounded strained.

"Before you yell, I'm sorry I didn't call you the second Gina told me about you finding me." I sighed and ran a hand through my hair. "I knew you'd yell and I—"

Jay had me up and off the ground before I could even blink. He held me tight to him and rocked me in his arms. My feet dangled. "You're okay."

"Other than the fact you're cutting off my ability to draw in air," I teased, hugging him back.

He set me back down and kissed my forehead. "I just had to see for myself."

"Do you want to come in and eat?"

He let out a soft laugh. "No thanks. Gina made sure to tell me that you left with a guy. I'm not here to cause problems for you, Lindsay. I just needed to know you were really okay."

"I'm fine, thanks to you." I tossed my arms around his neck and gave him a good squeeze. "Mmm, what would I do without you?"

"Probably bring home serial killers and try to feed them dinner."

Laughing, I let go of him. "Are you sure you don't want to come in and meet Exavier?"

"Nice name," he said, sarcastically.

"Jay."

He put his hands in the air in an "I'm innocent" pose. "I was just saying. I bet he's a *great* guy. A real pretty one. I'm sure."

"Are you done?"

"Done with what?"

Snorting, I put my hand on my hip. "Being an ass. I know you're mad about what happened. I swear to you it wasn't my fault, Jay. Like I'd purposely go and—"

He yanked me to him so fast that I yelped. "I never in a million years thought it was your fault that some sick bastards have targeted you! Never! I'm sorry I'm in a shitty mood, Lindsay. I had a hell of a night. I got back from a case that had me out of town for three weeks to find one of my closest friends, my ex, a woman I still care very much for, laying in a fucking parking lot, barely breathing and mangled!"

"Lindsay?"

The sound of Exavier's voice made me gasp. Putting my palm against Jay's chest, I patted it several times. "You better be nice. I mean it."

"I'm the nicest guy I know, darling." He slapped a rather fake smile onto his face and looked at Exavier. "Nice to meet you. *Love* the name. It's very pretty."

"Jay," I said in a warning tone.

"Lindsay, are you okay?"

Turning as much as I could considering Jay had a hold of me, I found Exavier standing there looking deadly. His stare was cold and directed at Jay.

I elbowed Jay and he let go of me. "I'm fine. Exavier, this is Jay. You'll have to excuse him. He's a little cranky today."

"Just today, huh?" Gina asked, running up from the back side of the diner glancing at Exavier and then me. I gave her a questioning look. She smiled. "I was, umm, hungry?"

"Bullshit, Harly called you the second he saw me pull in," Jay said, shaking his head. "Have I ever hurt Lindsay?"

"Nope, but you do tend to get loud and make scenes. I'm here to cut those down to a minimum." Gina came and stood next to me. "Wait, does that time you got caught out on a date with that blonde chick, while you and Lindsay were still a couple, count as hurting her?"

I tried not to laugh but failed miserably. "Or the redhead?"

Exavier snickered.

"Or that one who we were sure was really a guy?" Gina ducked behind me as Jay made a move to grab her. She peeked out from under my arm. "Ooo, how about the bimbo who kept trying to answer your door every time your pager beeped? God, she was stupid. Who thinks that's a doorbell? What did she do when it went off in the car, think God was trying to communicate with her?"

"Or, how about the chick who was more into you than him?" I winked at Gina. She laughed so hard that she squealed.

Jay made another move for her and I caught his hands. I began to move to music only I heard, making him my personal dance toy. Gina joined in, dancing around him and tickling his ribs. Jay snickered as he shook his head. "You two never stop. You're missing your third partner in crime."

I laughed at his mention of Myra. Gina gyrated down his side and Jay stared up at the sky. I'd seen that look before. He was horny. "Careful, Gina, or you'll be the next one we're teasing him about."

She leapt back and shuddered. "Oh that's just not right. It's Jay. Eww."

"Hey, I'm a great catch, if I do say so myself." His gaze raked over Gina slowly.

She bit her lower lip. "Is that why so many women have caught you?"

I couldn't help but laugh. Jay didn't seem to find it as funny. In fact, he looked hurt by Gina's comments. He rubbed his jaw, doing his best to appear unaffected but he was too late. I'd already seen it. Gina had always been able to strike a nerve with Jay. He seemed to value her opinion of him.

"He is a great catch, Gina," I said, coming to Jay's rescue.

"Uh-huh," she licked her lips, "is that why you tossed him back?"

Jay stiffened.

"I didn't toss him back. He was never mine to begin with. We had a mutual understanding."

She grinned. "Fuck buddies? Got it."

"Lindsay, can you tell me how it is you have never had a problem with me dating other women?" Jay asked, staring over the tops of his sunglasses at me. "Any other girl would claim they don't want any commitments but they'd be livid the second they realized other women were in the mix. I try to make you jealous and it backfires. You poke fun at the girls and go out drinking with them. Why is that?"

Grinning, I swayed my hips. "Easy. Myra says I think like a man."

"Oh, it makes sense now." He pointed at me. "You watch your ass. I do not want to have to tell you again that you cannot be out after dark without one of us, Lindsay. Hell, anymore, you should think of having at least two of us with you at all times. Day or night."

I saluted him. "Yes, sir."

"Lindsay, joke about anything other than your life."

Gina thumped her hip into Jay's upper thigh. "I'm with Playboy."

I arched a brow as Jay slid his arm around her waist. I could have sworn he inhaled deeply. His eyelids fluttered and for a moment I honestly thought he'd lift her up and kiss her.

She cringed and ducked out of his grasp. "Aww, I meant I'm with, uhh…never mind."

"Hey," Jay said, glancing around. "I like to think I'm an all-right looking guy. Lindsay liked me well enough. I must be okay boyfriend material."

I laughed so hard that I clutched my stomach and bent forward.

"It's that funny?"

I nodded. "Jay, your problem is you know you're hot and you suck at being a boyfriend. The very idea of being with one woman only makes you cringe. Why do you think I even started dating you?"

Crossing his arms over his chest, he gave me a hard look. "I take it the reason was not my award-winning personality?"

"Nope."

Gina raised her hand. "I got this one. It's because Jay isn't ready to settle down so you had no fear of being in a real relationship." She glanced at something over my shoulder and stopped laughing instantly. "Umm, but that's neither here nor there. It's water under the bridge. Let's go, Jay. I want to ride you…err…your bike with you."

Jay wagged his dark brows. "Oh, you are more than welcome to ride me, fiery one."

"Fiery one?" Gina rolled her eyes.

I looked over my shoulder at Exavier and shrugged. "Gina, have no fear. He's a nice guy but we just met and he's leaving after today. We'll never see him again so I hardly think we need to tiptoe around feelings he doesn't even have for me. Though, he does have an uncanny ability to just blend in and make me feel so comfortable I tend to forget he's there. Besides, he's a musician. All they do is groupies. I bet his list of conquests could wallpaper my office."

Gina's eyes widened. "Lindsay!"

"What? It's true."

"Exavier," Jay said, tilting his head a bit. "You want to go grab a beer or something? They can talk about us all the way through their next class. If one isn't dancing on a pole, the other is beating the shit out of someone under the guise of self-defense classes. I need that kind of life."

I beamed. "Aww, thank you. Even if he says no, thank you, Jay."

He growled. "Don't give me that 'what a good job' look because I fall for it every time and then you have me running around being a better person. I hate that. So, Exavier, what do you say?"

Exavier took so long to answer that I thought for sure he'd say no. "Yeah, I could go for a beer. My truck is at the center. I'll walk Lindsay back and meet up with you there. Gina could catch a ride with you then."

A knowing look passed between Gina and Exavier. She nodded. "That is a great idea. Come on, stud, I want a ride."

Chapter Five

"So, wanna tell me about your relationship with Jay?"

Putting my hands in my front pockets, I walked along next to him and shrugged. "There's nothing really to tell. He's a close friend."

"That's all?" he asked, tipping his head just enough that the sun caught the highlights in his hair, making them look almost purple.

Puzzled, I stared at him. "Correct me if I'm wrong, but didn't you come to me for help with something I don't even do anymore? Or was I mistaken? Did you come to ask me non-stop questions about my personal life?"

"I'm sorry. I was under the impression that we were bonding."

I snickered and rolled my eyes. "That would mean that you've shared things about yourself too. You've shared nothing. Who are you currently fucking?"

He came to a grinding halt. "Excuse me?"

"Oh, I could have sworn you were trying to find out if I was sleeping with Jay so I thought turnabout was fair play."

His brows drew together as he cleared his throat. "I've been in and out of situations with women that can't possibly qualify as a relationship. Currently, I'm not seeing anyone—yet," he added, locking gazes with me. "I'm pushing thirty-one, have been into music since I was kid. My closest friends are my band mates. Growing up, I had the biggest crush on this girl who had such a lust for life it was infectious. That's about it for me." He pointed at me. "Your turn."

"I'm not sleeping with Jay. Technically, I am if you count him staying over but he only does that on rare occasions and he's normally in the guest room. But as far as actual intercourse goes, we've not been using one another for sex for quite some time now." His eyes widened. I was on a roll so I went with it. "I have had a relationship that certainly counts as one. Any other males who have entered my life have been 'just browsing' without the option to buy. There, now we've bonded." I winked.

For a second he looked so serious, so deep in thought that I found myself instinctively going to him. I put my hand out to him. "Xavs, how much do you really want to bond?"

"You have no idea."

"Want to see my grown up version of dolls, or kind of see them, anyways?"

He laced his hand in mine and heat flared between us. "Yes, Linds. I'd like that very much."

❧❧❧

Exavier shifted awkwardly in the rocking chair and swallowed hard. "Linds," he whispered. "I've never held one before."

Smiling, I placed the newborn baby on his chest. The yellow gown they'd given him should have made him look ridiculous, but it didn't. His large hand came up and engulfed the premature baby's entire body. Exavier stiffened. I nodded. "You're doing great."

"It's so tiny."

"She is one month old today and she's doing really well now." I slid around to his side and bent down. Our faces almost touched. It didn't feel out of place to be that close to him. It should have. "Do you want me to take her?"

"No," he said, his voice low. "I mean, I don't mind holding her longer." He glanced at the machinery next to him. The baby was hooked to various cords, all of which had concerned Exavier when we'd first arrived.

"Then I'm going to go get her brother."

"Brother?" Exavier cast me a worried glance.

Running the back of my hand over his cheek, I held his gaze. The connection I felt to the man before me was so intense, I found myself blinking back tears of sheer joy. Seeing him holding a child felt so right, so natural to me that before I even realized it, I was leaning into him, kissing his cheek and brushing his hair back from the side of his face. "She was a triplet."

"Was?" he asked, not seeming to notice or care that I was treating him as if I'd known him all my life.

I closed my eyes slightly and drew in a deep breath. "They came too early. Way too early and, well, she and her brother survived."

Nodding, his gaze flickered to the baby. "Does she have a name?"

"I'm sure she does, but the nurses here don't tell me any of their names."

His brow furrowed. "Why?"

"Because I asked them not to, Xavs. They're fragile little humans. So precious. So new to this world that sometimes they don't stay in it very long. I can deal with a lot. I can't deal with that. I wish I could heal every last one of them. I wish I could make them stronger." Tipping my head, I averted my gaze and stepped away from him.

"Why come here if it's that hard on you?"

The tiny baby in his arms stretched, causing her little body to form a peanut-shape on him. She opened her mouth and inserted her fingers. The action left Exavier staring down at her with an expression so full of emotion that I thought it best to give him some privacy.

I backed out of the room quietly. Shutting the door, I turned to find a row of nurses standing there, each one looked more excited than the next. Jakki, a woman who had been working there since I'd been coming in, motioned towards the closed door. "Girl, you've got about two seconds to tell us why Exavier Kedmen is in our hospital, holding our babies, with our Lindsay?"

The rest of the line of miracle workers nodded in agreement. It had completely slipped my mind that Exavier was some hotshot famous front man. Apparently, that wasn't the case with the rest of the world. I knew the women wouldn't run to the tabloids and start vicious rumors. They were good people. I also respected Exavier's privacy and thought it best to change the subject if at all possible.

"He's an old friend of mine."

What made me say that?

Jakki glanced at Karen. "I told you she knew him from her days of dancing professionally. I bet he took one look at Lindsay and knew if he wanted to win his way to her heart, he'd have to understand what's in it."

"Pfft, umm, no. We're just old friends. I brought him down here with me because I missed the babies. Nothing more."

Being a liar was becoming a habit with Exavier around.

Karen went toward the observation window to the room Exavier was in. Her jaw dropped. "Oh my gods, Lucy is lifting her head and I think she just smiled at him." She rubbed her eyes. "I must be hallucinating."

"You must," I said, putting my arms out. I did my best to block the name Lucy from my head but it was impossible. "Brother, now. My arms ache."

Jakki didn't waste another second. "Go ahead back in with your boyfriend. I'll bring the little one in."

"He's not my boyfriend. I told you already. He's an old friend." Knowing it was pointless, I cracked the door open and took a step in to find Exavier humming and rocking Lucy. Her color looked so much better than it had only minutes before that I, too, thought my eyes were playing tricks on me.

"Exavier, how are you doing?"

He grinned and it melted my heart. "Lucy and I have come to an agreement. I'll stop being nervous holding her and she'll give life her all."

"You heard them talking about you?" I asked, shocked his hearing was that good.

"What?"

I pointed towards the door. "The nurses, they were shocked to see you here in their hospital so they gave me the third degree. They also slipped up and mentioned her name was Lucy."

Something I couldn't read passed over his face a second before he nodded. "Yep, the walls are thin here."

As I watched the premature baby who had seemed so fragile only moments ago, seem to thrive, I shook my head. "You've got the magik touch, Xavs."

"Umm, yeah, something like that." He winked. "I'd like to hold her brother now, if possible and then we should get back. I believe that I've stood your friend up."

It hit me then. "Jay."

Nodding, he lifted Lucy up towards me. "Here. She wants you now." The conviction with which he said it made me believe he was right, Lucy really did want me to hold her. It was ludicrous so I ignored it.

"Xavs."

"Yes."

"We've officially bonded now."

Chapter Six

Gina stared at me with wide eyes as she artfully juggled several bags of Italian food. "You took Exavier Kedmen to the Neonatal Unit?"

"Yes." I kept walking, carrying two pizzas. We'd decided to go for dinner together at the center since it was closed and we didn't really feel like sitting in a stuffy restaurant or going home quite yet. Besides, I was still a little worried about Exavier. He and Jay had left for a beer mid-afternoon and I hadn't seen or heard from him since.

Jay had called Gina to let her know that he still had "the rock star" and they were fine but wouldn't be back until late. Since I didn't own Exavier I had little say, but I was concerned about he and Jay getting into a physical fight. Jay was a were-wolf. Exavier was just a human. Serious damage could be inflicted.

Myra had spent the greater part of the evening trying to convince me that Jay would never hurt Exavier, especially since Gina told him who he was. I didn't put much stock in that theory. Jay was the type of man who could give a shit about someone's status.

"Myra, can you ever remember our girl dragging anyone other than Harly with her to the hospital?"

"Nope and I for one am happy. I hope Lindsay gives him a chance. She's never going to settle down and find Mr. Right if she's surrounding herself with Mr. Can't Remember Their Names."

I laughed. "Watch it, babes, or I'll be knocking one of those bottles of wine you've got there over your head."

Myra leaned forward, as if she was going to hand me a bottle. "I dare you."

"It's no fun threatening you. You aren't scared of anything."

"Yes, I am. I'm scared of bad hair days, leaving you in charge of your own schedule, finding out my mother will be visiting, watching movies of the week..."

Rolling my eyes, I snickered. My friends were so far from what people considered normal that I wasn't exactly sure what the baseline for it was anymore. Not that it mattered. I loved them for them. For some freakish reason, they seemed to love me for me.

Misfits. There's no other term for us.

"Oh, news on the Gina love front," Myra said, lifting a well-defined brow. "I think she has someone serious in her life."

There was no way I could hide my surprise, so I didn't bother. "No way."

Gina huffed. "Hey, don't act so shocked. I'm lovable too."

Myra and I exchanged looks and burst into laughter. "Oh, yes, extremely lovable. Snuggly even."

"Mmmhmm, like a rabid teddy bear." Myra snorted and we all began to laugh. She was always so proper. To see her letting herself go was a treat. It wasn't that she was opposed to having a good time. No. Myra was just driven and businesslike in almost all aspects of her life.

We turned the corner towards the center and I bumped Gina with my hip. "Spill it. I want to hear all about him."

"You're joking, right?" She lifted a handful of bags and used them to point at me. It was cute. I didn't bring that to her attention though or I'd end up wearing the contents of the bags. "I'm not letting you two anywhere near Paco."

She froze.

I gave her a big grin. "Oh, we've got a name. Paco. Mmm, is he hot?"

"The better question would be," Myra licked her lower lip, "is he hung?"

"Yeah because we've got a strict 'no guppies allowed' policy," I added, doing my best to keep a straight face.

Gina shook her head. "Huh?"

Myra began wheezing and I knew she got my reference to her ex-boyfriend, "The Shark". The memory of her walking around a party shouting "guppy" would be stuck in my head forever. It was a classic Myra response to an issue—attack with claws erect. I think it had something to do with the cat shifter in her. She was born to be a bitch.

"Hey, since when did the boys who hang here start leaving their stereo and stuff laying around the parking lot?" Gina asked, slowing her pace. "Aren't they afraid that it'll get stolen?"

I stared at the portable stereo sitting on the ground and glanced around the parking lot. It was covered in a blanket of darkness and hard for me to see too far out. It didn't matter that my night vision was nowhere near as sharp as Myra's. There was no way the boys would leave their things lying around unless something happened.

"I don't smell blood," Myra whispered, moving in close to me. "You head into the center. We'll check it out."

The idea of any of my kids being hurt ignited my already short fuse. "No. I'll help."

"Lindsay." Gina shook her head. "This isn't up for debate. Take the food in and we'll be in as soon as we know they're safe. Call Jay's cell phone. Let him know what we found. He knows these kids as well as any of us."

My protests would only waste time. Nodding, I turned, allowing Gina to pile her bags of food onto the boxes of pizza I held. She did and I made my way towards the front entrance. I was just about to call upon my power to assist with opening the door when I spotted movement out of the corner of my eye. Unsure if it was supernatural or not, I didn't want to risk exposure so I made sure to turn my body enough that they couldn't see if my hand actually touched the door before using my magik.

I made my way in and headed straight for Myra's office. Setting the food on the counter, just outside of her door, I freed my arms and lunged for the phone. The last thing I wanted to do was call a no doubt drunk Jay and drag him away from whatever he was doing, unless he was beating up Exavier, but I didn't have a choice. The kids in the neighborhood meant too much to me to risk them.

When Jay's voice mail picked up, I sighed. "Jay, Gina wanted me to call. Something's up at the center. Could be nothing though."

The second I hung the phone up, music began to play. It sounded like it was coming from the back of the rec center, near one of my dance rooms. It was dark, haunting and nothing I could remember using in any of my routines.

"What the…?"

Confused as to why anyone would be back there, I headed in that direction. I didn't sense evil so I wasn't concerned about that. I was more worried the kids might have made their way into the center and gotten into things they shouldn't have. The last thing I wanted was for one of them to get hurt.

Pushing open the door to the room I used for pole dancing classes, I froze as the music seemed to surround me. "Hello?"

No one answered.

Uneasy, but unwilling to lose my mind over the fact that music was playing, I kept a careful watch on my surroundings as I walked to the stereo. A man began singing and I instantly recognized the voice. It was the one that always seemed to call to me on some bizarre level. It didn't disappoint. No. His deep voice seemed to enter my body, carefully caressing me from the inside out. Before I knew it, I was swaying to the music.

"I thought you'd like this, my love."

My blood ran cold as a hand fell upon my shoulder. "S-Stan?"

He pressed his mouth to my ear and his body to mine. "You missed me, didn't you? I knew he was lying. I knew he wasn't your boyfriend. You were too scared of him to speak out, weren't you?"

"Stan?" My mind seemed be having issues wrapping around the idea that he'd not only gotten into a locked building but was directly behind me. "You're wrong. He is who he said he was."

Stan seized hold of my hair and tipped my head back. "Lies. I've been watching you. He just entered your life today. He means nothing to you. Nothing!"

"You're hurting me."

He wasn't but he seemed to be all about making me want him. Maybe he'd actually be concerned if he hurt me or not.

"You've left me no choice." A cold steely blade pressed against my throat.

So much for my theory that he wouldn't want to hurt me.

"Why are you lying to me, Lindsay? Don't you want me too? Can't you feel our connection? How we're destined to be together?"

Think.

"Yes. I feel it and it scares me, Stan. The feelings are too intense," I said, almost gagging on my own words.

He eased his grip on me and pulled the knife away from my throat. "I knew it."

I turned to face him. He stood there, dressed in black from head to toe. His light brown hair was barely there. For some reason, he thought going the way of the buzz cut worked for him. It didn't.

I let my gaze casually flicker over the twelve-inch bowie knife in his hand. The only vibe I got from Stan was that he wasn't stable. At this point, I didn't really care. The man had pushed me too far.

"I can get rid of him, Lindsay." Stan's eyes were glossy and his face paler than I remembered it being. "I can make it so that he never scares you again."

As his words sank in, my hands clenched. He would not harm one hair on Exavier's head. My power crackled around me, not giving a damn if I wanted to let it out or not. Good thing I didn't care.

Stan looked around. "What's that?"

"Don't you know? You seem to know everything else about me." I let more power out, mentally directing it to coat him. It did and he gasped.

"Lindsay?" The fear in his eyes spurred me on. I released more magik and let it move in on him, suffocating him slowly. Stan went to his knees and the strangest thing happened—I laughed.

I'm not a monster.

The thought jerked me out of the moment, giving Stan a reprieve from my magik. He lunged at me, knife in hand. I let instincts take over. I pivoted my entire body and jerked my arm out of the way while twisting. Time seemed to still as I watched his knife hand move in slow motion. I caught hold of his wrist with my right hand and brought my left arm up quickly, elbowing Stan in the face.

I felt it then. Evil moving in on us.

Stan's entire body convulsed. The minute I realized that the evil had centered on him, it all made sense—the pale face, glossy eyes, erratic behavior. Demonic possession. I took control of the knife, and Stan, or whatever was in charge of him, rushed out the door.

I ran after him, knife still in hand.

Suddenly, it sounded like the music was coming from every direction. It should have scared me. It didn't. It was oddly comforting. It made me feel safe.

I caught sight of Stan turning at the end of the hallway, into the lobby. Picking up my pace, I kept going. As I came around the corner, Myra and Gina were walking in. "Get down!" I shouted, sensing the highly charged buzz of demonic power in the air.

They did, just in time. A blast of negative power flared over their heads and bounced off the wall. It came hurdling back towards me. Jay picked that moment to come rushing through the door, followed close by Exavier. I did the only thing I could think of. I screamed. It worked. They both stopped and the power just missed hitting them. Instead, it kept coming at me.

The last thing I wanted to do was take a direct hit from the dark evil thing zipping at me so I dropped into the splits and pressed my upper body to the floor. It came so close to hitting me it moved my hair.

"Lindsay?" Jay asked, staring down at me with a questioning look on his face. "Uhh, what are you doing? And why did you scream? Why the hell do you have a knife like that?"

Talking bad. Fighting good.

Looking at Myra and Gina for assistance, I drew a blank. Jay was a were-wolf. He understood creepy things. Exavier didn't. Telling Jay would mean telling Exavier. Not good.

Gina got to her feet. "Uhh, didn't you see that huge rat?"

"A rat?"

I wasn't sure I heard that right but since something had just tried to kill me I wasn't really all that focused at the moment.

She glared at me. "Yeah, a *rat*."

My lips pursed as I realized she was doing her best to keep Exavier from knowing the truth. Forcing a smile to my face, I did my best to ignore the presence of evil all around us and appear normal. "Oh, right. It was big. Huge. Mongo. Uh, you should go with Myra and Gina to find it. Now!"

Jay's brow furrowed. "Why in the hell would you get down closer to it? Were you hoping to stab it with your Rambo knife?"

As much as I wanted to invent some creative reason for being on the floor, I came up blank. It didn't matter. The buzz of negative energy increased again. I locked gazes with Myra. "Return of the rat. "

Her gaze darted around as she shook her head. "I don't sense anything."

Gina nudged her. "You know that she senses shit way before we do."

"You're sensing rats now?" Jay asked, putting his hand out to me.

I gave him a droll look and made a mental note to slap him for being too stupid to figure out I wouldn't just drop into the splits for no reason in the middle of the lobby. He'd probably like the abuse and start begging me to spank him. It would be a very "Jay" thing to do.

Exavier moved up next to him and swallowed hard as his gaze raked over me. "You're *very* limber."

"What's with the music? Loud enough for you?" Jay grabbed my hand and lifted me to my feet with ease, still oblivious to the fact bad things wanted us dead. Some detective. Geesh. I kept the knife close to me. "Hey did you know that this song is one of—"

The power went straight at Jay's head. He didn't seem to notice it. The urge to smack him myself was great. Somehow, I managed to hold back, opting instead to go with a more subtle approach for keeping his head attached to his shoulders. "It's one of those songs that makes you want to bang your head." I grabbed him by the back of the neck and pulled hard. "Great, lesson one on having rhythm." The power whizzed past him and he stiffened.

Sniffing the air, he jerked to the side a bit and went on full alert. "What the fuck was that? It smelled like sulfur and evil."

Hallelujah, the man may not be quite the moron I thought him to be.

"That was her saving your ass from—" Gina stopped in mid-sentence as she stared at Exavier. "Why lesson one in rhythm of course."

Myra took me by the arm. She pressed her mouth to my ear and whispered, "We can't sense it until it's almost on us. How do we fight it?"

I stared around, waiting for any sign of its whereabouts. "I don't know but I do know that Stan is still in the building. He held a knife to my throat."

"Stan is here!" she shouted. "And he held a friggin' knife to your throat? That knife? Christ, Lindsay!"

Smooth. Way to keep a low profile.

Jay went for his off-duty weapon. "That's it. I'm going to kill that little fuck."

"Stan, the guy from earlier?" Exavier asked, crossing his arms over his chest. "I'm with him. I vote we kill him."

I let out a nervous laugh. "Would you believe me if I swore to you that Stan is, for the most part, harmless?"

"No," they said in unison. I wasn't sure if I was happy they seemed to be getting along or not. Having them gang up on me wasn't all that great.

Chuckling, I locked gazes with Jay so he'd know I was serious. "Would you believe that he's been possessed by a demon and isn't responsible for his actions?"

Gina snorted. "The *devil* made him do it."

I saw the protest start and then instantly stop as Jay registered what I was telling him. "Oh, gotcha. Explains the sulfur smell. Never thought the defense would hold water."

I sighed. "Well, I should really help Gina and Myra look for the *rat*. I'm sure Stan is long gone. In fact, I think I saw him running out the back door. But, if we run into Stan, we'll give a shout out. Why don't you and Exavier start eating? Everything's on the counter."

Jay shook his head. "Hell fucking no. You are going to take your entirely too cute ass over there and sit down. Exavier and I will go find Stan and escort him to the station or the nearest church."

I snorted. "You want to take Xavs?"

I couldn't hold my laughter in. Gina followed suit. Exavier arched a brow. "Something funny with the idea of me lending a hand in the extermination process?" The way he said it made me wonder if he was on to us. Considering that would mean he completely understood demonic forces *were* at work and doing their best to kill us, I highly doubted it.

Jay scratched the back of his head and appeared to be in pain. "Lindsay, Exavier and I might have gotten into a tiny scuffle. Umm, I can vouch for him. He'll be fine."

I slapped Jay upside his head and glared as I pointed the knife at him. I wouldn't use it on him but it did make me feel special in a scary kind of way. "You picked a fight with him, didn't you?"

"Ouch. No. Not exactly." He cast me an apologetic look. "Okay, maybe I did. But I'm telling you that—"

I smacked him again, suddenly more concerned with Exavier being attacked by Jay while I wasn't there to protect him than the evil that wanted me dead now. "You will go over there and get things ready for everyone to eat. I am going rat hunting. I can't have them running loose in the center. It's a safety and health hazard."

"Lindsay."

I glared at him. "I will deal with you later." Glancing at Exavier, my expression softened. "Did he hurt you?"

A tick developed in his jaw. "No. He did not hurt me. Thanks for the vote of confidence."

The last thing I wanted to do was placate a famous guy during a fight with evil but he looked like he needed it. "You're a singer, honey, I lowered my expectations significantly already."

Gina laughed so hard she squealed. I would have joined her but I sensed the evil again. Spinning, I watched both halls, unsure which it would come from. "Rat's back!"

"Shit, so are the kids!" Myra shouted. "Gina, I thought you told them they couldn't hang out here after dark."

"I did."

The evil picked up on our panic. I sensed the instant it decided to go after the group of teenagers who frequently spent an hour or so at night doing various forms of street dancing in our parking lot. With the flux of paranormal activity we had as of late, they'd have been better off taking their chances partying at the mouth of hell. Though, the center was fast becoming a candidate for a back door entrance to the land of eternal damnation.

The mass of evil appeared out of nowhere and ended up heading straight at Exavier. I let my power up, knowing it would want the lure of pure energy. It took the bait.

Myra gasped. "Lindsay, no!"

Shrugging, I grinned and took off running towards the other hallway. I didn't make it out of the lobby before Myra was on my heels. I sensed another wave of evil coming straight at me, while the one behind me remained constant I knew I was in trouble. I came to a grinding halt. "Oh, bad idea! Really bad idea!"

Seizing hold of Myra, I knocked her to the side, put the knife in my mouth and launched into a back handspring. The power went under me just as the other crossed above me. I slashed at it, catching it and making it break apart for a moment. Coming to my feet, I sensed it headed at my head and ducked, grabbing Gina around the waist as I went. The knife fell from my grasp, and scattered across the floor.

Gina screamed as it crashed near her head. "I can't see it, Lindsay! Where is it?"

"What do you mean you can't see them?" I asked, watching as the power formed two dark shadows. "They're huge! Like Exavier and Jay kind of huge!"

Myra grabbed Exavier and pulled him down. "Try to play along, Mr. Right. I can't marry you off to her if you're dead."

I kicked her ankle. "*Rats* aren't deadly."

She grinned. "Good to know you were more concerned with rats than me trying to marry you off."

Gasping, I watched as the power went for Jay. "Jay, two o'clock."

He dropped just in time. "Any idea how to stop it?"

"Mirrors?" Gina asked. "Can we trap its essence there?"

"No," I said, unsure why. "We have to find something that can absorb it without letting it consume them."

Myra rubbed the bridge of her nose. "How is it you know these things?"

"I don't know. Lucky, I guess. Why?" I glanced at Exavier and smiled. "Umm, rats. Hate 'em."

"Seriously, Lindsay, you always know things you shouldn't."

I shrugged. "I paid attention to the stories a little boy used to tell me about bad things and what did and did not work to stop them. He used to tell me the stories to make me feel better about monsters in the dark. Instead, he made me scared to sleep without a light on."

Gina snorted. "Only you would play with kids who would creep you out."

"Exavier never creeped me out," I said defensively.

"Exavier?" She glanced at Exavier and bit her lower lip. "Didn't realize you knew him *that* well."

"What? Not him. A different one. The one I knew was smaller. Much smaller and well, smaller."

She laughed and I sensed the evil trying to lock in on the kids again. I jumped to my feet. "Hey, asshole, you aren't touching my kids. You don't really want them when you could have what you came for."

"Don't you dare unmask yourself—" Myra's words were cut off when I kissed her forehead and let my power out again. "Dammit, Lindsay!"

"I won't let it hurt my kids. End of discussion. I'll find a way to at least trap it. We can call my dad and ask what to do if we have to. He'll lock me in a tower somewhere to keep me safe when all is said and done but this stuff won't be able to hurt anyone. Well, I'd love to stay and talk but," I glanced at the other hallway and sensed it coming, "it's really pissed right now. Umm, if I can't figure out how to contain it, you might want to call the voodoo guy."

Jay grabbed my wrist and shook his head. "You're leaving. Now."

"Let go of my wrist. I have a rat to contain."

"Lindsay, I'm not fucking joking. Exavier will back me on this."

Glancing at Jay, I let a pouty face come over me and blinked as if I was going to cry. Jay sighed and let go of my wrist. I grinned. "Damn, all these years and I really could have just gone with crying to get my way."

"Get back here. You're going to get yourself killed." He reached for me and I dodged his grasp, moving to the beat of the song still thumping through the center.

"It, like you, will have to catch me first." Stripping my outer shirt off, I wagged my brows as I threw it at Jay's face. "Duck!"

He did. The evil raced past his head before heading straight at me. Jay shook his head. "Goddammit, Lindsay, none of us are sensitive to it like you are. We can't help if we can't see it."

The evil sent things flying around me. Papers scattered about the lobby and one of the computer monitors tipped over. I'd have fun trying to explain it all to Exavier later. If he had too many questions, I'd call my dad and have him wipe his memory. Really, though, something as serious as that was a last resort.

The knife came hurdling at me. Gina tackled me just in time to prevent something ugly from happening and the knife stuck into the wall. I glanced at her and then the knife. "Can we file that under me showing up for self defense class today? I think it counts."

Something struck my stomach and sent my body into Gina's. The force sent us both sliding across the floor. Gina screamed. "Jay do something! I felt the force it hit Lindsay with. It's not playing games."

Exavier was suddenly next to me, touching my shoulder. Myra grabbed for him but he avoided her. "Linds?"

I smiled. "Sorry, slippery spot on the...umm...floor." I rubbed my stomach and glanced around the room, trying to sense the evil.

It loomed up behind Exavier and I did the only thing I could think of, I grabbed hold of his leg and yanked him to the ground. "Get down!"

The evil swept past, narrowly missing him. Panting, I stared down at him. Every ounce of me wanted to shout the truth about supernaturals but I liked the guy too much to lose him. If I could even keep him as a friend, I'd be happy, so I went with a lie. It certainly looked as though I'd need to call my father later. "Umm, hi. There was a big spider by your head. Sorry about knocking you over."

I rolled off him quickly and got to my feet. Myra helped him up and stared around the room. "Lindsay, why am I getting the feeling this thing was just toying with us?"

No sooner did she say it then the shadows merged into one and took shape. For a moment it looked like thousands of bugs crawling in and out of each other and then it took on the look of hundreds of snakes. Its outer form was of a man but it was grossly unnatural to see it composed of bugs and snakes. My stomach churned as my pulse sped.

I took a step backwards and bumped into Myra. "Do me a favor."

"What?"

"If that thing gets in me, behead me. Set my body on fire and whatever else is standard protocol. I don't want to be brought back after that thing..." I did the "creepy crawly" dance and shuddered. "I hate bugs and snakes. Eww. Myra. Eww. Ohmygod, maggots. I'm going to throw up."

"Maggots? Lindsay, what is it? Where is it?"

The demon smiled and I cringed. "Call the prince to you now," it hissed.

A stray snake leapt free of it and landed on me. Screaming, I spun in a circle to get it off me. It slithered up my arm, around my back and I couldn't stop the heebie-jeebie quiver that tore through me.

The demon laughed as Myra tried to calm me down. "Honey, what's going on? Where is it?"

I threw the snake free of me and shook. "S-snakes. It threw one on me."

"Baby, you freak at the sight of a spider," Jay said, sliding up behind me.

I stared at the demon before me with wide eyes. "Jay, tell me you can see it. Please. Tell me I'm not crazy. Right?"

Jay reached for me. "Tell us where you see it, Lindsay. Exavier can help. We just need to understand. It's attacking under our radar. You're about ten times more sensitive than all of us put together and it knows it."

The demon smiled. "Yes, he speaks the truth. It is how it must be for the mate of the prince."

"What? Why do I have to be so sensitive? I'd be perfectly happy not having to stare at your ugly ass."

"Lindsay, what did it say?" Myra asked.

I forgot about attempting to hide what was going on in front of Exavier and simply spoke. "Something about me having to be this sensitive because of the prince guy." I let out a nervous laugh. "What? Am I supposed to just know when the prince of darkness is pissed off and head it off with a good joke? A nice massage? Sex?"

"Yes," it said, making me take a huge step back. "That is exactly what you were made to do, Lindsay." The way it said my name was pure evil.

I shook my head. "Fuck that. I'm no man's mood ring. And I'm not scared of you." I swallowed hard. "Okay, not *that* scared of you."

"Lindsay, tell us where it is. We can stop it," Jay said.

The demon tossed snakes at Jay and I lunged forward, using my body to block his. Several of them bit down on my arms and I screamed out. Gina's breath caught. "Holy shit! You're bleeding."

The demon laughed. "Take me to the prince."

Knocking the snakes free of me, I stomped on each one. I should have been screaming hysterically. How I wasn't, was a mystery to me. "I don't know where he is."

"What?" Myra asked. "What are you talking about?"

"T-the prince. It wants the prince."

"Lindsay." Exavier tried to move in front of me but I wouldn't let him. It was bad enough I'd have to beg my father to wipe his memory. Letting a creepy crawly demon kill him would never do.

"No, I'm good. It's just a really big rat who seems to be looking for, umm, royal cheese? I'm an animal sensitive in addition to being a witch. Did I forget to mention that?"

Why I even bothered to keep up the charade was beyond me, but I did.

The demon centered its gaze on me and smiled. Maggots crawled through its mouth. "You lie. Take me to the prince or I will destroy your friends."

It was my turn to glare at it. "Listen, you maggot infested, snake tossin', bug crawling piece of demonic defecation—I'll," I took a step towards it, letting my power flare, "give him to you. Come on."

"Lindsay?" Gina asked.

Another snake came at me. I pointed at it. "If that thing touches me, I'll…"

"You'll what?" it asked, not seeming impressed with my threat.

"I'll open the gates to heaven, like a good little wife of a dark husband would do to calm things down."

It took a tiny step back, enough for me to know it feared good.

"Can you open the gates?" Gina asked before covering her mouth.

Myra snorted. "Yeah, well, always good to try to bluff."

"Who is bluffing?" I asked, glancing at the demon. "Now, do you want me to take you to him?"

"Yes."

I glanced at Gina. "It's getting hot in here. I really hope a fire doesn't break out."

"Huh?"

Myra's gaze went to the fire extinguisher. "Oh, right. Fire. Bad to have with rats. For sure. I think we have some added protection in the back."

"Funny you should say that because I just happen to have the address this particular rat needs in the back as well. It's in my day planner. In my locker. Near the showers."

I didn't really have it but the demon didn't know and I wasn't about to point out the fact I was lying.

Gina snorted. "You? Organized?"

Myra shot her a nasty look. Gina shut up.

"Lindsay, where is this rat you're talking about?" Exavier asked, picking me up and setting me behind him before I could get a word out.

The demon moved forward and just missed touching Exavier. It hissed as it stared at him. "Interesting. This one reeks of—"

I let my power flare. "No! You will not touch him."

The overhead light sizzled and a bolt of energy shot out of it, hitting the demon. It screeched and I smiled. The smell of burning flesh filled the air. Still, I smiled.

Gina gasped. "Holy shit, I told you. See, Jay! I said she can make lightning bolts. You didn't want to believe me."

"Don't," I let another bolt of energy fly at it, "be silly, Gina. No one can create lightning bolts. I bet the rat chewed through something vital and now we'll need to call someone to fix it as soon as our little problem is taken care of."

"Lindsay, you're doing the scary voice thing we talked about," Jay said, glancing over at me. "The one you used when you locked me out in my underwear and it just happened to pour down rain with lightning that night. Tell us where it's standing and we'll take care of it. No more. You were sick for weeks after the last stunt. It drains you too much. Just tell us where to aim."

The demon moved again, apparently wising up that it shouldn't stand in one place too long. It watched Exavier with hate in its eyes. In an instant, it was tossing snakes and bugs at him. Spinning, I kicked them away and stood before Exavier protectively. "I said that you were not to touch him. I am positive I didn't stutter. I can and will bring the wrath of some heavy shit down upon your head if you continue to push me on this. He is not to be touched. None of them are."

"You lie," the demon hissed. "You do not have the power to call upon—"

"I don't? Really? Hmm, news to me."

I used my power to change the music. The sound of monks chanting filled the air, as did the sound of thunder. The demon looked around, hissing and snarling, clearly taken aback by the newest revelation. It threw a handful of snakes at Exavier. I shot another bolt of electricity out, unsure how I was controlling it as well as I was but not really caring.

Myra looked up. "Gina, isn't this the same chanting music that kept playing while Lindsay was healing from the accident?"

"Yes."

"What is it?"

Exavier put his hand on my shoulder. "It's an ancient chant used to call upon the protectors of good, of life. It asks them to protect the ones you love and to keep them safe from the evil that surrounds them."

We all glanced at him. He shrugged. "Music lover."

I laughed. "It's gibberish. Something that a little boy I once knew taught me. It's not Latin it's…" I stopped just short of saying ancient Fae.

Myra stood tall. "Same guy I sent a guitar to? Same guy who taught you about creepy shit? Same guy who is named Exavier too?"

"Yes, why?"

She snorted. "What do you mean why? You wrote a note with this on it for him. I stuck it in the package with the guitar."

"Note?" My eyes widened. "No, Myra. That wasn't my card to him. That was something I dreamt about. Something I couldn't stop thinking about. Not…Oh, shit, you sent him that?"

The demon tried to go to black mist again. I thrust another bolt of energy at it. "I'm trying to talk to someone here, asshole. I get that you have no respect for anything but you will stand there and allow me to finish. Understood?"

"Who are you talking to?" Jay asked, holding his off-duty weapon. "Just point in the general area. The last thing I want to do is carry your limp body out of here tonight, Lindsay. I can guarantee Exavier doesn't want that either. We spent the afternoon getting to really know each other, Lindsay. Trust that he can handle whatever comes our way—mentally and physically. Please, just glance at the damn rat. All I need is a hint."

Ignoring Jay, I stared at Myra. "Tell me you didn't send that with it."

"Why? It's nice. Kind of pretty."

"In an embarrassing sort of way. Sure. You're right."

"Lindsay Willows, how is this more important than the other thing?" Jay asked, clearly annoyed with me.

The demon hissed. "The prince now, bitch."

"Bitch? Me?" I rolled my eyes. "Oh please, Gina calls me worse by the time I'm through my first cup of coffee in the morning. Be a bit more original." I could feel my power waning. Drawing in a deep breath, I readied myself for what I needed to do. "Myra?"

"Yes?"

"Battery's about out of juice."

She, Gina and Jay did a collective deep breath and Myra lunged for me. The demon extended its arm. Snakes reached from it towards Myra. She came to a grinding halt. "I hear hissing."

I did the only thing I could think of, I began to speak in Fae to it. "No. I'll take you to him but if you harm any of them, the deal is off. I will see to it that you're in a place I've been told he roams. You have my word and my life should I forfeit."

Exavier thrust an arm out and seized hold of my waist. I glanced at him and smiled. "What's wrong?"

His expression didn't lighten. If I wasn't positive that no one but a fellow Fae and the demons that hunted them could understand ancient Fae, I'd have thought he understood me.

"Why is Lindsay speaking French at a time like this?" Jay asked.

"That's not French," Myra said, glaring at me. "What did you just say?"

The demon backed away from Myra. "I shall follow you. You are now bound to honor our agreement."

I nodded and spoke in Fae to it. "You have my word, a place I've been told he roams."

"Very well. We agree to your terms."

"*We*? There are more of you?"

It attempted another sickening smile. "Your knowledge of the old language is extensive. It is true. You are the prince's mate."

I pointed towards the opposite hallway. "He went that way, guys!"

Everyone but Exavier ran off as I stood facing the demon. It began to circle us slow at first, seeming to eye us up. "He watches over you as though he were your mate. Who is this man?"

"A friend of mine from childhood," I said in Fae and then shook my head. What had possessed me to say that yet again? I glanced at Exavier to find him staring at me with a shocked expression. Did he understand me?

My power began to drain again and Exavier picked that moment to pull me to him and hold me close. In an instant, I felt my strength gaining. Puzzled, I stared up at him. A slight smile played over his lips. I wanted to explore this more with him, see if it was a fluke or not but the demon had other plans.

"Give me the prince or I will have the others attack your friends."

"Fine, but I'm only showing one of you so they better be ready to follow," I said, in Fae as I pushed off Exavier.

"Linds?"

"Tell me you're not like me." I held his gaze. "Tell me you're not scared of the dark."

"No. I'm not. Why?"

I glanced up at the lights and let my power free. It shut them all down, rendering the center in a state of complete darkness. My night vision was better than the average human but nowhere near a shifter's. I took off running down the opposite hall I'd sent Myra and the others down.

I could feel the demon, hot on my heels as I ran. Another wave of evil came directly at me and I knew then it was one of the demon's buddies. I came to a grinding halt.

"The prince, now!"

"She lies," the other said.

I let out a nervous laugh. "No. I didn't lie so much as I stretched the truth. See, everything that comes looking for him talks about his power over the demons and the things belonging to hell. I'm just thinking of a creative way to send you back to hell." I shrugged. "See, technically not a lie. Just not a 'hand you the prince' either."

"Kill her," the demon said coldly.

The power slammed into my stomach and lifted me up and off my feet. Screaming would have required air, of which I currently had none. I struck something solid and instantly had a pair of large, warm arms wrapped around me. The evil shrieked and then dissipated as if it was never there. There was also no pain. There should have been pain.

"Huh?"

"You okay?" Exavier asked, hugging me close to him. The lights flickered back on but it wasn't my doing. "That floor's pretty slippery."

"Slippery what?"

He turned me in his arms to face him and the second he did, heat flared through me. We were so close that my lips feathered past his. He tightened his hold on me. Every ounce of me wanted to wrap my legs around his waist and demand he fuck me. I held back.

"Um, thank you," I whispered, my lips still close to his.

His blue eyes seemed to see through me and for a moment, I forgot anything but him existed. "I can't have my choreographer breaking her leg or anything. I need her," he paused and crowded me against the wall, "to be in," he exhaled deeply, "perfect health."

"I never agreed to be your anything."

Exavier ground his body to mine just right, leaving his thigh between my legs. As he leaned in, his leg rubbed past my clit, causing a deep shudder to move through me as moisture flooded the apex of my thighs.

"You like me, Linds. As much as you don't want to, you do."

Opening my mouth to object, I found Exavier's finger pressed to it, silencing me. "No. You said it earlier. We officially bonded. Don't analyze it and don't second guess it." He smiled. "And don't assume because I'm a singer that I am useless in every other area of life."

"Xavs," I kissed his fingertip without thought, "I was only joking with you. I really don't think you're useless. I was just..."

Kiss me.

For a second I was sure I'd heard Exavier's voice in my head. The really strange part of it was how much I truly did want to kiss the man.

Touch me, Lindsay.

"W-what?"

Exavier moved his body against mine even more, his lips hovered just above mine. My nipples reacted, hardening. As my gaze raked down Exavier, I noticed I wasn't the only one having issues with things getting hard. I swallowed, trying to get the lump in my throat down as I stared at his clothed erection.

Kiss me.

My gaze went to his and I was powerless to stop myself. I brought my lips to his gently. The second I went to open my mouth, I sensed someone coming.

"Is it gone?" Myra asked, coming down the hallway at us. She gave Exavier a pointed stare. "Fuck her later. I need to talk to her a moment."

"Myra!"

"What? Like the attraction between the two of you isn't thick enough to slice. It's all I can smell. I'm about to make him take you to your office and take care of the problem."

My breath hitched. "Myra!"

"I refuse to apologize for wanting you to have a night or two or ten of mind-blowing sex. Oh, I'm not opposed to you making a long-term commitment to him. He's kind of cute. I could get used to seeing him around here more."

Mortified, I dropped my forehead onto Exavier's chest. "There's no place like home. There's no place like home." I glanced up and found Exavier smiling down at me.

"It didn't work. You're still here."

"Yeah, I know."

Myra grabbed my arm. "Time out. I need to know if any more rats are here."

"Rats?"

It hit me then. "Oh, rats. Got it." I felt out with my power but found nothing. I shook my head and Myra clapped her hands.

"Goodie. Let's eat."

Jay rounded the corner. His gaze met mine before going to Exavier. "There's no sign of Stan. He's gone."

Myra clapped again. "That settles it. Let's eat. Insane extermination attempts and possible crazed stalkers always make me work up a good appetite."

Chapter Seven

I stared up at the gymnasium ceiling and laughed. The wine had been going to my head for the greater part of an hour but that still hadn't stopped me from drinking more.

Gina threw a wadded up napkin at me and grinned. "Stop laughing at me, Lindsay. I'm not kidding. I really did want to be a marine biologist when I was little. That or Santa but his gig was already taken."

I snorted. "Ohmygods, I went to the zoo with you and you screamed when the baby shark swam past the glass in the aquarium."

"Hey!" Gina threw another napkin at me. "I didn't say I'd be good at it, only that I wanted to do it. It doesn't matter. Life had something else in store for me." She locked gazes with me. "Did I ever thank you for spending the first few weeks with me after I found out what I was? I was so scared, Lindsay. It was all so new, so terrifying. But you weren't fazed. You didn't even scream when that thing popped out at us."

Rolling onto my stomach, I thought back to when we were teenagers. It was the summer before our freshman year of high school when Gina had started experiencing weird hot flashes and strange bursts of energy. We took up running together to help blow off some of her newfound steam. It didn't take long before we not only figured out that Gina was a slayer but that creatures we couldn't begin to imagine lived among us.

Sure, I understood growing up that my father was half-vampire and half-Fae. I also knew my mother was a full Fae. That didn't mean a thing. In my mind, they were special. End of story. I had no idea that horrible, evil things with similar powers existed and thrived off death and destruction.

Gina let out a soft laugh. "That thing that popped out at us was huge. He kept talking about all the horrible things he was going to do to us. I remember being terrified but what I remember most was how you told me it was okay to be scared."

I snickered. "It was all I had at the moment. I was too scared to think of anything earth shattering."

"You talked your dad into letting you spend almost every night at my house for weeks because I couldn't deal with what I was, what I was expected to do. At least not until I took my first one to…"

I closed my eyes and nodded. "To protect me. I remember. You switched gears. Stopped over-thinking and just started doing. It was amazing, Gina."

"Thank you for being there for me, Lindsay."

"Don't thank me, Gina. Don't ever thank me. So much of what you've done has been for me. It's me who owes you a thank you."

"No," Myra said, lifting her heels in the air while she lay on her side. "It's the male currently known as Prince that owes Gina a thank you."

"He owes you one too, and Jay," I said with a tiny laugh.

Jay let out a choked snore and opened his eyes slightly. "Huh?"

I winked at him. "Go back to sleep. But could you lie on your side? You're snoring—again."

He rolled onto his side and tossed his arm over Gina. She tossed it right back at him. "Nice try."

He smacked his lips. "I thought so."

Myra nudged Jay. "Don't go there. She has a man. Paco."

"Paco?" Jay asked and let out a deep, throaty growl. Myra glanced at me. It was something a supernatural male typically did to lay claim to what was his. When Myra lifted her brows, I knew she was wondering the same thing I was—was Jay into Gina?

It made perfect sense. He originally gravitated towards me to inquire about her but she'd paid him no mind. Ignoring hot men was a very Gina thing to do. If she wasn't in the mood to screw them, she didn't really bother with men in general. Killing things seemed to satisfy most of her basic needs.

"We are not bringing Paco into this discussion." Gina went to smack Myra on the butt but ended up falling onto Jay instead. He tried to bear hug her and she pressed her fingers to his windpipe. "Hug me and die."

Jay looked all too pleased with the idea of being "punished" by Gina.

Exavier chuckled, drawing my attention to him. Since I had Myra on one side and Exavier on the other, I decided to slide back a bit so I could see them both. Glancing over at Exavier, I found him staring at me. He lay on his side with his head propped up on his hand.

"What?" I asked, unsure why he was looking at me like that.

"I've missed you, Linds."

"Well, I only spent like five minutes in the bathroom. I had to pee and then there was hand washing time on top of it."

Myra snorted. "Such a lady. Your mother would die if she heard you say the word pee to him."

"My mother can't die. She will live forever—telling me what a loser Tim was and how I need to move on and get over him."

"You and Tim weren't an item. He was one of your closest friends. How the hell can she say you need to get over him?" Gina asked, pushing Jay's hands off her once more. "Boy, I'll rip off whatever touches me next."

Jay actually looked as if he were entertaining the idea of risking life and limb to touch her again. I shook my head, hoping the man would be smart enough to leave well enough alone. He tried to make contact once more and she made a quick move. He jerked his hand back and licked his lips. "Mmm, such a fiery one."

"Because," Myra said, sighing, "Lindsay will take some secrets to her grave and knows it's better to let her mother and father believe her troubles come from Tim's death—and only Tim's death. Can you even imagine what her father would do if he knew the truth?"

Not wanting to discuss it any further, I focused on Exavier. "Okay, you know about us. Tell us something about you."

"I don't just sing." He touched my chin and smiled. "I also play guitar."

Gina put her hand up. "I knew he played the guitar already. New one."

"I'm trying to convince Lindsay to go on tour with me."

Myra shook her head. "Nope. Can't use that one because I already knew you wanted her to."

Jay tilted his head back and stared at me. "I didn't."

"Still doesn't count. So, hush up Mr. Wanted to Be a Cowboy When He Was Little." Myra snickered and Gina actually spit wine on herself.

"A cowboy?" she asked, doing her best not to choke.

Jay groaned. "It's not that funny."

She leaned in and kissed his cheek quickly. It was a very un-Gina like thing to do. "Oh, but it is."

I couldn't help but laugh too. "She has a point. It is funny. I'm guessing that's what's up with the motorcycle. You were too urban for a horse."

"Ha, ha, I love being teased by a woman who wanted to be a princess ballerina when she was little."

"Hey, technically, I did accomplish the ballerina portion of my dream, Wild Jay Hickock." I pushed to my feet and swayed. "Whoa."

Exavier was on his feet in the blink of an eye, steadying me. He laughed. "You okay there?"

The music in the stereo advanced and the song that came on was signature Gina style. She jumped to her feet. "Let's dance. You can tell me all about Ruland."

Jay groaned.

Ruland was the artist playing now. Gina absolutely loved everything he did. He had a hip-hop, crunk style. He also wasn't too bad on the eyes. This song in particular had been a source of contention between she and I ever since she found out I spent a summer touring with him.

"Come on, Lindsay. I know you know who this girl singing with him is. Tell me."

Grinning, I began to dance to the slow, rhythmic, thumping beat. "I've got no clue."

Liar.

"You have to know. Whoever this is shows up on some of the discs you brought back from…umm…well, the ones you had when you retired."

I appreciated her reluctance to talk about Tim. That being said, I didn't want to tell her the truth. It was too embarrassing for me.

"Please."

"I have no idea. Stop bothering me about it."

Gina tossed her hands in the air. "Fine. Tell me everything about him."

"Ruland is a nice guy. He's not nearly as tough as he portrays. I'm not saying wimp. I'm saying nice guy. He was probably my favorite artist to tour with because he's a natural dancer. He gets into whatever you tell him to do and takes it to another level. Many a night he'd come to me with an idea about what we could do with the dancers. His ideas were phenomenal."

She danced her way over to me and grabbed my wrists. "If I beg will you whisper it to me? I've only been asking non-stop for five years."

Jay grunted. "For the love of my sanity, would you please just confess it's you?"

Exavier laughed. "Yeah, right. Linds doesn't sing."

"Yeah, nice try, Jay." Gina rolled her eyes.

Getting to his feet slowly, Jay yawned and closed the distance between us quickly. He pulled me into him and began to dance with me. He had to be the best dancer out of all the men I'd dated in my life. I loved to tease him about having no rhythm but that wasn't the case. The man could do amazing things with his pelvis.

Tilting my chin, he forced me to look into his dark brown eyes. Since most of what Ruland did in this song was say the words, not sing them, Jay didn't hesitate to jump right in. I couldn't help myself. I began to hum. Soft at first and then louder.

Jay rocked our bodies and leaned into me. Getting lost in the moment, I let my guard down and dropped the one thing I rarely did in front of others, I started to sing. All I really did was repeat Ruland's lyrics. It had originally come about during a late night rehearsal. It ended up being something he asked me to put down on a track with him. I still wasn't sure why I gave in.

When Jay got to the portion of the song about having sex, he slapped my ass and made me yelp. I stopped singing and tried to find enough skin to pinch his sides. I failed. "I'm so going to let Gina beat you up."

"Promise?" he asked, looking hopeful. He stepped back and winked. "I'd like to present the mysterious voice."

Gina and Myra gave me dual shocked looks. I shrugged. "What? Stop, he tricked me. I wouldn't have subjected you to that under normal circumstances. The only reason Jay knows is because I," my cheeks flared red, "apparently like to sing in the shower."

"And I," Jay said, cocking an eyebrow, "apparently like sneaking up on you while you're showering."

Exavier cleared his throat and Jay took a giant step back from me. "Wait, did I say that? I meant to say I'll never again be near you while you're showering. Ever. Ever. Nope. Never. Can we go back to Paco? Who the hell is Paco and why haven't I met him yet?"

"Jay?" I'd have questioned him further but the reality of it all hit me. My face fell. "Oh, shit. I just sang in front of a guy who is famous." I glanced at Gina. "He is famous, right?"

"Huge," she said, putting her arms out for effect.

"Jay, hide me and then take me home so I can slit my wrists."

"No can do, Lindsay. For one, I like your wrists. For two, the only man who will be taking you home from here on out is that one." He pointed at Exavier. "Trust me when I say that any other man who dares to try will not even live to get to regret it."

Myra put her hand on her hip and gave me a pointed stare. "Got something you want to share with the group?"

I shook my head. "No. I'm as lost as you are. I just met the man this morning."

It was Jay's turn to laugh. "He's looking a little jealous. My guess is because he didn't know you liked to sing. Tell him why it is you keep it a secret."

"Cuz, I can't sing."

"Lindsay."

I rolled my eyes. "Fine. Because when I was little the boy I told you about, my first crush, used to tease me for it. So, I hate doing it around anyone."

Exavier gave Jay a hard look. "Nice. So happy I filled you in on everything."

"Oh, like you had a choice," Jay spat back. "Now, the question isn't how pissed you are at me. It's how long are you going to stand there? You could be home bedding your woman."

Shocked, I took a step backwards. "Well, by all means, Mr. Kedmen, don't let us hold up a booty call."

"In that case," he stormed towards me, "let's go." Exavier ducked down and swooped me up and over his shoulder with ease. He smacked my ass cheek and turned to head out of the gymnasium.

"Put me down!"

"Can't do that. I need you for the bedding of my woman to work."

I wiggled, doing my best to break his hold. "What the hell am I supposed to do? Tell her you're a really nice guy under all that rock star shit?"

"Nope. You're supposed to tell me you're looking forward to being bedded."

My stomach dropped as his words sank in. "I'm not sleeping with you."

He slapped my ass again. "Who said anything about sleeping?"

Chapter Eight

Turning, I snuggled into the warmth Exavier was letting off and sighed. I should have been freaked out by the fact I was sleeping with a man I just met. I wasn't. It helped that we were just sleeping. No sex, sadly enough.

Exavier shifted slightly and I knew he had to be uncomfortable. At six-foot-five, he didn't exactly fit in the back end of his SUV, even with the rear seats down. When he'd first plopped me into the front seat, claiming to want to bed me, I wasn't sure what he was going to do. After driving around for a while and talking about nothing in particular, I dozed off for a bit. When I woke, we were parked far off the highway in the country.

I didn't even want to think about how long Exavier must have driven to get us out of the city and somewhere secluded. I didn't care. It felt good to be away from it all for a bit. It felt good to be with him.

He'd been asleep too, with his head back, still sitting in the driver's seat. I think I shocked him almost as much as I shocked myself when I woke him and suggested we climb in the back and rest. I would have suggested a hotel but he looked exhausted and there was something carefree and fun about what we were doing.

As I lay there, snuggled close to him, I did my best to ignore the fact that I had to urinate. It wasn't like it was convenient timing. Giving in, I went to open the back door and Exavier wrapped his arm around my waist.

"Hey," he whispered. "Where are you going? It's dark out there and you hate the dark."

I slid my hand over his and yawned slightly. "I know, but I have got to pee."

The laugh that came from him was deep and sexy. "You are so unaffected by being around famous people."

"Oh, what? Famous people don't pee?"

He chuckled and went to sit up.

"You aren't coming with me. I, unlike you, can't just whip it out and go. I'm not exactly sure how I'm going to pull this off but I know that I can't wait much longer. Ah, man, I can't not wash my hands. Forget it. I'll hold it."

"Lindsay, I can drive us to find a rest stop or something."

Smiling, I touched his cheek. "Honey, you're tired. I can feel it. Sleep. I'll be fine."

Something passed over his face and the dimly moonlit vehicle prevented me from fully soaking it all in. "Baby, I don't mind."

Baby?

It hit me then, I'd called him honey. I huffed. "I can't believe I pet named you. What the hell is that about?"

"You like me. Admit it."

I nodded. "Fine. I like you. Happy now, Mr. Rock Star?"

A shiver moved over me as cool air seemed to settle in near me. Exavier reached for me. "Linds?"

"Hmm, you throw some serious heat off when you sleep. I move away from you and then I'm suddenly freezing." I shivered again.

Exavier sat up as best he could in the tight space and pulled his tee shirt over his head. The lighting may have been dim but it was good enough for me. It also helped me get a look at his upper body. I drew in a sharp breath as my inner thighs tightened. He was chiseled perfection.

I bit my lower lip and willed myself not to reach out and touch him. It was hard but I managed.

"Here," he said, pulling his tee shirt over my head and dressing me as if I were a child. It seemed to radiate heat, much the same way Exavier did. "I'll find us a place to stay for the night. Somewhere with a bed, blankets and a bathroom."

"Xavs, I don't need your shirt. I'm…"

He pressed his finger to my lips. "You were cold. I'm hot. Works out well. I had an excuse to shed some clothes. I was going to roll a window down but when you snuggled against me I felt the goose bumps on your arms."

I couldn't help but smile. "Thank you."

He winked at me.

"This is nice. In case I forget to tell you that."

His brow furrowed. "What? Lying in the back of my SUV? I get that you've no idea who I am or what my status is but trust me when I say I could spring for nicer accommodations."

Laughing, I shook my head. "No. This is nice. Being out in the country, away from the hustle and bustle of the city. It reminds me of camping. I used to make my father take me and my friend camping. My father hated every second of it. He's not the outdoor type. Definitely more the lap of luxury kind of guy but he did it because I liked to look at the stars and he wasn't keen on letting me and a little boy camp out alone—regardless how much he liked the boy."

Exavier propped his head up and lay lengthwise, watching me close. "What did you like most about it all?"

I laughed. "Well, I can tell you what I didn't like. I didn't like it when a snake wandered into my sleeping bag. I was so scared, I couldn't even scream. I just lay there paralyzed with fear. Xavs crawled over my father, who was out cold, reached into my sleeping bag and grabbed the snake like it was nothing. I have no clue how he knew it was there or that I was terrified. He just did. He took it away from the tent and then came back in, worried I was still scared."

I shuddered at the thought of snakes and the demon we'd encountered earlier. "I still hate snakes. You know, most little boys would have laughed and probably chased me around with them. Not him, he even got rid of his pet one because he knew it scared me. That was sweet."

I rubbed my inner arms, where the snakes from the demon had bit me, and shivered. "Eww, I hated the bug and snake part of camping. I'm very glad nothing creepy can get in here with us now."

"You never outgrew that fear, did you?"

I shook my head. "No. I did try to get used to them because he seemed to like them so much, but I couldn't." I smiled down at him. "Want to know what I liked most about camping?"

"Yes."

I went to answer him but stopped as I sensed evil nearing at an alarming rate. Closing my eyes, I swallowed hard. "I really need to pee. I'll, umm, be back in a little bit."

It wasn't a complete lie but it wasn't the complete truth either. I needed to lure the danger away from Exavier.

"Linds?"

I smiled. "I'll be right back." I didn't wait for him to respond. I climbed out of the SUV and looked into the darkened wooded area. Shutting the door behind me, I let my power run over the SUV, coating it with protection. I also assured the doors were locked and bound with my magik so Exavier couldn't get free and get hurt.

He tapped on the window. "Lindsay?"

Glancing over my shoulder, I found him struggling with the door, looking puzzled as to why it wouldn't open. His eyes widened and I knew without looking something bad was in front of me. "Lindsay, get in the car! Now! Open the door! Now!"

Something growled and I forced myself to look ahead. The minute my gaze fell on three wolves, I backed up fast, hitting the SUV.

Exavier pounded on the glass. "Open it, Lindsay! Stop blocking me!"

Stop blocking me?

Did he know I was using magik to keep him in?

The wolves growled again and I knew from the buzz of energy they were emitting they were not only evil but lycans as well. I put my back to them in order to be able to face Exavier. Drawing on the quarter of me which was vampire, I pulled those powers forward and let my magik run over him. I was powerful enough to mesmerize some mid-level demons and had done it before. Yet, the idea of doing it to Exavier killed me on the inside.

"You do not see this as it happens. You forget I was here with you, that I even exist. You were driving back to meet your band, got tired, pulled off. You'll leave here now and not look back. Go!"

I didn't have time to force more power at him. He was human. He wouldn't need it. The wolves began to circle me. I turned and pressed my back against the vehicle.

"You can do this, Lindsay. Gina, Jay and Myra spent the last three years teaching you what to do," I said to myself, not caring who heard. "Calm down."

I couldn't seem to follow my own advice. I was scared beyond words. All I did know was I needed to move away from the vehicle. I took a tiny step forward and one of the wolves picked then to morph into a man.

He stood there, staring at me with glowing eyes of burnt orange and claws emerging from his fingertips. I stiffened. He laughed as he drew in a deep breath.

"Fear. It's divine."

I couldn't help but stare at all of him. It wasn't like he'd opted for clothing or anything. He laughed again as he took one clawed hand and stroked himself. "Yes, your fear is divine. As are you. Stories have been told of your beauty but we believed them to be greatly exaggerated. We were wrong."

Gina's words rang in my head. *Lindsay, don't see them as monsters. See them as dance partners.*

Myra's voice was next. *Regardless who they are, they're still men.*

Jay even snickered at the comment and how true it was.

Deciding to take a different approach to my normal running, since I was in the middle of nowhere and couldn't outrun lycans, I called upon my power. The minute I felt the first raindrop, I knew it was working. Thunder sounded in the distance. The other two lycans took human form as well, both naked and looking all too horny at the idea of having found me near the woods.

The one with the orange eyes stepped closer to me. "You know what we've come for—the prince."

Exhaling, I chased away my fears and let my gaze rake down him slowly. "Pity. I was hoping you came for something else."

Thunder boomed and lightning flashed as the rain increased. Pulling Exavier's tee shirt over my head, I made sure to take my red tank with it, leaving me in only a tiny, red stylish sports bra and black, boot cut stretch pants. They rode low on my hips and I tugged them lower as I locked gazes with the main man. My long hair clung to me as did my remaining articles of clothing.

The man tipped his head back and howled. I wanted to cringe and run. I didn't. I held my ground.

"Dispose of the human in the truck and then we can see what the female knows," the man said, arching a brow and licking his lower lip.

Dispose of the human? Exavier!

I went to glance over my shoulder and the man used the opportunity to advance on me before I was prepared. He jerked me to him, grinding his erection against my lower stomach.

I heard a car door opening and tried to look back. The man before me made his move. He went to slide his hand down my wet pants and my power surfaced to protect me. A bolt of lightening struck right next to us. The force threw us apart. I went high into the air and hit the SUV with a thud. My knees sank into the muddy ground and rain continued to pour around me.

The man charged at me, growling, his eyes ablaze. I waited until he was directly in front of me before giving in and rolling to my side. I got to my feet and leaned back quickly, narrowly missing taking a clawed hand to the head.

"You will beg me for mercy, bitch," he spat. "You will watch as we kill your friend and then you will beg for your life."

He came at me again. I spun, stepped to the right and watched as he went right past me. Turning, he glared at me. "Oh, yes, you will beg me for mercy."

Something inside me snapped. A sick sounding laugh erupted from me. Tipping my head to the side, I let the rain wash over me as I smiled. "You are oh-so-very late on that threat, asshole. I spent four days begging. First for the life of another and then to die. I'm all begged out."

I let my power out more, recreating the sound of the music Gina often played while she taught me to defend myself. The man looked around, clearly taken aback by the development. "What the…?"

"This," I smiled, "is what Gina calls ass kickin' flavor. And you," I winked, "are what she calls expendable."

He came at me and I moved my body as a full unit, countering his advance with a kick to the back of his knee. He went forward and I wasted no time in leaping into the air, anticipating his strike before it came. The whoosh from his clawed hand just missing me was a reminder of how very deadly a game this was.

Drawing one leg up, I extended the other and kicked him in the side of the head, knocking him away from me. I landed on my feet and watched as he tried to come at me again. I went into a jumping front kick, holding my arms firm and waiting to strike until I was almost to the height of my jump.

As my foot came into contact with his chin, I couldn't stop the surge of power that moved through me. Lightning crashed around us again, this time launching me high into the air. I tucked into myself and did my best to sense the ground coming up on me. I landed on one knee, my breathing ragged and my pulse racing. The music stopped as I felt my power waning.

The sound of growling caught my attention. Glancing up, I watched as one of the other men was attacked by the biggest black wolf I'd ever seen. It took him down with ease. The man with the orange eyes advanced on me again.

The black wolf lunged at him, striking his throat and ripping it from his body. The wolf turned, setting its sights on me. I froze. The closer it got, the more the pressure in the air around me increased. My fingers slid over material on the ground and I glanced down to find myself clutching Exavier's wet tee shirt.

127

Looking up, I swallowed hard as I willed the gods to hear me. "Please keep him safe. I don't care about me, just keep Exavier safe. Please."

I closed my eyes, preparing for the inevitable. A huge wave of thunder boomed. I gasped and opened my eyes to find myself sitting in the back of Exavier's SUV. I was completely dry and still dressed. Exavier was lying on his side with his head propped up, smiling at me.

"So, what did you like best about camping when you were little?" he asked, staring up at me with beautiful blue eyes.

I glanced out the window but found no sign anything had happened. Confused, but relieved to see him in one piece and safe, I scrambled towards him and threw my arms around his neck.

"You're okay."

Laughing, Exavier went to his back, allowing me to lay on top of him, hugging him tight. I clung to him, savoring the sound of his beating heart. The hardness of his chest and the warmth of his body left me feeling safe in his arms. Rubbing my cheek against his smooth skin, I exhaled deeply.

"Linds?"

"Hold me," I said, so low I wasn't sure he heard me.

The second his large, muscular arms wrapped around me and held me close to him, I gave in to the trembling that had wanted to overtake me. Whatever had made me hallucinate an attack was enough to let me know if anything happened to Exavier I'd be devastated. That should have scared me. It didn't.

Exavier kissed the top of my head and caressed my back. "I've got you, baby, nothing can get you with me here. I promise."

"Huh?"

"Snakes, they can't get you in here," he said, not sounding extremely convincing but I didn't care. "So, how about I get us somewhere so you can use the bathroom?"

"No." I hugged him tighter. "This is good. Right here, with you is good."

"But, Linds..."

I eased my grip on him long enough to go for his lips. Pressing mine to his, I silenced him. A tiny chuckle escaped him. "That's one way to shut me up."

Moving down next to him, I kept my arms around him and he did the same to me. "I'm tired, Xavs."

"Get some sleep, baby."

⚜️

"Feeling better?" Exavier asked as I came out of the restaurant's restroom.

I nodded, my eyes wide. "Yes. Much."

He handed me a cup of coffee and leaned against the wall. A table full of women kept glancing in our direction, their attention focused solely on Exavier. He didn't seem to notice or care. "What do you want to do today?"

Holding the coffee like it was a precious artifact, I stared up at him and shrugged. "What do you mean? I thought we were heading back. I need to stop in at the rec center and—"

"Lindsay, I called Myra. Everything is running smoothly there. You don't have any classes today. So, what do you want to do?"

I gave him a droll look as I sipped my coffee. "I need a shower."

"I think I spotted a lake down the road." He arched a black brow. "We could go for a dip."

"Exavier!"

The table full of women converged on us, crowding Exavier against the wall. "It is him. I told you it was."

One of them thrust her chest out and tipped her head a bit, doing her best to look sexy and alluring. She looked like an idiot to me but I wasn't a man so it might very well work with them. The way Exavier glanced at me told me he was concerned with how I'd take the fact he had fangirls.

Arching a brow, I took another sip of my coffee and smiled. One of them touched his arm and went to ruffle his hair. Instantly, my calm disposition went south.

"Ohmygod, look at him. He's even more gorgeous in person."

Gag.

I rolled my eyes.

One of the women gave a strained smile as she tried to fit her hands around Exavier's biceps. "He's huge."

"We have tickets to your show," another said, reaching up to pet him, too. "He is solid. Mmm."

A short brunette glanced at me. "Are you his sister?"

My eyes widened as I choked on coffee. "Umm, no." I guess I could kind of see why they would ask. My hair was almost black but Exavier was tan, bronzed almost everywhere I was pale white. His eyes were royal blue and mine emerald green. Never mind. I couldn't figure out how the idiot came up with the idea of us being siblings. I did know it made my stomach turn, almost as much as seeing Exavier be pawed.

"Sing something for us, please."

"I can't get over how big he is. All muscle."

I'd had more than enough of it all. Setting my coffee cup down on an empty table, I rubbed my temple, doing my best to chase away the headache that was looming. "Oh, you should see how big his cock is. Giant. Rip you in two kind of thing. I'll be walking funny for weeks. Now, if you're done petting my husband...erm...Exavier."

They jerked back from Exavier and his gaze flickered to me. A slow smile curved over his lips. In a flash he was on me, lifting me up and wrapping my legs around his waist. He walked us towards the bathroom I'd just come from, ignoring the gasps from the women and pushed the door open.

The minute it closed behind him, he set me down and locked it. Grinning, he leaned against it. "Husband? Rip you in two, huh?"

My cheeks reddened. I wanted to crawl under a stall and die from embarrassment. "Sorry. It popped out. I didn't mean it. That made me sick to my stomach the way they were acting. I'll go tell them I was just being a bitch. Move."

"Hey, claiming the rock star guy is brave. People will no doubt come to pin medals to your chest." He put his hand out to me and I went to him, unsure why I did.

Kiss me.

Looking into his blue eyes, I tried to make sense of the voice in my head. It sounded very much like Exavier.

Kiss me.

My entire body lit with the need to be closer to him. I leaned into him and he wrapped his arms around me. The second I felt his clothed erection, my breath hitched and I did what my mind seemed to want. I went to my tiptoes and kissed him. It was long, drugging, intoxicating.

My nipples hardened as Exavier slid his hands up and under my red top. His fingers skated over my sides slowly, followed close by an almost searing heat. He claimed my mouth fully, taking lead of the kiss and making it fierce.

Touch me.

I obeyed, running my hands up his torso and groaning into his mouth out of a need to have him filling me. Exavier turned us, pressing his body to mine and pinning my back to the door. His tongue plunged into my mouth and I ate him eagerly, wanting even more.

Exavier ground his body against mine, continuing our fiery kiss. I couldn't make up my mind if I wanted to run my fingers through his hair or take his shirt off. I gave in and went with the shirt. It hit me then, what we were doing.

I was about to have sex with him in a public restroom.

"Xavs," I whispered, breaking our kiss and panting. "We should probably separate now or…"

His breath came fast and hard as he nodded. "I end up taking you against this door and giving those girls an earful while I," he ran his hand down my body and stopped just shy of putting it down my pants, "fill you. Rip you in two."

I moaned as I kissed his jaw line. "We can't do this here. We can't do this at all. I'll hurt you."

The manly chuckle that came from him only served to add moisture to my already soaked pussy. "Hurt me, huh? Mmm, we'll see about that but you're right about one thing. We can't do this here. But we will do it soon. I promise you that."

He took a step back and then came at me fast. He captured my lips with his and kissed me tenderly. As he broke away, he planted a tiny kiss on the tip of my nose. "Okay, now we can go."

Shaken from the raw display of attraction, I let him take my hand. He opened the door and nodded at the women still standing there. "My wife reaffirmed her assessment that I'm huge all over."

Exavier didn't give me time to protest, not that I would have. Instead, he spun me around and kissed me again. My toes curled and my stomach tightened as I clung to him, powerless to do anything but accept all he had to offer.

As he drew back slowly, his lust-filled gaze stayed locked on me. "We should eat before I take you back into the bathroom and have you instead."

I nodded, wishing he would turn me around and march me into the bathroom.

He smiled. "I love you."

That did it. It snapped me out of the sex-craved stupor I'd been in. My gaze darted around and I tried to pull away from him. He held tight to me and pressed his lips to my ear. "Oh, come on, they're eating this up, Linds. You can say it back to me. I'm your *husband* after all."

Cupping his face with one hand, I forced a smile to my face. "I'm starving. If you don't feed me soon, I'll be too worn down to let you have your way with me again."

"I love you," he repeated, not giving an inch.

I grinned. "Feed me."

"I love you." He kissed my neck.

"Yes, but will you love me when I leave you for a chef because he'll feed me?" I asked, artfully dodging repeating the phrase to him.

He slapped my butt playfully. "I don't share. Let's go eat."

"We should really get going. You have dinner with your parents tonight," Exavier said, his hand on my lower back.

133

Groaning, I picked my head up from its rather comfy spot on his shoulder and stared at him. "I don't want to. This is nice. I like smelling bad with you and doing nothing."

Exavier chuckled. "I smell bad?"

Burying my face in his armpit, I wrinkled my nose. "I think we could both use a shower but I don't want to leave here. In fact, leave me here. This shady spot is perfect. All except for the ants I'm trying really hard to ignore. I haven't been this lazy since I was a little girl." My brow furrowed as I looked up at the oversized maple tree. I was thankful Exavier had selected the spot. It was shady enough to keep me from having issues with my eyes. "In fact, I seem to remember wasting many a day under a big tree similar to this one."

"You do, huh? Was it with your friend? The one you had a crush on?" Exavier asked, picking blades of grass with one hand while caressing my lower back with the other.

I nodded. "Yep. As soon as the sun was at its peak, he'd insist we go hang out under this big tree he had in his backyard. I think he knew the sun bothers my eyes after a bit. So, needless to say, lots of time was spent under a tree. What about you? Anything stick out for you?"

Exavier reached down and adjusted himself. "Around you, sticking out *is* my number one concern."

I couldn't help but laugh as I snuggled closer to him. "You know, when you showed up at the rec center yesterday morning, I never imagined I'd be hanging out under a tree in the middle of nowhere with you, begging you not to make me go to dinner with my parents."

"What did you imagine you'd be doing with me?" he asked, adjusting himself again.

I licked my lower lip and did my best not to dwell on the fact that all I wanted to do was stroke his cock. "Stop doing that. I can't quit picturing you naked. I thought we had this talk already."

"Yes and the entire time you were yelling at me to stop drawing attention to the fact you have left me with a permanent hard-on, all I could think about was sinking into you so I blocked most of it out."

I let out a soft, shaky laugh. "Yeah, I had the same thoughts running through my head. I guess you're right. I need to get home and get cleaned up. I can hardly show up for one of my mother's horrible attempts at marrying me off smelling like this with ants crawling on me and grass in my hair."

"You smell wonderful and look beautiful. I think the guy will be more than happy to get the ants off you and pick the grass from your hair." He kissed the top of my head.

"Exavier?"

"Yeah."

"Have you ever felt this comfortable with someone you just met? I don't know if you picked up on Myra teasing me when you first arrived but I'm not known for this. In fact, by this point, I'd have fucked you and kicked you out of my place already. Kind of ironic considering you're a rock star and they're notorious for the same behavior."

Exavier stiffened. "Don't, Linds. I can't hear about other men and you."

I snorted. "Umm, Xavs?"

"Hmm?"

I glanced down at his hand on his clothed cock and bit my lower lip. Giving into the desire to touch him, I ran my hand down the length of him and slid my hand under his. My palm came into contact with the bulge in his pants and I cupped him. Exavier jerked, bucking me off.

Laughing, I rolled onto my back and stared up at Exavier as he held his clothed cock, his jaw slack. "Good gods, Linds, are you trying to get me to make a fool of myself and come before I even…"

I yanked my shirt over my head and slipped my shoes off. He stared at me with wide eyes. I kept going, sliding my pants off and then glancing at him. "Are you going to sit there or are you going to use that thing you've been sporting all day?"

"Linds?"

"What? If you don't want to, that's fine." I went to my hands and knees, being sure to position my body just right so my ass was aimed in his direction. I glanced at him and slid a finger under the back of my thong. "I hate it when they ride up like that. Where are my shoes? We can get going. I need to meet my parents and all."

Exavier moved up behind me, growling softly and pressing his body to mine. "I was trying to behave myself. This isn't helping. I think I have enough control for you to get dressed and to get you home without taking you but you're going to need to stop wiggling your ass in my direction."

"Hmm, that's a plan or you could just shut up and fuck me. Then you could take me back to the rec center so I can get my car, go home and get cleaned up."

"Lindsay." He rubbed against me.

"Consider it a parting gift, Exavier. For your time and company."

"You're coming on tour with me so there will be no parting, Linds," he said, moving his hand around and onto my stomach.

"I'm not going on tour with you. I'm retired. Now, I'm horny and know I have to say goodbye to you soon, so if you don't want to fuck me, please let me know. I'll get dressed and we can head back."

He held me to him and kissed the shoulder that had been injured in the panther attack. "Don't try to shut me out, Linds. It won't work. You can't flip a switch, toss a wall up and think you won't feel."

Taking his hand in mine, I slid it down, under my thong and over my mound. He stiffened. I let out a soft laugh. "Mr. Kedmen, I believe that's exactly what I'm doing."

Exavier sighed. "Get dressed, Lindsay. We've got to get to dinner."

"We?"

"Umm, I have dinner plans tonight too." He moved away from me. "Get dressed."

Shrugging, I went to grab my pants. A tiny green snake slithered through the grass near them. I screamed and threw myself into Exavier's arms. He chuckled and kissed my cheek. "It's okay, baby. It's a garter snake. It's harmless."

I shook as I clung to him, both of us on our knees, me clutching him for dear life.

He pointed at the snake. "Go. She doesn't want you by her."

I laughed at his antics but stopped the second the snake switched directions. It slithered off as though it had not only heard Exavier but understood him. "Xavs?"

"Hmm?"

"I'm sorry I tried to treat you the way I treat every other man in my life. I just, umm, you make me nervous in a good way," I whispered, ashamed of my vulnerability. I thought I was past that. Past the need to ever crave a man to the point I just wanted to be close to him for the sake of being close. I was wrong.

He kissed my forehead. "Please know, all I want to do is be in you. Trust me on this but I'm not letting it start and stop here, Lindsay. I want you with me. Agree to come with me. I need to hear you promise to be with me for longer than here and now."

Pushing off him, I grabbed for my clothing. "We should get back. We smell funny and other people are going to be required to try to digest food near us."

"That's a no on coming with me, isn't it?" he asked.

"I had a really nice time this last twenty-four hours. I don't think I've felt this safe and laughed this much since before the accident. Thank you for that." I slipped my shirt over my head and did my best to hide my emotions. The man behind me had somehow done the unthinkable, he'd breeched my defenses.

"Linds."

"We should get going."

Chapter Nine

I hit the lock button on my keychain and stood tall. With the three-inch stiletto taupe heels I had on, I now hit six foot exactly. I smoothed my hands down the front of the floor-length dress I'd decided on. The shiny satin insets on the shaped bodice kept me from looking like a tan bean-pole. My matching handbag barely fit my cell phone, ID and extras in it but it had the all important lip gloss so I couldn't complain too much.

Two long black waves of hair hung down the sides of my head while the majority of the rest lay in a loose upswept style. I headed up towards the restaurant's entrance and stopped the minute I sensed something in the area with me. The hair on the back of my neck stood on end and my heart beat fast.

"Not tonight. Please not tonight."

My pleas sounded pathetic, even to me. I could still feel it. The evil watching me. Hunting me. A dark shadow moved past me, fast. The stench of evil rode it. Gasping, I turned to run. I slammed into something massive and solid. I brought my power up fast and readied myself to use it. Whatever I hit felt safe but I knew *we* weren't.

"No," I whispered, jerking backwards and almost falling. I didn't care. Looking behind me, I tried to find the dark shadow. My chest rose and fell rapidly as I closed my eyes, not wanting to know what would attack me now. "I can't do this anymore. I can't."

A warm hand cupped my face and I couldn't hold back the tear that fell down my cheek. When the man before me ran his thumb over my cheek, wiping the tear from me, I calmed just a bit.

"Hey, it's just me, Linds."

Joy surged through me as the sound of Exavier's voice ran over me. Opening my eyes, my mouth dropped and I couldn't have formed a sentence if I tried. Tossing my arms around him, I hugged him tight. I wasn't sure I'd see him again after the way I'd left things at the rec center. I'd told him again I wouldn't be going with him and wished him well. He'd been reluctant to leave but in the end, he did. My chest had ached the rest of evening.

His strong arms circled me and he caressed my bare back lightly, making me shiver with delight. "Well, it's nice to see you too. I'm glad to see you missed me."

Pulling back, I collected myself and laughed softly. "Wow, sorry about that. I guess you can add that to my crazy file. It expands by the second you know. And I did miss you, more than I should have since I only just met you and we've only been apart about three hours." I took a good look at him and arched a brow. He wore a tan turtleneck with a black dinner jacket and black slacks. He looked amazing. If I didn't know better, I'd have thought we'd coordinated our outfits. "Hmm, I didn't realize front men for bands clean up so well."

His blue eyes raked over me. Suddenly I felt very self-conscious. I pushed a loose curl behind my left ear and shifted a bit. Exavier's gaze moved back up me and stopped on the hand near my ear. His brows drew together as he tipped his head slightly. "You have your upper ear pierced. I didn't notice it with your hair down."

I nodded, unsure why he seemed shocked by that. Touching it lightly, I smiled. "Yeah. This heart used to be a charm on a necklace someone special gave me. When I grew too big to wear it anymore, I had a friend of mine convert it to an earring and had my cartilage pierced with it."

"You look beautiful, Lindsay," he said in a hushed tone.

The feeling of being watched moved over me again. Turning my head slowly, I glanced around for signs of trouble. The minute I noticed another dark shadow, I knew they'd found me and wouldn't stop until I drove them away.

"It was nice running into you tonight, Exavier. You should probably go ahead in and meet with—"

Something growled.

"Meet with…umm…I think I forgot something in my car. Take care and enjoy your evening." I turned and bravely took a step forward. There was no way I was going to let them hurt Exavier. No. They would follow me. I knew that much about the enemy.

Exavier slid his arm around my waist and leaned down to me. "I'll walk you to your car and escort you in."

"No!" Panicked, I stared at him with wide eyes. "I mean, no, thank you. Go ahead and meet your party. I'm fine."

"If it's all the same, I'd rather stay with you."

It was plain to see that he wasn't planning on leaving me alone. Giving in, I nodded and turned around fast. "Right then. Let's get in there."

"I thought you needed to get something from your car?"

Another growl sounded. I took hold of his hand and walked as fast as I could in my heels. "It's not that important."

"Linds, is something wrong?"

"No. Don't be silly. What could be wrong?"

"Oh, this and that," a male voice said from behind us.

Turning slowly, I found myself staring into a pair of grey eyes. Their owner was my height and extremely pale. His white-blond hair hung to his shoulders. He smiled and I caught the hint of a fang. "Lindsay, how good to see you again."

Again? I didn't know the vampire but apparently, he knew me.

"Is this a friend of yours?" Exavier asked.

The vampire smiled, waiting for my answer. Patting Exavier's hand, I nodded. "Mmmhmm, do you think you could do me a favor? Could you leave a message for the Willows party? Tell them that I'm running late and can't wait to see what their surprise is. Make sure they know how much I *love* meeting new people." If my father didn't catch on that something was wrong with that message, he never would.

Exavier nodded. "Sure. I'll see you later then?"

"Mmmhmm."

Probably being carted out in a body bag but hey, it counts.

Exavier headed towards the entrance and I took a deep breath as I stared at the vampire before me. He smiled wickedly at me. "That was a very good girl, Lindsay. I thought I might have to kill your date as well as you. Even I tire of needing to dispose of so many humans."

"Who are you? I'm positive I don't know you."

He shrugged. "That is not important. All I wish to know from you is the identity of the dark prince."

I stood still, keeping my power near the surface and masking it from the vampire. "Why does everyone think I know the identity of this prince guy?"

He laughed and waved a hand of dagger-like nails at me. "Do not play games with me, Lindsay. You are his mate, his chosen one. You know who he is. Tell me."

"No."

The vampire appeared taken aback by my stance. "What?"

"I said no."

"Do you wish to die?"

I bit my lower lip to keep from either laughing or crying. At the moment it was a toss up. "That's a rhetorical question, right?"

"You have a smart mouth for a mortal woman. I shall enjoy cutting your tongue from it." Taking a tiny step towards me, he licked his fangs for show. "Tell me what I wish to know or I will unleash my legion of demons on you."

I snorted. This guy was full of shit. I, for one, wasn't feeling like dealing with his crap too. I'd have enough to deal with when I got to my mother. If I got that far tonight. "Since when did three shifters become a legion?"

He froze. "How is it you know this, human?"

"Mmm, going out on a limb here but I'm thinking I'm not as human as somebody told you I was. And let me just say that the last thing I want to do is get my hair wet right now so don't go pissing me off. Bad weather tends to follow."

Laughing, he took another step towards me. "You are terrified. I can smell it."

"Yeah, and you're dead. I can smell that too. Now that we have that out of the way, tell my why you want to know who the prince is?"

He snorted. "Simple, to challenge him and win is a great honor. Defeating him puts one in a position to rule."

"If you think you're powerful enough to take on the prince, why is it you need me to tell you who he is?"

Narrowing his grey eyes, the vampire snarled. "I grow tired of talking to you, woman. I shall kill you and then the date you seemed all too willing to keep out of harm's way."

"No you won't." It was childish, but completely called for.

"Yes, I will."

"Ooo, here's where I say 'no you won't' and we go back and forth until I call your mother something offensive. Let's skip all of that."

I waved my hand in the air and released a small amount of my power. Giving my voice an added "push", I spoke to him, "You will not harm the man I was with. When you see him again, you will look away, uninterested. He is not a target, not a threat, a simple human unworthy of your time. And you will issue the command to your slackies that he is not to be harmed or they will face your wrath."

Moving closer, I smiled as I continued to let my magik ride over him. "As you stand there, you're forgetting why it is you're even here. Did it have something to do with a woman? No. A prince? No. It will bother you, fester in the back of your mind until you can no longer stand it. It was something. You're sure of it. But what? Ask the shifters you brought. Ask them and force them to tell you. Don't listen to their lies of some prince you know nothing about or some woman. There is no mate. No position of power—just three lying shifters who will need to be dealt with. When you're finished, go to your master and tell him he is a liar. No such thing exists. Don't stop until he believes you."

Easing my power back, I smiled. "You were saying?"

"I was, umm, saying," he stammered. "You are…?"

"Gee, did you lose your place? I hate it when that happens."

He nodded. "As do I. Enjoy your evening, *madame*."

"You too."

Turning, I found Exavier standing there. His blue eyes held my attention as he shook his head slightly. My stomach dropped. "How long have you been there?"

Exavier put his hand out to me and the compulsion to go to him was great. So great I found myself almost running to him. The moment he took hold of my hand my power flared and rushed out of me. I yanked back fast as I tried to pull my hand free of Exavier's. He didn't let go or let on that he'd just taken a heady dose of my magik. Either he didn't notice or he absorbed it.

He pushed the doors to the restaurant open and whisked me through them. Drawing me close, he stared down at me with bedroom eyes, leaving me breathing heavily and clutching onto the backs of his arms.

"Ah, Ms. Lindsay, your father is expecting you. He is at…"

Exavier pulled me down the corridor, towards the main eating area, paying no attention to the man's attempts to seat us. He took his jacket off, released my hand for a brief second and handed the jacket to the man attempting to steer me to the table.

"Xavs, I need to go meet my parents for dinner."

"I know," he said, yanking me out onto the dimly lit dance floor. Small orchestral music played as other couples moved together around the area. Exavier drew me into his arms and held me close as he began to dance slowly to the music.

I stopped fighting and let him lead me. Staring into his eyes, I seemed to lose myself. Suddenly, all that existed was him. He kept his head bent a bit, allowing us to dance eye to eye. The intimacy it created left me sighing in his large arms. I drew in a deep breath, savoring his musky, fresh, morning dew scent. Our lips brushed, fire ripped through me and I firmly believed Exavier was going to kiss me. When he didn't, I was disappointed.

"Have you decided yet? Will you come with me?" he asked, his warm breath blowing over my lips.

Leaning up, I tried to capture his lips with mine but with the height difference he had the upper hand and kept them just out of reach. "Exavier."

A slight grin splayed over his handsome face. "Tell me your answer."

"Exavier, I already did."

He brushed his lips over mine quickly. "Are you willing to be mine? Will you leave with me?"

Closing my eyes, I tried to block the overwhelming surge of emotions tearing through me. I couldn't. Our lips touched again. This time I whimpered softly.

"Say yes, Linds. Come away with me."

"I can't."

Exavier feathered his tongue over the edges of my mouth gently, making moisture pool to my inner thighs. His tongue darted out and over my lower lip, leaving me to melt in his hands. "You can. Say yes."

Our tongues touched for one fiery second and it was pure ecstasy. "Please."

"Say yes. Swear you'll come with me, Linds."

"Xavs, I can't—"

He cut me off quickly by dropping his mouth down onto mine. He slid his tongue in and explored the inner edges of my mouth. Instantly, I did the same to him. It was his turn to moan as I tipped my head and nipped at his lower lip. Exavier jerked my body to his. The feel of his hard, clothed erection against the thin, silky material of my dress was too much. He rocked his hips against me as we moved in a circle. The hard bulge dug into my lower abdomen as if it knew exactly where it needed to go for pleasure.

"Say yes, Linds."

This was all too much. I'd never wanted a man as badly as I did Exavier. Every inch of my body craved him. I couldn't do this. Not now. Not in the middle of the restaurant. Pushing on his chest, I managed to put a tiny bit of space between us. It wasn't much but it was all he gave me. "Xavs, this isn't the time or place to…"

Pressing his mouth to my ear, he licked the heart-shaped earring, making me jolt slightly in his arms. Chuckling, he whispered, "To throw you down, tear the clothes from your body and bury myself in you just like I wanted to do earlier today?"

The very vivid image he painted flashed before my eyes and I wanted it more than I'd ever wanted anything. "Yeah, that would be a good example of what should not happen here."

"Promise you'll think about it."

"What? Sex or helping you?"

"Both."

Pulling back fast, I did my best to right myself and glanced nervously around the restaurant. Thankfully the lighting was dim or the entire place would have been able to witness our erotic dance. He moved to put his arm around me and I stopped him quickly. "No. No more. I refuse to be putty in some singer's hands."

"Some singer?" he mused.

"Oh, I have no idea how famous you are. More importantly, I don't care. Now, I need to meet with my parents." Touching my swollen lips, I silently wondered what I looked like now that he'd turned me on to the point I had almost tossed him down and torn his clothes off.

"Stop fidgeting, you're beautiful. Nothing is out of place. Though, I have something that is now painfully enlarged but other than that, we're good." He kissed me quickly, catching me off guard. "Go to your parents now. We'll finish this later. You aren't getting rid of me that easily, sweetheart."

In a flash, he was moving in the other direction. Stunned and very horny, I made my way slowly towards my father's regular table. As I approached, my mother waved and my father stood, pulling out my chair and smiling. "You look lovely, Lindsay. Thank you for joining us."

I sat down and forced a smile onto my face when all I really wanted to do was chase after Exavier. My mother looked beautiful with her long chestnut hair wrapped in a bun. Her high cheekbones were dusted with the tiniest bit of blush. Her pale rose-colored strapless dress looked stunning on her. She smiled, not looking anything close to the age she wanted people to believe she was. Only, in her case, she wanted to look like my mother, not my sister.

My father sat down next to her, adjusted his tie and pushed his shoulder-length, jet black hair behind his ears. His green eyes locked on me and he smiled, careful not to reveal any fangs as he did. "I was afraid you would not show, Lindsay."

My mom laughed. "He's checked his watch every two minutes since we arrived. I'm going to take it away from him if he does it again. Our surprise still isn't here so I have no doubt he will."

"*Je t'aime*," my father said, lifting her hand and kissing it tenderly.

I looked away, allowing them a private moment.

"Tiennot, you didn't spoil our surprise did you?" my mother asked. "I know how bad you are at keeping things from Lindsay. She has you wrapped around her little finger."

"As do you, Olivia."

"Guys, can we possibly wait until I'm gone before you start going at it like two horny teenagers? I'm not sure I can handle that just yet."

My mom's mouth dropped. My father burst into laughter, only to find himself being elbowed in the stomach. "Tiennot, she is just like you."

"I know. Let us go home and try for another one."

A wave of nausea hit me. Sure, they both looked like they were in their mid-to-late thirties but I did not want to think about them having a baby. "Could you wait until I'm married at least?"

My mother scowled. "Darling, we are immortal and will *still* die of old age before you get to that."

"Okay, looks like the mystery date is a no-show. Who wants to order and pretend like we enjoyed the food?" I asked, tapping my glass of water. "His loss, let's eat."

"Don't cut me out of the running just yet."

Mom looked behind me and smiled wide. My father did the same. I didn't move. "Ah, Exavier, it has been too long. Look at you," my father stood and reached his hand out, "you are a man now. Gone is the little boy who chased our Lindsay around. Please sit."

My fists clenched as Exavier put his hand on my shoulder. I wanted to knock him on his ass. I held back by a thread.

Mom nudged me. "Look, honey. You remember Exavier Kondrashchenko, don't you?"

"Mmmhmm."

"Lindsay?"

"Yes, mom?"

"Look, he's all grown up now. When we received a call from him last week we couldn't believe it. Can you believe it?"

"No. I certainly can't believe it."

Exavier slid into the chair next to me and reached for my hand. I glared at him. His lips twitched and his eyes twinkled with amusement. As he lifted my hand, I pulled it back and struck him across the face.

My mother gasped and my father shot up fast. "Lindsay Marie Willows!"

Exavier kissed my palm gently, chasing the sting out of it. His blue eyes settled on me. He no longer had the amused look on his face. "I deserved it, Mr. Willows."

"You have not seen one another for twenty years. Tell me how it is you warranted such a response." My father exhaled deeply. "And it is Tiennot and Olivia to you, Exavier."

"Thank you." Exavier stared at me. "I'm sorry I didn't tell you it was me. It was nice to get to know you without that being between us and to be honest, I wasn't sure if you'd be happy to see me or not. I'd been told you requested I stop calling or trying to contact you in any way when I was younger. And every time I got up the nerve to do it anyways, someone who I plan on having a serious talk with assured me you didn't want to see me."

I shook my head, trying to make sense of what he'd just said. I'd never requested he stop calling me.

My mom laughed. "That's ridiculous, Exavier. I sat, stroking her hair and pretending not to notice she was crying for years. Lindsay would never ask you to stop calling her."

I rolled my eyes. "Thanks, Mom."

"Well I did, Lindsay. So did your father."

"It does not matter, what matters is that he is here now. Tell me again what brings you to the area." My father was always one to elegantly smooth things over. I seemed to have missed getting that trait from him.

"I came to ask Lindsay to take the position of artistic advisor for my tour and videos for our new album." He looked at me and I could tell that he was more than worried I'd say no again.

"Oh, Lindsay, tell me you said yes. I hate knowing you're wasting your talents away at that center of yours." After a very elaborate sigh, my mother laughed softly. "You're almost twenty-eight, darling. You're throwing away the best years of your life there."

My father took hold of her shoulders and gave me an apologetic look. "Olivia, she will come out and face the world when she is ready to. Do not push."

"Please, Tiennot, she has no intention of leaving the security of that place. Myra and Gina even gave up everything, allowing her to continue staying tucked away. They feed into her need to hide. I wish they would push her to move on. Heaven knows I have. Exavier was my last hope. See how she greets him? She slaps him! I'm out of things to try. That worthless thing she shacked up with dies and she cuts herself off from the world."

"Olivia, enough."

"No, Tiennot. It's not enough. Someone needs to tell her. Someone needs to stop letting her hide away. She needs to get over it and move on. It's clear it was meant to be."

Meant to be?

My father gasped and threw his napkin down on the table. "Olivia, you know not what you speak of. To say such things to your own flesh and blood is unacceptable."

She rolled her eyes. "Oh, and you do know about it? She keeps secrets from us, Tiennot. You have to hire people to spy on our own daughter just to know what she's doing with her life."

I locked gazes with my father. "Daddy, say it. Tell her what I'm sure you know by now."

"*Non*, Exavier is here now." He glanced around the restaurant. "It is not the time nor the place, Lindsay."

I glared at Exavier. "I don't really give a *rat's* ass what he thinks of me, Father."

"Ladies do not speak like that, Lindsay," my mother said. "This is ridiculous. Really, had I known losing that vagabond would leave you this way I would have—"

My father put his hand up and let his power ride out and over the table. "Silence! You will not speak of this matter any further, Olivia. The man you speak of gave his life in an attempt to save my granddaughter's. I believe you misjudge their relationship as well."

He knew I'd been pregnant at the time of the attack? Myra, Gina and Eion were the only ones who knew, or so I thought.

It felt as if someone had kicked me in the gut. I gasped and did my best to draw in air. My mother shook her head. "Tiennot, watch the slip of the tongue. You mean your daughter, right? It will be a cold day in hell before we get any grandchildren out of Lindsay."

My hands shook as tears filled my eyes. The second my father reached for me, I jerked my hands back and shook my head. "How long have you known?"

I had to hear. I had to know.

"Tiennot?"

He ignored my mother and gave me a supportive look. "Did you honestly think you could hide something of that nature from me, Lindsay? You are my child. My baby girl. There is nothing I would not do to assure your happiness. There is also no way I would allow you to travel about the world alone—in that condition."

I clutched onto the tablecloth. "Daddy, I didn't know how to tell you. *He* wanted to tell you. He wanted to come to you so you could know him. I didn't let him. I thought you'd kill him. You never liked the idea of me being around any man, except for Exavier and I honestly thought you'd hurt him." A choked sob tore free from me. "After it happened, I was scared you'd blame him."

I still feared my father would kill Eion. I would always love him and just because I'd cut him out of my life didn't mean I wanted harm to come to him. We'd almost had a life together. We'd almost had a family.

"Shh, *he* did come to me, Lindsay. I got to know him and I know it was not his choice to be separated from you—but yours. I know his feelings for you were far greater than a father could hope for his daughter. His love was real."

My eyes widened as I grabbed for my handbag. My mother arched a brow. "What are you doing?"

"Finding my phone. Daddy, tell me you didn't...oh gods." I couldn't think straight. Thoughts of Eion being harmed flooded my head. I didn't want to think my father would do it but I couldn't help but be concerned.

My mother snorted. "Even your father does not have the power to kill a dead man. Tim is gone, Lindsay."

Tim? It was clear my father had never told my mother Eion and I were a couple or that we'd gotten pregnant. She'd always assumed Tim and I had a relationship that extended into the bedroom. We didn't. It was easier to let her believe it than to confess the truth.

I dropped my bag and Exavier caught it. He placed it in my hand and wrapped his around mine. I couldn't help but stare at him with tear-filled eyes. "Xavs?"

"Yes," he said, using one hand to cup my cheek. "I'm right here. I'm so sorry it took me so long to get to you, Linds. I thought you were married with children."

"That is absurd," my mother said.

Exavier ignored her and kept his gaze trained on me. "Lindsay, I had no idea they were looking for you. I didn't know."

My father's breath hitched. "Exavier, is it true? Is my daughter your true...?"

Nodding, Exavier kissed the top of my nose. "Lindsay, if you cry, I'm fairly sure I'll cry too and that would be bad for all involved. Locusts would pour forth from the skies. Tidal waves would occur. It's best we try to keep my emotions as in check as possible especially now of all times."

"Why now?" I asked. It was a stupid question but all I had at the moment.

It was my father who answered. "Because if he is who I have always believed him to be, then from the very moment he laid eyes on you again, he has had to fight to keep from doing what seems so natural."

"Tiennot?" My mother touched his arm. "What are you talking about? Please tell me you aren't going to discuss our daughter's sex life with her oldest friend?"

"Do you not recall how linked Exavier seemed to be with Lindsay's feelings when they were just children? I, for one, lost count as to the number of times he would show up on our doorstep at the very moment our Lindsay's mood would darken. The second I opened the door for him, she lit up. Happy again. Did you think it a coincidence?"

Mom laughed. "Really, Tiennot. Do not make more of it than what it was. Two children, extremely close. The best of friends."

Exavier kept his gaze locked on me but spoke to my mother, "Olivia, no disrespect but you are wrong. Lindsay is so much more to me than just a friend."

"Yet she slaps you."

He pressed his lips to mine and fire shot throughout my body. Dropping my bag, I put my hands on either side of his face and returned his kiss with all I had. Our tongues danced around one another. My entire body tightened beneath his tender touch. He was so soothing, so what I needed to regain my composure, so much the little boy who leapt away from me when I informed him I was going to marry him.

I broke the kiss and stared at him with wide eyes. "You lied to me!"

A soft laugh came from him. "Well, at least you don't look like you're about to cry anymore. You do look like—"

I slapped him across the face again.

My mother gasped.

Exavier nodded. "You're about to slap me. Yep. I saw that one coming." He put his hand up. "It's fine, Olivia. Don't start with her again. Lindsay is welcome to spend forever knocking me on my ass if she wants. It would mean she's with me so I'm fine with that."

My father clasped his hands together and drew in another sharp breath. "Exavier, your word my child shall suffer no more. That regardless what has transpired in her past you will accept and love her for her and hold nothing against her? She too, had been told you were wed and starting a family, Exavier. I believe her choices would have differed greatly had she known the truth, but I refuse to allow her to regret certain aspects, regardless."

Hearing my father say he wouldn't let me regret having been with Eion and pregnant meant the world to me. I'd always valued his opinion. His strength, love and support of me was never ending.

"You have my word, Tiennot. I will handle the reason for the misconceptions. You have my word on that as well."

I glanced at my father. "I'm sorry, Daddy."

He shook his head, sending waves of black hair spilling about. "My only regret is you did not trust in my ability to both accept and protect you, regardless of what decisions you made. I do not have to lecture you on what one will do to protect their children, do I?"

No. He didn't. I knew the extremes. I'd gone to them but still failed.

My mother made a disgusted sound. "Look, she actually responded to Exavier. How the man could stand being around her after she has continued to assault him is a mystery. I never thought I'd say this but I am glad it happened. Had the accident not occurred—"

My father growled. "Had it not occurred, Olivia, we would be sitting here celebrating our granddaughter's second—"

I put my hand up. "No! I can't do this. It doesn't matter what Mom or anyone thinks of me, Daddy. It doesn't. Let her believe what she wants. I can't do this anymore." I stood quickly and stared down at my mother. "You are never to interfere in my life again. You will never speak of the 'accident' again. Understand me? Never!"

My father tried to come to me. I gave him a firm look. "No. I'll be okay. I need to go clear my head."

"I'll come with you," Exavier said, rising and sliding his arm around my waist. "Just give me a minute with your parents, okay? Wait for me in the main entrance. I'll be right there."

I nodded.

He hugged me to him. "Do not leave without me. There is something your parents," he glanced down at my mother, "and I need to discuss."

Again, I nodded, knowing I wasn't going to wait for him. I wanted to be alone. Nothing I had to think about concerned Exavier. I could almost feel the center calling to me. It was the place I poured myself into in an attempt to forget my past. It's where I wanted to be.

Chapter Ten

I rushed towards the recreation center doors, not caring that my feet were getting dirty with my heels off. The feel of evil was all around me. That was no surprise. This area of the city was well-known in the underground supernatural community as a hot bed for paranormal activity. That's why I had the center built there. The kids needed a safe place to play and be kids. And the adults needed the safety of that as well.

A stone rolled past my foot and I knew then that the evil was with me, following me. I tried to reach out and sense how many and what exactly was there. A powerful magik pummeled me, knocking me down. Crying out, I tried to scramble to my feet, only to feel another wave of magic hit me.

"You dared to think you could take on someone my age, Lindsay. Your foolishness has earned you a long, painful death. I have brought many, many more than three shifters with me this time."

The vampire slammed another hefty load of power into me, making me scream. I thrust out hard with my power, knocking his magik free of me long enough to run toward the center doors with keys in hand. Something slammed into me, taking me down face first. White-hot pain shot through my leg as fangs sank deep into it. Kicking out, I drove my foot into my attacker's head.

It let go and hissed. Chancing a peek at it, I found a second vampire there, blood dripping freely from his chin while his eyes swirled with red and black.

"Ah, your fear is intoxicating, Lindsay. Are you willing to turn your prince over to us yet?"

The vampire near my legs slashed his dagger-like fingernails out and caught hold of my dress. He slit it from my waist down and went to slice my leg wide open. I threw power out in the form of fire. It hit his eyes. Hissing, he lurched backwards.

I pushed to my feet and ran full force at the center's front doors. I hit them hard and tried to find the right key. Giving up, I thrashed power out and shattered the glass. Pushing through the opening, I cried out as the glass sliced my arms, sides, legs, feet. I didn't stop to examine how bad my injuries were. No. I needed to get to my office and call for help.

"Give us the prince!"

I ignored the vampire and ran into the lobby. I heard the shifter coming a half-second before it actually arrived. Dropping down, I narrowly missed taking a direct hit from the were-wolf. It flew over my head and crashed into the cinderblock wall.

I used my power and retrieved the cordless phone from its base. I hit the button for Gina's cell phone. It ran twice before it beeped. Her voice mail picked up. "Gina! Center, I'm at the center. Lots of baddies! Help!"

Power slammed into my hand, sending the phone crashing into the wall. It shattered and I ran. Almost instantly, I found my body being lifted high into the air.

"I want the prince *now*, Lindsay. I am tired of playing your games."

I stared down at him and laughed. "Then kill me because you can't have him. He's mine."

Mine? Why the hell am I claiming a man who doesn't exist?

"You cannot win this, Lindsay. There are too many of us. You are bleeding so we can follow your scent anywhere you try to hide and you aren't powerful enough to stop us all. Give me the prince and I will kill you quickly."

"Fuck you."

With a flick of his wrist, he sent me hurdling towards the cement wall. I tossed my magik out to cushion the blow. Laughing hysterically, I slid down the wall. "For the love of a vampire with balls, would you just kill me already? I'm tired of fighting. I'm sick of it all. Do it!"

"Oh, I will, but you will give me his name before I give you the death you so desperately seek." The vampire appeared next to me. He yanked me off the ground and stared at me with his pale grey eyes. He licked my cheek and I shivered. "Do you like that? I can do so much more that will make you scream."

Slamming my forehead into his, my vision blurred as pain radiated throughout my head. He tightened his grip on my hair and slammed the side of my head against the cement wall. "I want the prince."

"No."

He did it again and my vision blurred. "Give me the prince."

"I don't have him on me. He didn't fit in my pocket."

The vampire snarled madly and threw me across the floor. I slid into the gymnasium and tried to get to my feet. Looking up, I found a large, half-shifted wolf coming at me. He hit me hard, knocking the wind from me as he pressed the length of his body to mine.

The vampire laughed. "That a boy, you can smell her fear, can't you? You want to be in her, fucking her as she screams out in terror beneath, don't you?"

I lashed power out, burning the were-wolf. He rolled off me, yelping, and I kicked out hard, slamming my foot into his stomach. I felt his ribs break beneath my foot. Rolling over, I went to climb to my feet. Something wrapped itself around my waist and pressed its body to mine.

Looking over my shoulder, I found a man with a panther's head behind me, pulling my tattered dress up, staring at my ass with pure need on its face. I tried to break free but he was too strong. Putting my hand up, I conjured the hunting knife I'd taken from Stan that had been locked in the closet of my office. Twisting, I thrust it into the were-panther and pulled it out quickly. It gave me the second I needed to break free of his hold. Crawling forward, I slipped in my own blood.

Power seized hold of me, jerked my body out wide and slammed me face first to the bloody gym floor. I lay there, spread-eagle on my stomach, desperately trying to fight the magik that held me.

"Give me the prince or I will give you to every male in attendance. They love the bloody, scared ones." He laughed. "Give me the prince."

"No!"

I heard a loud crashing sound and some of them shouting, but all I concentrated on was freeing myself from the magik that held me. I jabbed out, striking the source, the vampire, with my own power. His hold on me broke. Twisting, I watched as a very naked, half-shifted were-panther crawled towards me. Muscles rippled all over his back. He licked his over-sized mouth and stared at me with hungry eyes.

He pinned me. I screamed and tried to buck him off, with no luck. He bit down hard on my shoulder. Pain gripped me. For a moment, I couldn't draw in air.

The vampire appeared above me and laughed wildly. "Give me the prince and I will call him off."

I didn't answer. I just lay there with the beast's jaws locked tight on my shoulder.

"It hurts, doesn't it, Lindsay?" he asked, smiling at me. "I see no prince here defending his mate, assuring her safety—your safety. Why do you protect that which has never protected you?"

He stared at me for a bit more and ran his fingers over my neck. "You are so very beautiful even in the face of death. Offer me your prince and we can rule all of it. I can turn you into a creature of the night. Give you a chance at everlasting life. Allow you the privilege of having me in you." He ran his hand down my side and stopped just shy of my sex. "Give the prince to me and I can make this existence you've begged me to end, easier."

The colder I grew, the worse shape I knew I was in. I was losing too much blood, too fast. "Let's make...a...deal."

The vampire tossed his hand in the air. The were-panther let go of me. "I knew you would see things my way, Lindsay. What arrangement do you wish to make?"

My head was too heavy to hold up. Letting it rest on the floor, I stared up at him. "I want you...to kill me. And then, I want...you and your friends to...go fuck yourselves. I told you...once. You can't...have him. He's mine."

"Kill her."

A dark shadow appeared above me. The panther was ripped away. Then the vampire was thrust in the other direction. Deep blue eyes stared down at me. It took me a second to understand who was there. Even then, I wasn't sure if it was real or a result of blood loss. "Xavs?"

Nodding, he moved over me slowly and began to check my body for wounds. His eyes widened and he looked as though he were in pain. "Linds, baby, hold on for me, please."

"It's cold in here. Why is it so cold?"

"No, no, no, honey, it's not cold. Don't—" Exavier was ripped from my line of sight.

There was a series of howls and growls and then a wet thud. I drew in a deep breath and shook my head. "No!"

Exavier appeared next to me. He lifted me in his arms effortlessly and headed towards the offices. I felt the vampire's power wrap around us. Exavier continued to walk through it, paying no mind to the pull the vampire was using.

"We have no quarrel with you. Give us back the female and you may go on your way."

For the vampire to offer Exavier a deal, meant there was something big going on. My guess was that he was scared of Exavier. "You will not touch her again."

"Leave me. Go. He's not…hu-man," I whispered.

"Neither am I."

Puzzled, I simply stared at him. The vampire increased his power, doing his best to crush us with nothing more than air. The pressure was great. Exavier held me close and seemed to radiate an energy that countered the vampire's power.

"What are you?" the vamp asked, sounding concerned.

"I am the last person you should have pissed off."

"She is but a human with tiny powers. She is nothing to someone such as you. Stand with us and you can share in the power that will come when we bring the prince down. Killing her assures he can never have an heir and he will forever have a hole, a piece missing when his mate is dead. He will never be at full-strength and he will slowly go mad. Kill her and let the process begin. We can attack then, when he grieves and is weak."

Exavier came to a stop outside of my office door.

"If you do not have it in you to kill her, then hand her to me. She is all but dead now. Allow me to finish the task. She has already begged me to end her existence. Can you not feel her sorrow? She no longer wishes to walk among the living."

Exavier's eyes shifted from blue to black. I gasped as his nostrils flared. "You will not harm her, *vampire*. When I know she is safe, I'll deal with you and the rest of your men. You should know that I've sealed the building. No one can get out. You can't run."

The vampire laughed. "I am not afraid of one man. I will kill the bitch myself."

"My *mate* is not a bitch. She is a gift from the gods and I intend to see she understands that."

"No! You cannot be the—"

"Oh, I can and I am. And you just made yourself an enemy you can't run from, can't barter with, can't defeat. I suggest you prepare to die—again. My mate needs my attention before I kill you." He pushed my office door open and carried me inside. The door flew shut on its own.

The contents on my desk cleared away on their own as Exavier laid me on it. He ran his hand over my cheek and brought his face down to mine. "I'm sorry, baby. I stayed behind a few minutes longer to tell your mother to go to hell and ask your father's permission to claim you. When I got to the parking lot, you were gone."

"You lied to me."

He smiled as he pulled the top of my dress down enough to see the panther bite. "That's one of the things I've always loved about you, Linds. You can stay mad about the littlest thing."

I baulked. "It is not little. You let me sit there and tell you all about…umm…you. Not once did you stop me and tell me that I was right, that there was a legitimate reason why you reminded me of him…err…you."

He smiled again as a warm sensation came over me. "Little, little, little."

I glared at him. "Care to tell me how you conveniently forgot I was coming to visit you?"

"Simple," he said, as heat flared through me. "I was never told you were coming. I would have never picked some camp over you. There was nothing in the world I'd have selected over you, Linds. There still isn't."

"Are you happy?" I didn't add sarcasm to the question. I needed to know if he was happy in his life. That was important to me.

"That's hard to answer."

My mouth opened as a horrible thought occurred to me. "Ohmygod, I kissed you and you're married!"

"Lindsay."

"No, don't touch me. How can you do that? You should have told me it was you. I would have stopped." I stared at him, half expecting him to morph into a wildebeest or something. "Xavs, what happened to you?"

"Lindsay?"

I gasped. "Sex was brought up, Exavier. I would have had sex with a married man. Wonderful, I've reached whole new lows. Gee, I'm curious to see what's next. Will I do a lycan train? How about a den of vampires? I can't believe I felt bad for hitting you. I am such an idiot."

"Lindsay, stop!" He gave me a hard look. "I'm glad to see you still have a flare for the dramatics. For one, I am not, nor have I ever been married. Kissing and making love to you would not have qualified as cheating…"

My jaw dropped as I huffed.

"Lindsay, hear me out!" His face hardened. "Before I explain let's get one thing straight. You are in no way, shape or form doing a train or a den of anything. Understand me?"

Before I knew it, my power had lashed out at him, giving him a hard shove. "You jackass! I'm not worth your time of day so even if you were married I wouldn't count? Am I the token fuck? Don't answer that. I don't want to know. And I will do anyone I want to. You are not my keeper. You are a childhood friend who showed up out of the blue after twenty years. You obviously have a life and I have my own. Go on your tour and take lots of pictures. Maybe, in twenty more years you can stop by and show them to me."

His eyes flashed back to black as he moved his body over mine again. "Lindsay, you are not a token anything. I am way more than just a childhood friend to you."

"Mmmhmm." Letting out a very unladylike snort, I looked away from him. "What's up with the spooky eyes thing? You didn't do that when you were little."

"And you didn't dance on poles or sleep with my best friends."

"You have to be kidding me. You were engaged. I also had no idea Eion was your best friend."

Exavier's eyes widened and a low growl emanated from the back of his throat. "Eion? Eion was your first? You slept with my cousin? I can't believe you spent a summer screwing him. And for the record, I was never engaged."

I wanted to pummel him. Lucky for him, I was a little injured at the moment. "Hey, asshole, I spent more than a summer with him. We had a good number of years under our belt."

"What?" He dragged his hands through his hair and over his face.

"I was with him while I was choreographing for Tim."

Exavier's face paled considerably as he stood there. "Please tell me you didn't sleep with them both." He groaned. "Oh, shit, they're the two men at one time the women in your morning class were teasing you about."

"Maybe, we were all too drunk to remember. We woke up on the beach in a tangled heap. Who knows?" I was fucking with him but he didn't seem to catch on to that.

"Who knows?" His eyes blazed with onyx fury. "Any more surprises for me? Though, it'll be hard to top the fact that you didn't seem to care that you had a husband waiting for the right moment to come for you."

"Are you a virgin?"

Exavier jerked back slightly, clearly surprised by my question. "No."

"And of the two of us, you knew that you're supposedly my mate. I didn't. Tell me, Xavs, how many women have you been with? I'm guessing the numbers would blow me away. After all, you're the one on tour in a different city every night with women throwing themselves at your feet. Yeah, preach to me some more, jerk. You knew every time you sank your dick into another woman that she wasn't your mate." Turning my head, I huffed and clenched my teeth tight. "My mate, my ass."

"That is it. You are impossible to deal with."

I smiled wide. "Great, does this mean you're done asking me to handle that tour issue of yours?"

"No. That means you're coming whether you like it or not."

Laughing, I sat up as fast as I could and held my shoulder tight. "Uhh, you can't force me to do anything, Exavier. Now go away before one of the things trying to kill me actually gets you."

"They're trying to kill you to hurt me, Lindsay. Why in the hell didn't your dad go to the council about this? They would have come to me and I'd have gotten here long ago."

"Why did you wait so long?"

He looked down a minute. "My mother told me you were married with children of your own now. She also said you were happy."

I hopped off the desk, expecting pain to move through me. None did. Glancing down at my shoulder, I found it was completely healed. "Exavier? What did you do?"

"I healed you."

"You don't say? Wow, I would have never guessed that. Thank the gods you're the prince or we'd all be lost." I stopped and thought about what I'd just said. "Oh shit, you're the prince. Of course you are. You're an asshole now. It makes perfect sense you'd be a royal one."

"Lindsay."

"What?" I wrinkled my nose at him.

"You're even sexier when you're mad."

I threw my hands in the air and stormed towards my office door. Tossing power at it, I forced it to open. "I don't know if I want to hit you or hug you!"

Stomping into the hallway, I headed straight for the gymnasium. My hopes were to find the ass who had caused all the trouble and annihilate him. I rounded the corner and found Myra, Gina and Jay engaged in battle with the bad guys. As Jay moved, his arm muscles flexed, and his entire body rippled. Watching his caramel-colored skin as the lights reflected off it, I couldn't help but notice just how sexy he was. The wolf within him gave him even more mystic.

"What in the hell are you doing, woman? You almost died. You don't go..." Exavier stopped in mid-sentence and stared at everyone as they fought.

Gina's mouth fell open a second before she lobbed a were-lion's head off. "He's still around? Do you really think he should be here right *now*, Lindsay?"

"No. I think he should go."

Exavier growled and stood close to me in a protective stance. "And I think you should keep your ass in one spot, stay safe and let someone who knows what they're doing, do it. Gina was right. You weren't created to have to fight for your life. That's my job. You were made to look pretty and stay safe while I do it."

My jaw dropped. "Look pretty?"

A shifter charged at me and Exavier moved to cover me. Tossing my hand up, I let my power out. It circled the shifter, lifted him high off his feet. As I clenched my fist, his body twisted and contorted, smashing into pieces. He dropped to the floor and I stared at Exavier. "Make yourself useful. Make sure he's dead."

Grabbing my arm lightly, Exavier gave me a stern look. "Lindsay, this is ridiculous. You have to be the most stubborn woman ever to walk this earth. Would you please just stop and acknowledge that you're happy to see me? That you missed me? That you still love me?"

A vampire came swooping down at his head from behind. I aimed my magic that way and let it loose. Exavier's eyes widened as he ducked down. "Lindsay! Killing me is a bit extreme don't you think." The dead vampire fell at his feet. "Oh, sorry. Thought that was directed at me."

"I'm not only too low to count as cheating, I'm an attempted murderer too? Great. Care to add to the list or do you think you've screwed yourself enough, Xavs?"

Exavier sent several bad guys hurdling into a wall as he continued to stare at me. "Think about it, Lindsay. You are my mate. If you and I do anything, how is that cheating? You're the spouse! I can't cheat on you with you."

He had a point. I'd just been too upset to realize it. "Oh."

"Oh?"

I laughed. "I hope you aren't expecting me to apologize. I have been hunted, beaten, tortured and so many things I don't even want to talk about, all because some jackass upstairs thought I'd make a great Eve to your Adam." Tears flowed down my cheeks freely as I glared at him. "I can't have children now, Xavs. I can't give you that heir the vamp was so quick to bring up. Do you want to know why?"

He closed his eyes and tipped his head down.

"Do you?"

"Lindsay, don't do this. No one can change the past," Gina said, between killing bad guys.

"You wanted to kill the prince guy earlier." I motioned to Exavier. "Have at him."

"Lindsay."

I glared at her. "I can't have children because I spent four days having my insides ripped from my body repeatedly, Gina! They would let my body begin to heal itself and do it again and again, each time demanding I give the prince over to them. It's his fault! His fault she's not here, now." I swallowed hard, not wanting to go into further detail. "Where was he when it was all happening? Huh? I'll answer that, probably fucking some woman who wasn't his mate! I can hate him all I want."

Exavier swung his arms around and a loud, ear popping boom occurred. I didn't take my eyes off him. Everyone else gasped.

"Holy shit, he killed them all with one magikal blow," Myra said, sounding more than surprised. "He's a prince all right."

He moved towards me and wrapped me in his arms, tight. Pressing his mouth to my ear, he whispered, "I will never be able to say sorry often enough, Linds. Never. I will never be able to prove how much you mean to me. I'm just asking for some time. I want to get to know you all over again. I want to have you back in my life. I have loved you from day one. Let me show you."

"Didn't you hear me? I can't have..."

Stroking the back of my hair, he held me tight to him. "I heard you and I still love you."

"Pfft, you don't even know me anymore."

"Then say you'll come with me. Show me who you are now."

I couldn't stop myself, my rage was too great. Twisting, I slammed the back of my fist into the side of his head and made sure to slap a hefty dose of power behind it as well. Exavier jerked backwards and I went at him. "You son of a bitch! How dare you ask me to go anywhere with you?"

Coming at me fast, he took hold of my wrists and brought my hands to his chest. I could feel how quickly his heart was beating. He nodded. "Yes, my heart isn't carrying on like that because we were fighting evil. It's carrying on like that because of the way I found you—the shape you were in when I got here tonight. I thought I was going to lose you, Linds. I swear to you, I honestly thought you'd married someone else. Had I known different, I would have been here ten years ago! I have loved you from the first day I met you. Nothing will ever change that. Nothing."

"Exavier," I whispered, my voice caught in my throat.

"Come with me. Get to know me. You said it yourself at the hospital when I was holding Lucy. You said we'd officially bonded. Don't tell me you didn't mean it. I saw it in your eyes."

The shock of what he'd just said sank in. "You healed her. You healed Lucy!"

"I didn't heal her so much as I strengthened her. It was her choice to fight to live or not. She chose life. So did her brother."

I eyed him suspiciously. "Did you do that just to make me happy?"

"I would move heaven and hell for you. You love those babies, Linds. They love you. I love you. The choice was simple. It still is. Come with me."

"Fine."

His body stiffened. "Is that a yes?"

Was it a yes? Could I really just pack up and go traveling with him? Could I really watch him walk away and not know if he'd ever be back? My stomach clenched tightly. "It's a yes, Exavier. I'll come with you on one condition."

"Anything."

"You agree we're nothing more than friends. If we move past that on our own, fine. If not, we part ways on good terms."

"I am not going to agree to let my wife walk out on me."

Backing up, I laughed softly. "I'm not your wife yet. Agree or I never will be."

"You're asking too much of me, Linds."

"No, I remember the doll situation. You pulled through there. Pull through now, Xavs."

A wide smile broke over his face. "It's a deal, if you agree to give it a hundred percent, Lindsay. I know we'll be perfect together. You know it too. You told me you were going to marry me when you were five. And you told me you loved me then."

Laughing, I stepped closer to him. "And you fell off the park bench and acted like I had germs."

Putting his hands on my hips, he pulled me to him, pressing his forehead to mine. "Let the record state I was a moron."

Gina cleared her throat. "Umm, not to interrupt this feel good moment, but we're still missing a master vampire and two weres."

Exavier shook his head. "No, they aren't missing. I saved them for myself." Touching my chin, he moved his thumb up and ran it over my lips. "You don't need to see what I'm going to do to them so I put them somewhere to wait for me. They're trapped between two realms. I'll be back in a little bit. I can't leave you alone tonight. I'll go crazy with worry. I know you're physically fine now, but I'll still need to see it with my own eyes. I can help you get ready to go then."

"Hold up," Myra interjected. "Where exactly is Lindsay supposedly going?"

"On tour with me and, gods willing, she'll stay with me from now until eternity." The black which had been in his eyes faded away fast, leaving blue in its place. He stared down at me. "I'll bring some of my people in to help run the rec center. Plus, Brook and the girls will still be here to keep things running smoothly. Any one of the people I send will be able to get them to you in seconds if you need them or just want to see them, Lindsay. I want you to be happy."

I looked at Jay, Gina and Myra. All three of them nodded. Jay winked at me and it suddenly felt okay. Having their seals of approval meant a tremendous amount to me.

"What do you say, Lindsay?"

"I say, hurry up and kill the vampire. Before you go, let me give you my address. Contrary to popular belief, I do not live here."

Chapter Eleven

I shut the lights to the dance studio off and made sure the door was locked. As I turned to head up the stairs to the portion of the apartment I lived in, I heard a faint knock at the door. Putting my hand up to sense who was on the other side, I smiled as I felt Exavier's energy. I opened the door and sighed at the sight of him.

He'd changed from his turtleneck and dress pants to a snug orange T-shirt with an imprint of Elvis Costello on it and a pair of loose-fit dark blue jeans. The black leather combat boots he had on suited him nicely. His hair was still wet so I knew he'd taken time to get cleaned up. Thankfully, I'd done the same thing.

I glanced down at my faded grey T-shirt with a screen print of Elvis Presley on it and back at him. "Oh no, we're dressing alike now too."

"I don't think I'd look nearly as good in those pajama bottoms as you do."

The lightweight, grey cotton bottoms I had on were loose but comfortable. Laughing, I shrugged and stepped back for him to enter. "I don't know about that. I got them in the guy's section. You're looking at my absolute favorite comfy outfit. The one I toss on to binge on ice cream, play sad music or lay around and watch movies."

"Do you do that often?"

"No." I lifted the T-shirt a tiny bit. "That's probably why I've had this outfit since I was sixteen."

Chuckling, he stepped in and looked around. "Umm, do you have furniture?"

I flicked the light switch on and motioned around. "I do but this is my own private dance room."

"You own an entire rec center. Why do you need another place to dance?" Exavier walked over to the built-in sound system and turned it on. A slower, darker song came on. Exavier turned and gave me an odd look. "How in the hell do you dance to this one?"

"I don't know. I just do. It's one of the songs I listen to when I can't sleep."

"Me too. I, umm, think it was written because the guy couldn't sleep."

Rocking my head back and forth, I listened to it and smiled softly. "This band's discs should be the only ones in the player. They're the only ones I listen to."

"Hmm." He stared at the sound system.

"I have a question for you." I walked to the barre on the wall out of habit and began to stretch.

"What? Are you finally going to ask what kind of band I have?"

"No. I figure you'll tell me when you're ready. Plus, I'm still trying to picture you singing. You used to hum a lot. I loved it when you would walk around sort of singing. I didn't care so much for how you yelled at me when I pointed it out to you though." I laughed.

"Sorry about that. I'd like to say again, I was a moron." He chuckled. "What was your question?"

"Gina and Myra hear me listening to this song at work too. I've accidentally ended up with multiple copies of the same CDs. They tell me to write the names down so I quit buying the same ones. I tell them to bite me. It works out well all around." I winked as he glanced at me. "Anyways, they told me this one was about running from the horrors of your life. And about how the human mind manifests stress into nightmares, leaving you afraid to fall asleep."

"Yeah, I think everyone believes something along those lines."

Placing a foot on the barre, I bent the other leg down, careful not to bounce at all. "Hmm, I really need to get out more. I feel like I'm a hundred years old next to other people at times. I didn't get that out of this. I'm either crazy or not meant to be one who listens too hard to lyrics."

"What's your take?"

"It doesn't matter." I switched legs on the barre. "It's just always sort of bugged me. I end up laughing at myself because it's only a song but it bothers me when I hear it labeled that way."

"I really am interested in your take on it. I sort of know these guys."

I did a tiny *rond de jambe*, before moving my leg to the side and then out, following the music carefully. The beat changed a bit, getting harder. "See, I think the person who wrote this wasn't afraid to fall asleep, he was desperate to. So desperate that the harder he tried, the less it worked. I think he went through a spell when he connected in his dreams with someone he cared about. I don't know who—maybe a lost loved one, someone he couldn't get to while awake. I think he had a taste of it and then it was ripped away from him without warning.

"I think he blamed himself and felt like if he concentrated hard enough, set his mind to it and tried again and again, he'd be the master of his own dreams. The only problem was, he needed to focus on his inner demons first because his mind and his heart knew that should he connect again, he wasn't quite strong enough to keep the demons down. No part of him wanted harm to come to the one he was reaching out to and in the dream realm it's entirely possible to harm someone if you're not careful. So, naturally, he wouldn't allow himself to reach out while asleep regardless how much he wanted to."

Twisting slightly, I made a large circle with my leg and held my arms out before me, carefully making motions following the song. "But, that's just my opinion. I'm sure everyone you ask has a different one. Regardless, I like my version so I'm sticking to it. My version left me crying the first time I heard the song. I'm such a sap. I wanted to make it better for him."

Strong arms wrapped around me. My breath hitched as Exavier pulled me to him and began to move with me. He turned me slightly, held my hand while I moved out with a half-spin and then drew me into him once more. He rocked us back and forth gently as the song played on.

"Mmm, is this a pity dance for my pathetic attempt at relating to music with words?" I asked, jokingly.

"No." His blue eyes seemed to burn through me. "This is my way of telling you just how right you are about it. That is exactly what was going on in his life at the time."

"At the risk of offending you because I haven't heard your music yet, umm, could you pass on how much I like this one to your friend? Did he sing it too or is it someone else?"

"Why?"

I turned red instantly, and looked away. "I was just wondering."

"Linds? Tell me why you want to know." A slow, sexy grin spread over his face as we continued to dance.

"Swear you won't laugh at me or think I'm crazier than you already do."

His chest shook slightly as he laughed silently. "What? Are we five?"

"We were when we knew each other best."

"Okay, I swear."

"The first time I heard this guy singing I was in a stereo sound system place with Myra and her boyfriend of the moment. A song, not this one though but by the same group, came on and the second he began to sing, I passed out cold."

"You did what?"

Laughing, I nodded. "My power surged through me and I couldn't get control of it. It literally knocked me out cold for about a minute. I was so embarrassed. I had to lie that I'd been in the sun too long. Please keep in mind that too much sunlight burns my eyes and makes me tired so Myra believed it. And she bought the CD for me for my birthday. I put it in, recognized the start of it and braced for impact. It didn't happen again. Instead of overloading me, my power simply wrapped around me, kind of like a warm blanket, and that's the whole boring, humiliating story."

"Umm, so are you saying you don't like it or you do?" he asked, tentatively.

"Well, every time I'm scared or as of late, terrified, I play this row of discs. When I'm lonely, I play them. Umm, the list goes on but it's safe to say they cover all moods. Even PMS. See, now you have to tell me what it is you sing and what sound your band has so I can begin the near impossible task of replacing those CDs with yours." I closed my eyes and screwed my face up not wanting to think about getting rid of it all. "Okay, I lied. Tell me what you do so I can set it along side this guy."

Exavier looked slightly shocked. "So, you're telling me you aren't willing to toss this even for me—your mate and best friend from when you were little?"

"You do realize you're bringing up issues that will weigh in heavily on the whole marriage thing. I think I'll need a prenuptial stating my CD collection is safe from you."

"A pre-nup, huh?"

"Yep. You get to keep your underworld and all its perks and I get to keep my CDs."

He bit his lower lip, trying not to laugh. "My underworld and all its perks? You're a perk. That means I get to keep you regardless if you want to keep me or not."

"We'll have to iron that point out then." I leaned into him and stood on my tiptoes. "That or I could just swear to love whatever music you make too and ask you very nicely not to chuck these out of the window."

"Hmm, I'm going to have to make a list of all my demands and if you don't meet every one of them, I'll be forced to make room in the player for my stuff." His warm breath moved over my face lightly, making my entire body press even closer to him. "If we don't find something else to do, right this second, you are going to end up pinned to the floor with me deep inside you, Lindsay."

Nodding, I drew back from him slowly, not wanting to let go but not wanting to surrender myself to him completely before I knew him better. I owed that to the both of us. Twenty years was a long time to be apart. "Okay, are you hungry? I know for a fact you didn't eat dinner.

I cupped his cheeks and felt stubble starting. Rubbing it lightly, I giggled like a school-girl. "Exavier, you grew into a man."

He rubbed his jaw and laughed. "Want to move those hands lower? I've got even more proof I'm a big boy now."

If he only knew how very much I did want to look lower, he'd have run. The need to offer myself to him was so great, I almost blurted it out several times. I took his hands in mine and pulled on him gently. "Let's feed you, to put my mind at ease and then let's go to bed. I haven't been able to sleep in weeks and I think it picked tonight to catch up to me. I'm tired."

"No, your body understands who I am to you. It's relaxing and knows I'm close and will protect you at all costs."

"Xavs?"

He smiled. "I am hungry and a bit tired myself."

I yanked him up the stairs with me. He waved a hand, using his power to shut the lights and stereo off.

The second I heard the exterior door locking, I sighed.

"Are you okay?"

"Yes, I'm just realizing how much I missed you and how safe you've always made me feel."

He rubbed his index finger over my wrist. "I love you, Linds."

"I love you too." The second I said it, I stopped fast. My pulse sped up and heat flared to my cheeks.

Exavier wrapped his arms around me. "Breathe. It's okay. I'm not going to lay claim to you here and now. I promised you time. I'm just happy to know that at least you give the automatic response when I tell you I love you."

"I didn't say it just because I'm used to answering that way. Other than my father, you are the only man I've ever said I love you to. In fact, my lack of saying it was the reason for the majority of my relationships ending. So don't stand there thinking it was a shallow automatic response, Exavier. It wasn't. No part of me has ever stopped caring for you. This is all very sudden. That's all."

Closing his eyes, he looked so peaceful, so content. The minute he looked up at me, he smiled. He tapped my butt cheek playfully and wagged his brows. "Feed me, woman or I'll feast on you instead."

"You might want to stop bringing that up." I opened the door at the top of the stairs that separated my living area from the dance studio below and stepped back so Exavier could enter.

He brushed past me, let his hand linger over my hip and then took my hand in his. "Lindsay, I can see it in your eyes. You're thinking of telling me I can't touch you since we're doing the starting-off-as-friend's thing. I'd like to remind you that we held hands and were close when we were little too."

"Yes but I never once wanted to beg you to throw me against the wall and fuck me, Xavs. Now I do."

His gaze skimmed over me slowly. "Baby, begging doesn't even need to come into play. Trust me on this."

My eyes lit as I stared at his mouth. "We should eat."

Taking his hand in mine, I pulled him into the upper level. He tugged on me and pointed at the tub. "Lindsay, you have a tub in the middle of your," he glanced around, "umm, is this the living room, kitchen or dining room?"

I beamed. "Isn't it great?"

"Does it work?"

A tiny laugh escaped me. "Of course it does. I soak in it every night when I get home. It relaxes my muscles. It, and the oversized downstairs, was the reason I got the place. I love it."

Exavier appeared to be in pain. I slid into him. "What's wrong?"

"I'm picturing you soaking in the tub and it's not helping with the urge to claim you. Did you have to tell me that? I'm going to be staring at it all night, knowing you're naked in it nightly." He groaned. "Ah, Linds, I see water on the faucet. You were already in it. Weren't you?"

I nodded and did my best not to laugh. "Mmmhmm, with bubbles too."

"Bubbles?" he asked, a tiny whimper coming from him. "Feed me now or so help me gods I will be in you in a matter of seconds. Yes, food now and then point me to that other room Jay sleeps in when he stays over. You might want to lock me in for your own protection."

I woke with a start and stared around my bedroom. I wasn't sure what had pulled me from the deep sleep I'd been in. Something tugged on my gut, telling me to get up. I followed it, sliding out from the warmth of the bed. I continued to allow it to pull me and the second I found myself in the hallway headed towards Exavier's room, I broke into a run. It felt as though I were swimming in molasses. The harder I pushed onward the slower I went.

I tried to open the door but found it was locked and hot to the touch. Hissing, I jerked my hand back and hit the door with my fist. "Exavier!"

He didn't answer.

My heart leapt to my throat as I pounded again and again. Still, he didn't answer. Frantic, I thrust my power out, splintering the door to the point that I could see through it. It took a minute for my mind to register what I was seeing. Black shadows sat hunched on Exavier's chest and abdomen. Though they were only shadows, I could still make out talons, fangs, monstrous figures.

Exavier shifted restlessly beneath them, still asleep. The shadows directed their attention to me. Glowing red circles were where eyes would be on each one. Three pairs of red flames stayed locked on me. I felt it then, something evil lurking behind me. I turned just in time to find a fourth shadow demon crouched against the wall, hanging at an impossible angle.

Screaming, I flung power at it only to hear its tormented laughter running across me as I missed. The shadows swept out and through me, chilling me to the bone, leaving evil streaks of power in their wake.

"Exavier! Wake up! Please."

He didn't move. One of them leapt upon his chest again and seemed to draw in a deep breath. I watched as a faint, sheer, ghost-like image of Exavier began to rise from his body.

His soul.

"No! Get off him, now!" I charged at the demon only to fall through it. A helpless feeling consumed me as I continued to charge it and it kept on sucking Exavier's very soul from his body.

I flung power out madly, desperately trying to get it off him. I gave in and practically lay in the demon itself, doing my best to try to wake Exavier. He didn't budge. "Please wake up, Xavs. I can't get it off you. Honey, please. I can't lose you now." I hit him hard with my fists, repeatedly. His eyes shot open. They were filled completely with black. His mouth opened and a row of jagged teeth greeted me.

He's a were-wolf.

"Xavs? It's me. It's Lindsay." No part of him seemed to understand. I backed up fast, scurrying to get away from him.

He shot out of the bed with incredible speed and had hold of my neck before I knew what hit me. Lifting me high in the air, he stared at me with soulless eyes.

Tears ran down my cheeks as I clung to his arm to avoid suffocating. "It's me. It's me, Xavs. Fight back. Fight—"

He ripped at my neck and all went dark.

"Lindsay." Something shook me.

My eyes shot open and I found myself staring up at Exavier. Screaming, I tried to crawl away from him as I clutched my neck. He reached for me and I screamed again.

"Lindsay, it's just me. I won't hurt you. You were dreaming, baby."

"You tore my throat out!" Touching it and feeling that it was smooth made me rethink that a bit but I didn't rescind the statement.

Exavier's face wrinkled in confusion. "No, I would never hurt you."

I motioned around my room still trying to make sense of it all. "They came, the shadows with the red eyes. They could crawl on walls and looked like demons but I couldn't touch them without going through them. They came and they pulled your soul out of you. I tried to stop them and your eyes were pure black, not like they are when they swirl but pure black, Xavs. You attacked me and ripped my throat out. I tried to make you understand it was me. You didn't care. Your teeth were like Jay's when he's partially shifted. You weren't you anymore." I shook my head. "It was your body but it wasn't you anymore."

Something passed over his face as he backed away from me quickly. "Get away from me, Linds. Run to Myra, Gina, your dad even. Just go."

Confused, I shook my head. "You said it was just a dream."

"It was a warning."

My eyes widened. "No. Xavs, you wouldn't do that. Would you?"

"No, baby. I would never hurt you. The evil I carry in me would if it was set free."

"Evil within you?" I let out a nervous laugh. "No part of you is evil, Exavier."

"Think about it, Linds. I'm powerful enough to control all breeds of evil. It takes evil to do that. I have just enough to make me more powerful than them and that's it. If something is trying to remove the portion of me that you know, the human portion, then nothing stands in the way of the evil I carry. It's part of being the prince of darkness, baby."

"They can't force you out. You were a man, a normal man before you came into your powers."

He nodded. "I know. I think that's why I'm not sensing the attack. I have a good deal of control over my darkness. In fact, it's never been an issue for me. So, I'm not expecting them to attack me that way. You're sensitive to evil. You felt the attack the second they launched it. Your screaming woke me from a sleep so deep, I actually staggered out of bed."

"But why could I wake you here when in my dream, I couldn't?"

"I don't know. But I'll be damned if I ever hurt you. I need to get away from you. I love you too much to let anything happen to you. Go to your father. He'll be able to protect you from me. Tell him that I can be killed. It's hard, so they tell me, but it can be done. Tiennot carries a darkness in him as well. If anyone could kill me, it would be him. He'll protect you."

"No. I'm not leaving you." Everything I'd ever learned about the Fae, demons and supernatural creatures came flooding to me. I searched frantically for a spell, something that would protect him. My eyes widened as it hit me. "Exavier Wesley Kondrashchenko or Kedmen, if you prefer now, I claim thee. I offer my soul, my heart, my love and my body to you for all eternity. Take this gift and make it yours."

Exavier tripped over nothing and hit the wall with his shoulder. "Lindsay, don't do this. Don't tie yourself to me because of this."

Putting my hand out, I used my power to pluck him from his spot and bring him to me. He wore only his jeans, unbuttoned, showing off a thatch of dark black curls and his amazing obliques. I bit my lower lip as need slammed through me. Exavier clawed at the air in an attempt to keep his distance.

"Please stop, Lindsay. If I counter your magik you'll get hurt. I can't do that to you."

"And I can't lose you, dumbass, so stop fighting me."

"You're calling me a dumbass in the middle of a shadow demon attack? In the middle of what you're trying to make our wedding night?"

I nodded. "Well, you're attacking like one in the middle of it. Two hours ago, you would have accepted my offer of marriage. Accept it now, Exavier. We'll get to know each other still. I'll be fine. I promise. The alternative—losing you—is not acceptable."

"No, I'll get a handle on this and keep my promise to you."

"Think about it, Xavs. They're attacking at an alarming rate. They don't want us to merge essences. Somehow they know we're close. They won't let up. You know it. Do you want them to figure out a way to use me against you or vice versa? Do you want to be left no choice but to kill me?"

"Gods, no."

"If you want me, even the tiniest bit, take me now or I will run as far as I can and when they attack again I won't fight back." I looked at the wall, ashamed of myself for what I was about to admit. "At the rec center, the vampire wasn't lying. I told him to kill me. I begged him to end it. I was tired of fighting. I'm still tired. I can't do this anymore. Fix it, Exavier. Make it so they can't keep trying to stop us from being together, or walk away and let me end it."

"Lindsay? No. Baby, we'll get past this." He moved towards me slowly.

"Make it official. Pull the rug out from under them, Xavs."

"You'll resent me for it, Lindsay. You'll blame me and claim I did this to have you."

I pushed to my feet and rushed towards him faster than I ever thought I could move. Pulling my hand back, I slapped him hard across the face. "Did that knock sense into you yet? I love you, you idiot! I loved you when you were clumsy and nervous around me. I loved you when you spent every free minute you had with me. I loved you when you broke down and gave in to the doll request. I loved you as I cried every night, thinking about you. I continued to love you, thinking about you daily, wondering if you were okay, if you were happy, if I'd ever be happy without you. I fell fast for you when you showed back up in my life and I didn't even know it was you, dumbass. Do you want to know why I walked out of the room when you were holding Lucy? Something inside me clicked, it felt perfect, you me, babies—all of it. My body knew who you are to me. It just took a minute for my head to catch up. It has. I love you. Now, step up to the plate, make this official or wish me the best against the creatures that keep coming for me—coming for us."

Something passed over his face. He nodded. "Lindsay Marie Willows, I claim thee. I offer my soul, my heart, my love and my body to you for all eternity. Take this gift and make it yours."

The room was instantly bathed in bright, blinding white light. My eyes stung. Tears filled them as the quarter vampire blood I carried in me screeched out madly as the light seemed to sear right through me. Exavier was suddenly there, pressing his body over mine, shielding me from the light as a wind began to circle around us. It ripped at my T-shirt and bottoms. Knowing it wouldn't stop until we were both nude, I waited without fear, letting Exavier protect me.

Exavier's body was suddenly lifted from me enough that, except for his hands on my eyes, I could no longer feel him there. I reached out, frantic to find the rest of him. "I'm here, baby. Right here. I won't leave you. I'm so sorry. I didn't want this to be our first time."

The unseen force pushed me backwards on my bed and spread my legs wide. Exavier's body settled between my legs. The feel of his naked, firm body pressing me to the bed made cream flood me instantly. I ached to be filled by him. To feel his muscles move as his body artfully pumped in and out of me. I wanted it all. I wanted him.

I felt him stiffening, trying to fight it. "I don't want to hurt you, Linds. This isn't how I wanted this to be. I'm sorry…"

"I know."

The power circling us aligned our bodies perfectly, setting the stage for the act that had to be performed to complete the bonding. The second I felt the head of Exavier's cock pressed to my entrance, I readied myself for him as best I could. Instantly, his body slammed down into mine, ramming his shaft to the hilt. His girth spread me to the brink. Hot, searing pain ran through me as he stretched me fully and struck my cervix with the head of his penis. Each spearing movement left me panting, clawing at the bedding, doing anything to separate myself from the pain of it all.

Crying out, I grabbed hold of Exavier's shoulders and held on tight, doing my best to relax for him. Without thought, my body clenched around his. He cried out then.

"Ah, baby, you're killing me."

Letting go of my eyes, he dropped his head down and captured my lips with his. As his tongue ran over mine, my body loosened a bit, allowing Exavier some play to continue to move. And move he did. It took only a second before he was hammering into me, impaling me with his ridged cock. Our tongues danced around one another as my entire body lit with need. My nipples hardened into tiny pebbles and my sex continued to produce the much needed lubrication for the event.

Soon, we'd struck a rhythm, a comforting counter partnership that left my body climbing, seeking that pinnacle point. The one where we would forever be locked to one another—our souls intertwined and our fates sealed.

Exavier ran a hand down my side and cupped my ass cheek as he continued to drill into me. His lower abdomen rubbed against my clit as he worked me towards new heights. Moaning, I clawed at his shoulders as he filled me so full, so right, and continued to stake his claim on me.

"Linds, you're so tight."

Tiny animal noises came from me as Exavier fucked me so thoroughly that he ground my body into the mattress and still kept going as if he would never tire. I prayed that was true. Wrapping my legs around his waist tight, I allowed him to take and fill me even deeper than he'd been. He no longer hurt me. Each thrust left him rubbing my swollen bud, filling my sex and leaving indescribable amounts of pleasure branching throughout me.

"Exavier."

Hot magic moved through my lower abdomen rapidly and seemed to stay there, pulsing, teasing, elevating me. My inner thighs tightened. A tingling began in my toes and worked its way up me slowly, taking care to caress every inch of me. Arching my back I clawed at him. "I'm coming. Fill me now."

"Ahh, uhh, I claim you," he stammered as he slammed down into me. "Mine." His eyes shifted a second before his mouth did. I'd seen Jay shift into wolf form enough not to scream. Though Jay had never done even this small of a shift while on me.

Arching my neck back, I offered it to Exavier, knowing he had to mark me to seal the deal. The second his teeth broke my skin, I cried out. It wasn't painful. No. Whatever he was doing made pleasure strike in bursts.

"And I accept you, from now until eternity," I whispered as an orgasm tore through me. I kissed him fast and furious as his hot jet of semen shot into me. Another moment of bliss hit me as I peaked yet again.

Exavier continued to shoot long waves of come into me. I held tight to him, an ache in my chest wishing with all my might that the seed he'd given me could find a home but knowing it would never be able to.

He released his hold on my neck and kissed it gently. "I love you so much, Lindsay."

"I love you too, Xavs." As the last bit of his come filled me, the bright light surrounding us faded away and the controlling wind of magik dissipated.

Exhaustion hit me hard as I cupped Exavier's head in my hands. He made a move to withdraw from me and I clung to him. "No, stay for a bit."

"Did I hurt you?"

"Mmmhmm, and in the best way possible. You can hurt me again after I get some sleep."

"Promise?"

"Yes. And if you're a good boy, I'll hurt you too."

Moaning, he kissed my neck and kept hold of me as he moved us to our sides. Hiking a leg over his hip, I kept our bodies locked. The very idea of falling asleep with his member still resting in me not only excited me, it reassured me that we were now one.

I clung to him as I traced lazy circles on his upper arm. "They can't take you from me now, can they?"

"No," he said, chuckling. "I almost feel sorry for anyone who tries it. You're the scariest thing I've come up against when your mind is made up."

"Xavs?"

He kissed my forehead. "Yes."

"Why didn't you ever tell me you could change into a wolf?"

Drawing in a deep breath, Exavier kissed me again. "Probably because I didn't know I could until right before I turned eighteen. Man, Linds, it scared the hell out of me. I had the weirdest dream. It was about you. You weren't the way I remembered you, you were about fifteen and asleep in your bed. I could see you through your window but I wasn't me." He hugged me to him. "When I looked down at myself, I was covered in fur, long claws from my fingertips, the works. The compulsion to break through your window and claim you as my own was so great that I howled out."

I kissed his chest and let out a soft laugh. "About that same age, I dreamt that a wolf was trying to get into my room. I woke to find my radio on and that chant, with the monks, the one I played at the rec center, was playing. I wrote it down, verbatim and that's what Myra sent with the guitar."

"Lindsay," he whispered, as he held me to him. "I think I was really there. I think you sensed my struggle to control my beast and gave me the power I needed over it. I think I went to you to take you as my mate because I'd reached the age to take one. I think the only reason I didn't burst through and do it was because you weren't that age yet."

I planted a kiss on his pec and cupped his cheek. "I think you'd have scared me to death at that age."

"Mmm, I know. Jay told me how many years it took for you to be comfortable with the idea of what he was."

"I take it Jay found out you were my mate while the two of you were having a beer."

Exavier kissed the top of my head and laughed. "Oh, I'm not even going to give you details. You'll just get mad at us both. Just know that we came to terms with each other and have an understanding."

Arching a brow, I looked up at him. "And that is?"

"That I'm eternally thankful for all that he's done for you, keeping you safe and caring for you but that you're mine. And that I am the only man you will ever be with again."

Much to my surprise, I didn't pick a fight over his comment. "Does that go for you too? Other women?"

"Lindsay, you are the only woman I will ever be with again." He shifted slightly and I felt his cock stirring to life. "I think we might have a problem."

"What's that?" I asked, a sly smile on my face.

Rolling onto his back, he took me with him, leaving me straddling his waist and his cock buried deep within me. My eyes widened as I took him to impossible depths. "Exavier."

He ran his hands up my sides and took my breasts in his large hands. "You're beautiful."

Staring down at his dimpled chin and lush lips, I smiled. "You're not so bad yourself, prince." As soon as it came out of my mouth, I snorted. "I'm sorry, Xavs, but it feels ridiculous referring to you in that way. You're just my Xavs."

He tweaked my nipples, rolling them between his fingers. I began to ride him slowly. His jaw went slack as we locked gazes. His body gleamed with sweat and I couldn't help myself. Leaning down, I licked a line up his chest, savoring his salty taste. As I came to his neck, I glanced up and found him staring at me with a shocked look on his face.

"I like the way you taste."

"I like that you weren't just taking the scenic route," he said, one eyebrow raised.

Scenic route?

It hit me then, Susan's comments about my leaning down while I ride a man or staying upright. I also thought about her comments regarding my avoidance to kisses. Continuing my leisurely ride on Exavier, I captured his lips with mine and thrust my tongue in.

His hands went to my ass. He cupped my cheeks and began moving me up and down faster on his cock. A shiver of delight moved through me as Exavier slid a finger dangerously close to my anus. He teased it, rimming it as I took him deep within me.

The angle that I lay on him left my clit rubbing just right against his body. The sounds of our lovemaking were only slightly masked by my panting. Taking all of Exavier was a feat even I found daunting. I was stretched to the brink, taking him to the hilt while he continued to toy with my anus.

Increasing my speed, I moved up and down on him, leading with my left side. My pending orgasm built. Exavier seized hold of my hips and stopped my movements. I broke our kiss and gave him a questioning look.

"I'm going to come. I need a second," he whispered, the slightest tinge of red to his cheeks. There was no reason for him to be embarrassed by his need for release. It told me that I was doing my job well.

I tried to move but Exavier held me in my spot. "Xavs, please."

"Just a minute, honey. I just need a second. You feel too good. All I want to do is explode the minute you move."

A sultry laugh bubbled up from me. "That's the idea. You're supposed to want to fill me so full of your come that we lose track of where I stop and you start. You're supposed to want to fill me to the point you can't anymore. You're supposed to want to fuck and be fucked by me as much as possible."

His stomach muscles tightened as his jaw dropped. "Lindsay!"

The second I felt his cock twitch, I knew he was going to come. Slamming my body down, I took him deep and let my magik out. It ran over us, caressing my nipples and clit, stimulating me to the cusp of culmination.

Exavier's hot seed filled me just as I gave in to the pleasure. My pussy tightened around him as my orgasm struck. I collapsed on him, my breathing ragged and my body spent.

"I love you," he whispered, running his hands up my back. "My princess ballerina."

"Huh?"

He chuckled. "Nothing. Sleep, Linds. You're tired."

I went to slide off him but he held me in place. "Xavs?"

"Stay. I want to fall asleep holding you, while I'm in you."

Snuggling up to him, I couldn't help but laugh. "Exavier, I'm not very good at cuddling."

"You're doing just fine."

His earlier words came back to me. "Princess ballerina?" As that realization sank in, my eyelids grew heavy. I yawned and froze. "Ohmygods, you're the prince of darkness and we're married."

"Rest, Lindsay," he said, his power dancing over me.

Sleep consumed me, not allowing me to explore my thoughts anymore.

Chapter Twelve

I stood in the back corner of the production studio and waited for any sign of Exavier. He was here to film a video. Every ounce of me wanted to ask him if the mating was real or a dream. I wouldn't have questioned it but when I'd woken I'd found him cooking breakfast. He was fully dressed, as was I, in clothes I knew had been shredded. My grey Elvis T-shirt was not only on me, it was in one piece.

There were no signs anything had transpired. Exavier didn't act any differently. He didn't kiss me or touch me in an intimate way. He merely smiled, told me about the long day we were going to have and then mentioned how happy he was I'd decided to join him.

I kept a close watch on him, waiting for him to give me anything that would hint he and I were now husband and wife. He offered nothing. I expected to be sore, wet, even slightly sticky after that heated sex session. I was none of the above. We both showered, in the bathroom with a door, allowing us each our privacy, and he helped me pack for the trip.

We'd stopped by the center so I could say my goodbyes. Now, as I stood in the studio, waiting patiently to at least catch a glimpse of him, my body felt empty and my chest tight. I'd not only mentally prepared myself to be his wife, I desperately wanted it to be true.

The director, a short man who appeared to be permanently fused to the dingy brown cap he wore, came walking past with one of his assistants. "Let's hope he responds better to the dancers this time. Christ, I thought the guy was dead from the neck down. How can you have six women pawing and clawing at you and not react?"

The assistant snickered. "Maybe he's so used to it that it's blasé."

I knew they were talking about Exavier and the thought of him being with so many women in his lifetime hit me hard. It hurt. It wasn't like I considered myself a jealous person but when it came to Exavier, I was. I could hardly point fingers and lay blame when I'd lived my own life as well. We both had a past and we'd both need to learn to live with that. If understanding wasn't possible then my arrangement with him would be terminated. That was the only good thing about waking to find our mating was nothing more than an erotic fantasy I'd dreamed up.

Crossing one, khaki-color, stretch knit-clad leg over the other, I clicked the heel of my boot and wished us home. It didn't work. The compulsion to continually touch the three-quarter length matching khaki blazer was maddening. Whenever I was nervous or on edge, I seemed to take great solace in fidgeting. Now was one such moment. Nervously, I smoothed the tight knit tank top I wore under the open blazer.

Shock of all shocks—it didn't calm my nerves one bit.

The director clapped his hands and cupped them around his mouth. "Okay people, time is money. Get Loup Garou out here. Extras, dancers, take your places."

I perked up and watched the dark set, made to look like a Goth-like prom setting, filled with people. The female dancers all wore corsets, long, layered shirts and heeled, old-fashioned looking boots. Their hair was swept up in various styles. Each one held a burlesque—beautiful quality that would look amazing with the right lighting.

Male dancers wearing black suit bottoms, suspenders, white cuffed dress shirts and top hats began to fill the area. It looked like a vampire ball. It was stunning. Near the back of the set was a raised stage where the band would no doubt be. Its backdrop was that of a cemetery. Vines and large stone pillars flanked it. Gargoyle statues were littered about as well as blood red velvet fainting sofas.

I watched carefully as three men walked out and instantly went to the stage. It was a little hard to see the raven haired man who seemed to be swallowed alive by the massive drum set but for a brief moment, he'd looked familiar. A tall man with long chestnut brown hair, tanned skin and a dangerous edge about him held a bass guitar and stared at the female dancers with nothing short of rapture on his face. The other tall guy with short, spiky hair, suspenders, an open shirt and a snug pair of vintage pants went towards a large triple keyboard set up.

The lights dimmed and smoke began to cover the floor, giving the stage a fog covered graveyard look. Someone bumped into me. I tripped and staggered a bit. Regaining my balance, I found myself staring at a woman who was my height with white-blonde hair that was styled high onto her head. She wore a bright red corset that left her breasts thrust obscenely to the surface. Her skirt was black where all the other dancers' were white.

Her light blue eyes flickered quickly and I knew then she was no ordinary dancer. She was supernatural. It didn't shock me.

The woman sneered. "Watch where you're going."

Me?

I just nodded, not wanting to argue with her. She needed to get her pasty ass out there and perform. Getting the shit kicked out of her by me wouldn't help Exavier get his shoot over with today.

Turning her nose up, she laughed. "That's what I thought."

As she stormed off, I considered using my power to trip her. I held back. It was hard.

Whoohoo, for me.

The director stopped the bitchy dancer and smiled. "Hyde, you look lovely. What's the matter?"

She looked back at me as a small grin spread over her face. "Exavier's latest conquest is underfoot. I almost broke my neck because she walked right into me."

The director glanced at me and shrugged. "At least she isn't throwing herself at him every chance she gets. It's rather tiring to have to continue to tell him not to bring his flavor of the week in, but you know him. He does what he wants."

"I can't work with her here. She's disrupting my muse."

Flavor of the week? Always dragging women in?

I shouldn't have been jealous. I had no rights to Exavier. The only thing I had was an overactive imagination and a hell of an erotic dream. Nothing more.

Glancing around, I scooped out the nearest exit and headed in that direction. Someone grabbed hold of my arm, stopping me in my tracks.

"Hey, where are you going?"

I looked up at Exavier and for a moment could only stare at him. They had his hair done so it looked stylishly messy. More so than normal. Black eyeliner circled his blue eyes, drawing them out more. It was faint but needed, to keep him from fading in the camera's eye. All of his stage make-up was subtle.

The black, long-sleeved, crew-neck mesh shirt he wore showed off his chiseled chest, making my entire body tingle. The snug black leather pants and boots only served to add to the dark sex appeal.

He arched a brow. "See something you like?"

"Yes, your eyeliner. What brand is it? I think it's divine."

Rolling his eyes, he chuckled and pulled me into his arms. "Ha, ha. Now, why were you leaving?"

I cast a wary glance towards the director and Hyde. "I think I'm underfoot. I'll walk around and check back in a few hours."

"Like hell you will." His jaw hardened. "I want you here, with me."

"Pull out your black book and call for backup. I'm sure one of the other 'flavors' will be more than willing to jump at your every whim. I'm not one of them." Unsure where the outburst had come from, I looked away from him and forced a pleasant look to my face. "Sorry, I think I'm tired still. I had some rather odd dreams and didn't sleep very well. I need some air."

He kept hold of me and raked his dark blue gaze over me. "Dreams? What kind of dreams? And what the hell are you talking about with flavors?"

I shook my head.

"Linds? What sort of dreams?"

Heat rose to my cheeks. "They were nothing. Demons, death, do or die situations. You know—always with the spooky stuff."

"What's with the flavor comment?"

"Exavier, play with your little girlfriend later. We need to get this rolling," the director said.

"Really, Exavier, I'm sure you fucked her in your dressing room like you do every other one you drag in with you so you should be okay for at least twenty minutes." The very sound of the bitch's voice made me want to send heavy objects pummeling towards her head.

I backed away and smiled at him, letting my fury show in my eyes. "They're waiting."

Exavier closed his eyes and shook his head slightly. "Linds, I, umm, I..."

I thrust power out at him, sending him stumbling towards the stage. I didn't back down once. Finally, he gave in and walked backwards of his own accord, all the while staring at me with a hurt look on his face.

Oh well, I hurt too.

Hyde ran to him as he walked and tossed her arms around his neck. As she went to kiss his cheek, he put his arm up, pushing her away. She looked like someone struck her. I wished they had.

"Are we all set then?" the director asked.

Laughing at my own stupidity, I turned and headed towards the exit. How could I have been foolish enough to think I was anything more than another conquest? The one he needed to come into his full power. After he fucked me, he'd probably cast me aside and go back to fucking everything in his path.

As I went to push the door open the music started, as did an ancient chant of the Fae. I knew that voice. It was the one I lost myself in while dancing. The one who talked of wanting to dream to get to his loved one. Shaking my head, I glanced over my shoulder slowly. Exavier stood on the stage, holding the black wolf guitar I'd given him as a gift, with his mouth near the microphone, singing the deep chant and looking directly at me.

I tried to back up but I couldn't, something held me in place. As I listened closer to the chant I knew why I was unable to move. It was used by the ancient Fae warriors to call their mates to them. To assure that they continued the race and found happiness. Covering my mouth with my hand, I fought back tears as his blue eyes stayed locked on me.

The dancers all moved fluently around the stage, dancing in the fog, dipping one another and caressing as they went. It was sexy, dark and alluring. Hyde came onto the stage and went to Exavier, pretending to be in awe of him. She made tiny motions to touch him and pulled her hand away fast. It was clear she was to act as though he was untouchable and powerful.

He was.

The lights began to simulate lightning and Hyde went to grab him. He stiffened and shrugged her off.

"Cut!"

Exavier stopped singing and the rest of the band instantly stopped playing. "What's the problem, Pat?"

"I don't know, Exavier. It could be that you look disgusted by the presence of the love of your life."

We locked gazes. Fire ignited in my body, instantly making me feel as though he was buried deep within me. I gasped and fought to stay upright as the feeling of being fucked by Exavier continued. I could almost feel his cock sliding in and out of me, stretching me, filling me so completely that I knew I'd never long for another.

"Pat, I am far from disgusted with her presence. If anything, I'm obsessed." Exavier licked his lower lip and it felt as though he were licking my pussy, tracing his tongue over my clit. I moaned and fought to stay upright.

"That's funny because you just shrugged her off like she was a fly on your shoulder."

"I did not."

"Hyde, did he ignore you?"

She nodded as she glared at me. "He did. I think his newest screw is distracting him. We're professionals here and need to get a job done."

Exavier burst into laugher. "Oh...ha...you were talking about Hyde. I misunderstood since you said love of my life. Umm, yeah, Hyde's touch makes my stomach turn. Always has."

His band mates and half of the dancers started snickering. Hyde's mouth dropped. She glared at him as though she was trying to burn a hole through the back of his head. "I will walk out on this project. Don't think I won't. I'm one of the highest paid models in the world. I agreed to do this because—"

"Agreed?" the man on the keyboards asked. "I heard you begged to get close to Exavier."

"Children, we have a video to shoot and a schedule to keep. The studio will not be happy if we go over budget."

All of them stared at the director like he was a moron. I agreed with their unspoken assessment. They nodded and the guys started to play again. The director mumbled something about lip syncing and Exavier flipped him off. I just stood in my spot watching the events unfold, doing my best not to laugh when Exavier growled as Hyde neared him again.

Two female dancers grabbed their stomachs and ran off the set. A few seconds later another ran off. Exavier glanced at me, clearly puzzled. I shrugged. The minutes ticked on as the director and his assistants spoke quietly amongst themselves. The second I saw the director throw his clipboard, I knew it was bad.

Storming out, Pat put his hands in the air and shook his head. "Apparently, some of these women were out late last night and decided to eat and come straight in. Too bad they ended up at an all-night dive. It looks as though they have food poisoning. I'm going to need two hours to get the other set prepared to do stills. I've got crew members over there now. I need the two of you," he pointed at Exavier and Hyde, "to act like you are in love. I can't have you clawing one another's eyes out while you're naked on the top of a crypt."

Exavier's eyes widened. "I never okayed naked on her with anything!"

"The rest of the band did it for you when you were late for the last meeting."

His band mates laughed. He looked livid. Shaking his head, Exavier backed up from the microphone. "No. Forget it. I'm done. Call the label and bitch. I don't care. Tell them to kiss my ass while they're at it."

"Exavier," Pat said in a tone one would use with a child. "Your fans can't get enough of you. You ooze sex appeal. Give them this. We can't show any full frontals and to keep this playable prior to nine at night, we won't show more than your upper body, hips, back, a profile of you from an angle that we won't catch a glimpse of anything we shouldn't."

Exavier gave Pat a rather nasty look and smiled. "Well, Pat. I'm still going to have to go with no."

"If it's about your body I have it on good authority from the dancers and crew that it is more than acceptable."

For a minute I thought Exavier was going to catapult the guy to Mars with his power from the look he gave him. Thankfully, he didn't. "This has nothing to do with me. I'm fine with the way I am. I'm not lying on Hyde in a fucking snowsuit let alone naked."

Hyde marched towards him. The long-haired bass player caught her around the waist, stopping her in mid-motion. "Let me go! I'll have you know, Exavier, that men all over the world would die for two seconds with me. They—"

Turning his head, Exavier glared at her. "They can have you. I heard the shit you said to Linds and I don't appreciate you putting your nose where it doesn't belong."

"Linds is just another flavor of the week for you and she knows it. I've know you a long time, you are a *royal* pain in the ass, and you've made using women an art form."

"Are you pissed that I've had whoever I've wanted or are you pissed that I've never wanted you?"

My gut clenched tight as I listened to them go back and forth. I couldn't deal with this. Not after spending a night dreaming that I'd not only taken him into me but had claimed him as my own. I didn't wait to hear the rest. I moved quickly through the set, down the hall. I didn't bother with the exit. It would only draw attention to me leaving and I wanted to be alone.

After running past several studio doors, I gave in and slowly opened one. Instantly, I was hit with the sound of hip-hop music. I knew the artist and couldn't help but smile. I needed to see a friendly face. Slinking along the back of the set, I watched many of the dancers I used to work with move in unison behind Ruland.

Gina is going to be pissed she missed this.

With no shirt on, his cocoa-colored chest glistened, no doubt squirted with enough water that it itched. They had a tendency to want him to glisten. I knew why. Ruland kept his head shaved and treated his body like a temple. The man could move as good, if not better, than any male dancer I'd ever worked with.

The baggy light-colored jeans they had him wearing rode low on his hips as he did his portion of the dance. I covered my mouth to keep in the squeal that wanted to come out. I knew that dance. When he'd been the opening act with a group I'd toured with, he and I would spend endless hours dancing and talking. Ruland was amazing. His voice could go from hardcore rapper to angelic in seconds. We'd gotten along instantly. When I discovered his father was a were-jaguar, I knew then that supernatural attracted supernatural.

He looked directly at me and stopped moving. The director stopped everything and called for a break. Ruland smiled wide, making joy surge through me. I raced towards him as he held his arms out. Bear-hugging him, I laughed. "How are you? I can't believe you're here."

He chuckled, holding me tight. "You can't believe *I'm* here? You drop off the face of the earth three years ago and reappear in the middle of a torturous shoot and you can't believe I'm here."

Dancers instantly flooded us. After the first hug and freak out for me being there, I lost myself in the rest. Ruland just laughed as he kept his hand on my shoulder protectively. A barrage of questions from the dancers followed.

Putting my hands up, I silenced them. "No, I am not here to take over. I'm here to say hi to everyone."

Ruland's music continued to pump all around us. It had his lyrics still in it. He, like most artists, gave into the demand of letting the studios and the labels have their way by making him lip sync while he danced for the video. Taking hold of my hips, he pressed his body to mine and began to move. "I say we break her back in."

The dancers all started laughing and agreeing. I took my blazer off and tossed it aside. "Mmm, trust you to have a song all about sex."

"Hey, it's one of my favorite things to do. Is it still one of yours?" Ruland asked, rotating his hips as if he was taking me from behind.

Countering his moves, I leaned forward for him. "I have to admit that I still love it."

Ruland began to sing along with his music and I shut-off, listening to the music and following his every move. He rubbed my right ass cheek, close to my hip as he sang about how he couldn't get enough of the view of the girl from above, from behind. Pressing my palms to the floor, I thrust my ass in the air, knowing that it was aligned perfectly with his groin.

We'd known each other a long time and we followed the other's lead without question. He made quick thrusting motions as he continued on with his song. Sliding down, I did the splits until I was all the way the to the ground. Ruland followed my lead, knowing I'd turn to him and crawl up his leg.

I splayed my hands out and over his thigh and bit at his leg gently. His hand came to my head. I let him lead it around in a small circle before bringing it close to his leg and upwards. The second I got to my feet, we both launched into the dance steps. I went at him, backing him up a few feet while the dancers spun, gyrated and slinked their way around us. Ruland then came back at me with harder moves. He wrapped his arm around and hooked me to him. Tipping my head back, I felt his hot breath on my throat. I brought my head up slowly and the second our lips would have touched, I heard someone applauding.

"That is exactly what I was looking for. Kim, did you get all of that?"

The director was there with a skinny little blonde in pink tights and blue shorts. She began to mimic our steps from memory. I knew then that she was the one responsible for the dancing in the video. Ruland laughed and shook his head. "Damn good thing that was the end of it. I might have been forced to kiss you, Lindsay."

"Well, you know me, ever the arm twister."

As soon as the words left my mouth, someone grabbed hold of my arm and twisted it. Turning, I found Exavier, his gaze hard and his jaw tight. He nodded towards Ruland. "Excuse us."

Ruland stared at him with wide eyes and it was then I knew that Ruland understood who and what Exavier was. Knowing I had little choice but to follow him, I let Exavier lead me into the hallway.

The second the door slammed shut, he turned me to him. "What in the hell was that?"

"What?" I glanced behind me. "Are you upset about me dancing? Correct me if I'm wrong but isn't that what you wanted me to come along for? Or am I here to play fill-in flavor? Wait, you've already had every one you wanted to have. Let me know. I'm a little lost. Clear it up for me, Xavs."

He put his arms out, pressed his palms to the wall and pinned me to it. "Lindsay, I love you and only you. I'm trying really hard to stay calm about the idea of you with other men. It's not going so well for me but I'm trying. Try to understand that I had a life before you too."

Laughing, I shook my head, sick of hearing him. "One small difference, Xavs."

"What would that be?"

"I had no idea who and what you are to me. Can you say the same? Don't skate around the question again."

Dropping his forehead to mine, he sighed. "I knew. I knew from day one who you were to me. I let my mother fill my head with lies. But I think part of me knew...hell... I wouldn't have come for you if I believed her fully that you'd found someone else, had children and a happy life of your own. I had to see it with my own eyes. I got ahold of your parents and didn't even need to ask about you. Your dad just began to tell me all about you, your career, the center and how your mother refused to let up the quest to marry you off. I couldn't get to you fast enough, Linds. Did you wonder why I showed up over an hour early for our appointment?"

"To be honest, I thought you'd come late in the day. I thought all rockers slept until at least noon." We laughed softly. "I'll do my best, Xavs. This is just a weird day for me."

"Hyde's a bitch."

I snorted. "I caught that. It just started off weird. I didn't sleep right."

Exavier caressed my cheek gently. "You mentioned that already. Tell me about the dreams."

What was I supposed to say to that? "Oh, hey, I dreamt you ripped my throat out after soul-sucking demons had at you. You gave me a story about carrying pure, unadulterated evil in some condensed form and that if they succeeded you'd be the devil himself. There was no way in hell that I'd let that happen to you so I claimed you and then yelled until you did the same. But hey, let's not forget the binding-induced sex that, while being controlled by forces bigger than us, was mind-blowing. Then I get brought along to have some painted whore with a god complex tell me again and again how I'm just like the endless string of women before me. Oh, fun. I can hardly wait to tell you all about it, asshole. Yeah, I don't think telling him that will go over well. I'll just end up killing him and saving all the other bad guys the time."

Exavier's chest moved up and down rapidly. He did a half-cough, half-laugh. "Umm, Linds?"

"What?" I asked, taking a chip and planting it firmly on my shoulder.

"I love the fact that you still talk aloud when you're upset and thinking too hard." He pressed his thigh between my legs and spread them. "In fact, I love every single thing about you."

Love the fact I talk aloud?

My eyes widened. I pushed against his chest. "Get off me! You...you...you."

Laughing, he pressed himself to me tighter. "I'm a what? From what you're telling me, I'm your husband. How do you like the sex?"

"I said it was a dream."

He grinned and kissed my lips quickly. "You didn't answer my question. It was mind blowing, huh? Good to know."

I almost choked on his arrogance. I would have if I wasn't laughing so hard at it. "Please, it was a dream. If it was real I'd still be clinging to you for dear life, scared to death they'd hurt you again. Gawd, Xavs they were horrible. Just cold, empty evil. I tried so hard to wake you up. I even hit you. I laid on you screaming and crying but they just kept drawing your soul from your body."

Looking at my hands, I shook my head. "I went through them. Right through them. Then when you finally did wake, I begged you to understand that it was me. You didn't care. Then you," touching my throat, I looked away, "grabbed me. I thought I woke up. I thought you were there telling me it was a warning. I was so terrified for you, not of you."

Pulling myself together, I took a deep breath and let out a shaky laugh. "It was so bad that I'm still shaking. Sorry. Crazy moment again. Those happen a lot. It's a good thing I didn't force you to take me. This way you'll have more time to observe my oddities. And I'll have time to tell you..." I stopped, unable to believe I'd almost let him in on something that only a tiny handful of people knew about.

"Time to tell me what?"

Cupping his face, I kissed his lips gently not caring what sort of policy I'd instituted. "I promise to sit down with you and talk about it when you're done today. It's for the best. Going too far from home is silly when I know you'll want me to leave you alone."

He baulked. "I get that something big went down. I was there when you found out your father already knew. I'd never send you away, Linds."

"Oh, for this you will. If you were just any other man, you'd get over it, maybe not even have an issue with it. But you're not ordinary and this isn't something you'll get past."

"Linds?"

"Hey, Exavier, Pat's about to have a heart attack. He wants you back in there!"

Exavier stared coolly down at me as the sound of Eion's voice moved around us. Turning slowly, I found Eion standing at the end of the long hallway. He'd let his black hair grow longer and now wore it tucked behind his ears as it brushed over his wide shoulders. I knew then why the drummer for Loup Garou looked familiar. He was my ex-boyfriend.

When in the hell did he and Exavier start playing together?

Exavier picked then to slide his hand partially under my shirt. My skin flared with need and I came so close to hissing that it was almost pathetic. He kissed my cheek, putting on a show for Eion. Finding out about Eion and I had no doubt been eating at him from the moment I told him. "I love you, Linds."

"I love you too," I whispered back. The second it left my mouth I knew what Exavier had done. He'd gotten me to say what he knew I'd never told anyone else. He'd gotten me to confess my love for him in front of Eion.

Eion's blue eyes locked on me, his face paled. He said nothing. He only shook his head and stared at me with complete disbelief in his eyes.

My heart shattered as I realized he had no clue who Exavier was to me. The truth was, he wouldn't even care. "Eion?"

He turned quickly and went back through the door. I went to go after him and found myself still pinned beneath Exavier. I pressed on him. He didn't move.

"Please."

"Let him go. He needs to get used to it—to us. I know how he feels. Trust me. But you're my mate. He needs to understand that. And he needs to know there will never be any casual sex—or sex period—between the two of you."

"I get you feel vindicated now but what you just pulled was wrong, Exavier. He didn't deserve to find out this way."

He snorted. "No. I didn't deserve to find out you'd ever been with him let alone spent years with him."

I let my eyes go hard as I glared at Exavier. "I need to go to him."

"What makes you think he's hurting more than I am? Do you think I'm fine seeing the way the two of you just looked at one another? I'm not. You sure the hell didn't look at me like that when I showed up at the rec center." He shook his head and let out a soft laugh. "It's killing me knowing he was there with you the entire time it should have been me, Lindsay. It should have been me."

"Let me go to him."

His hot power pushed against me. "Did you hear me?"

Doing my best to keep hold of my temper, I nodded. "He's what I need to talk to you about tonight. Don't try to make me leave him like that."

"What more do you have to tell me? I get he was your first, that you kept seeing him. What else is there?" The look he gave me told me he already knew my secrets. I wasn't surprised. He'd been there when my father confessed to knowing I'd been pregnant. Though it had never been spelled out for Exavier, it didn't take a genius to figure it all out. Apparently, he just wanted to hear the whole truth from my lips. I couldn't blame him. He deserved as much.

A surge of Eion's pain hit me. Crying out, I clutched my heart and stared at the end of the hall. "Let me go to him. Please. I need to make him understand."

"How the hell are you picking up on his emotions?"

I stared at Exavier. "How do you know what I'm feeling?" I would have waited for him to answer but another wave of Eion's grief struck me hard. For a moment, I couldn't breathe. "Let go of me. Don't make me choose because you will not win this one, Xavs. He needs me right now. He needs closure."

"You're taking him over me?"

"Don't make me. Let me go to him. Let me explain us to him. It has to do with what my father and I were talking about at dinner. It's him, Exavier. When we sat at dinner and my father talked about talking with a man, it was Eion. It was never Tim. I won't leave Eion like that. If you push me, I'll pick him over you because I couldn't live with myself for leaving him in this much pain."

Exavier pushed off the wall and moved far away from me. I didn't wait to assure he would be fine. I ran straight for Eion. When I opened the door, I didn't see him anywhere. Spotting the exit, I took it.

The bright sun shone all around me. I didn't have sunglasses on and it burned my eyes as I ran in search of Eion. I could feel him, his pain, his confusion. I spotted him standing near the corner of the building, slamming his fists on it over and over again.

"Eion, stop!"

Turning, he looked at me with tear-soaked cheeks. "Go away. Go back to him."

I rushed up and took hold of his face. He pushed me off and I did it again. We continued until he gave in and dropped his head down to me as I pulled him into my arms. Rocking him gently, I ran my fingers through his hair. "I should have come straight to you but I just found out the other day. I swear. I didn't know you'd be here or I wouldn't have come. I never meant to hurt you."

He snorted as he cried harder. He wasn't a weak man. Eion's tears were more than warranted. "Three years, Lindsay. It's a long time to keep the door slammed shut in my face only to open it for me to see you with my cousin— my best friend. Why? Do you hate me that much?"

I shook my head. "No, Eion. I don't hate you. I never hated you."

He pointed towards the doors. "Why him? It's to punish me, isn't it? I swear to you that I didn't know it was happening. I didn't. Myra and Gina showed up, and took me looking for you. I didn't know. You said you were going to be busy, not to worry and that we'd meet and finish going over plans for the wedding. I didn't know, Lindsay."

"Stop. Don't do this to yourself." I hugged him tighter. "No one knew. Do you think Tim would let them do that to him? Do you think he'd let them do that to me? To us? To himself?"

Eion shook as he lifted his head. "No. He would never let them hurt you. Never. If they hadn't—"

"If they hadn't sent one of their people in to get to know us, make us trust them then he wouldn't have died. He didn't know. How could you have? You have many, many gifts, Eion. The gift of foresight isn't one of them."

Confusion covered his face. "But if you don't blame me then why shut me out? We spent almost eight years together. Eight fucking years and you just end it all with no explanation, no goodbye. You just leave, don't take my calls, use magik to keep me away and pretend I don't exist. Why? What was I guilty of? Was it loving you? I won't apologize for that. Was it pushing you to marry me?"

He thrust magik out and let it hit the cement building. "I should have forced you, Lindsay. I gave you too much space. I thought you just needed time. I thought you'd come around. I thought when you told me about the baby you'd finally accept me fully. You didn't. You never once could even bring yourself to say three little words to me. 'I love you' never once fell from your lips. Don't think I didn't notice. I did, Lindsay. I noticed everything."

"*Shh*, Eion. Stop."

Thrusting more power out, he shook his head. "No. I won't stop. You were so excited when you found out you were pregnant. When you called and told me you needed to see me as soon as possible I thought something was wrong. When I got you and found you in tears I thought you were going to tell me goodbye. The second I realized you were crying because you were happy, I gave up that last piece of my heart I kept protected, shielded, from the knowledge that you didn't love me like I loved you. I surrendered to you."

Looking down at the ground, I fought hard to keep myself together. It was a losing battle. "I was there, Eion. I know."

"Do you know how fucking happy I was? I wanted to shout it off the rooftops. I wanted everyone to know that the woman I loved had my child growing in her. You said no. You didn't want it to ruin my 'image.' You let everyone think you were dating other men. I know you weren't. Tim knew you weren't. Hell, he even laughed up the drunken threesome ordeal the tabloids ran about us. He acted like it was more than it was just for the sake of keeping the two of us looking like we were available for the female fans. He never touched you and we all know that."

I tried to calm him down. He ignored my efforts, not stopping long enough to pay me any mind. "I agreed. I hated it but I agreed. The tabloids did their bit and got out, it made you happy. It never made me happy. I wanted you on tour with me. I wanted to crawl into bed at night, hold you and know our baby was safe. You refused to let that happen. Why?"

I didn't have an answer and I wasn't sure he really wanted one. "Why didn't you tell me that you went to my father?"

He snorted. "Because I knew you'd be pissed. You love him so much and he loves you with all his heart, Lindsay. He deserved to know his daughter was going to have a baby and I owed it to him to ask for your hand—not sneak around like we were children. We weren't!" He smacked his chest. "We had nothing to be ashamed of, Lindsay. We created a life! That's a miracle, not something you keep from your best friends even."

Blinking back tears, I nodded. "I know that now. I just couldn't—"

"Couldn't what, Lindsay? Couldn't love something I helped make?"

Anger shot through me. I let my magik up and used it to give him a good shove. "Don't, Eion! Don't you dare accuse me of not loving her. I was terrified and I didn't know why. The entire pregnancy I had this sick feeling in the pit of my gut telling me something would go wrong."

He tried to hug me but I pushed him away. "Lindsay."

"No! I knew, some part of me knew something horrific would come and take her from me—from us. I didn't want to tell you about being pregnant but I couldn't keep it from you, Eion. It meant everything to me. You meant everything. I couldn't ask you to give up all that you had in your life for me and I didn't understand the nagging in my gut not letting me say yes to your proposals."

Something passed over Eion's face and he gasped. "Oh, sweetie, every time you'd wake up in a cold sweat, clutching your stomach you…"

I let him pull me into his arms as I nodded. "I was dreaming someone would take her from us, Eion. I didn't know there was a real threat out there. I didn't. Had I known, I would have stayed with you or even went to stay with my father through the pregnancy. I thought I was overacting because of how much I'd always wanted children and was finally going to be blessed with one. I thought it was normal anxiety. I was wrong to keep it from you—to push you to stay away."

"Dammit, Lindsay. When Myra showed up out of thin air I knew something was wrong. She hates borrowing power from outside sources. I thought you'd miscarried. I never expected to have to search for you—that she and Gina only came to me because they knew I could track you. She'd sensed you were pregnant and knew without you confirming it was my baby. She also knew that for Fae, it meant we were linked now. That we'd merged essences. For a pair that aren't destined mates, that's a hell of a thing to pull off. We did."

I held him tight.

He continued, "I still can't get the images of you, of those sick fucking bastards, of what they did to you out of my head. They did," he closed his eyes, "the most horrific things to you. I've seen evil. It's in my bloodline. Hell, Exavier's father, my mother's brother, is notorious for his torture techniques, but I have never seen evil like that."

He openly sobbed as he clung to me. "They knew the baby couldn't survive that. That you would. They took you to the point that if they stepped even a bit further you would die and they pulled back—let you heal and then…"

Eion kissed the top of my head. "Lindsay, I will never, ever get that image out of my head. I'll never forget you begging me to kill you." He cried harder. I joined him. "You begged me to let you follow her. To let you be with our baby. I couldn't. I was selfish but I couldn't let you die too. I'd lost her and I couldn't lose you too. I should have known! I should have stopped it!"

"Shh, Eion. They'll never hurt me again, you saw to that. I remember that much. I remember waking up to find you there, standing over me." I touched his cheek. "I remember begging you to let me go and you telling me that if she'd have needed me to be there too, she would have waited." I lost it as tears fell openly down my cheeks. "You told me you couldn't sense her soul lingering, that she was safe. I remember. I clung to your every word and I remember what happened to you once you knew Myra and Gina were there to watch over me. I saw what you did to them, Eion. I saw you shift for the first and only time that night."

"Lindsay, I shut off. I don't remember killing any of them. I couldn't think. I knew before Myra said anything what they'd done and that I'd have to look you in the face and tell you the baby didn't make it. That she was gone. And I knew she was the only thing still holding you to me. Those bastards attacked you for no reason. And then you shut the door in my face. You built a fortress around you, disappeared from the public eye and were gone. Myra and Gina acted like guard dogs. They wouldn't let me near you. Why? I'd never hurt you. Ever."

Taking a deep breath, I locked gazes with him and confessed the truth. "Those monsters that took me had a reason, Eion. They told me I was the mate of a powerful man and they wanted to hurt him through me. I thought they were talking about you." Running my hand over my lower abdomen, I bit back more tears. "They laughed as others pinned me down and ripped my body to shreds. I couldn't stop them. There was too many and I didn't understand how to use my powers fully. I begged them to stop. They didn't. They just kept talking about the need to destroy my mate's line, his chance at happiness and weakening him to the point he didn't fight back anymore." A choked sob ripped free from me as the memories of it all hit me.

"Lindsay," Eion whispered as he reached for me. "Don't. I'm sorry. I should have left the past in the past."

Shaking my head, I let him hold me. "No. I lay there trying to stay awake through the pain, trying to heal what they'd done. I tried. The entire time I blamed you. I couldn't understand why you wouldn't tell me about them wanting to hurt you. Why you wouldn't give me all the facts. How you could let that happen to your family. I even thought you held back from telling me the truth because you were upset with me for telling you I wasn't ready to get married. That I couldn't commit to you because something inside me wouldn't let me."

"Gods, why in hell would you think that?"

Taking a deep breath, I cried against his chest. "I thought you were the one they talked about because…because they talked about my blood and the baby's…I can't talk about this. Just know that they told me they could taste the royal blood in me now. They celebrated that they took a royal heir, and fully planned on taking me after they finished. I thought *he* was you and at the time I hated you for that. It took me a long time to understand you couldn't have known and that if you had, you would have come to me, never letting it happen to begin with."

"If you understood that then why didn't you contact me?"

"Eion, something deep inside me wouldn't let me go back to you. It knew we couldn't last. I don't know how. But it knew."

Eion thrust another wave of power out. "Bullshit! We would have…Lindsay?"

"What?"

"Are you telling me that they thought the baby was this mate guy's and that her blood matched his royal line?"

I nodded.

"And I find you now with Exavier." His entire body went rigid. "Is he your mate?"

"Eion, I'll go. The two of you are family. He didn't know. He couldn't have. Exavier's not responsible for our losing her. He…"

Power leaked off Eion. I felt his hate, his rage as if it were my own. I tried to pull him to me. To hold him. He wouldn't let me. "He's always known they wanted to take over. It's common knowledge. And he has always known who his mate is. He wouldn't tell me. He didn't like talking about it because he 'missed her too much'."

His magik increased and I grabbed hold of him. "Eion, calm down. Don't take your anger out on him. He's your family. Don't do this. He'll kill you."

"Thanks for the vote of confidence, Lindsay."

Cupping Eion's face, I shook my head. "No, Eion. That's not it at all. I've had a peek inside him, in dreams, at what he carries and it's pure evil. He can't help it resides there and he'll never be free of it. You don't have that. No part of you is evil. I know that. You're more than a good man. If you go at him harboring nothing but hate and rage, his power will recognize it. It'll draw on the same source it takes from when dealing with evil creatures and it will destroy you. Not Exavier—he has no way to fight through it when it consumes him. He's on the edge already. I can sense it in him. It's not as bad today as it was but it's there."

Eion pulled a tiny portion of his power back. Not nearly enough to make me comfortable. "They hurt you. They hurt our baby because of him. How can you stand there and defend him?"

"Because he's my mate. Because a piece of me knows Exavier would have done anything to keep her safe had he known—his child or not."

Eion let out a soft laugh. "That means nothing. I have a mate out there and there is no way she'd come before you, Lindsay."

I ran my thumb over his lips, missing the touch of them. "You say that now but once you meet her you'll understand. It will all make sense."

"Do you love him?"

I closed my eyes.

"Lindsay, do you love him?"

"Yes, I've always loved him."

He made a move to go around me. Terrified he'd get himself killed, I took hold of his shirt and yanked him to me. "Lindsay, I—"

Clamping my mouth over his, I kissed him with all that I had, letting him feel just how much I really did love him. Eion wrapped his arms around me and moved his tongue over mine, thrust for thrust. I hated myself for what I had to do. Taking his memories was beyond wrong. Leaving him to live in his own private hell was worse.

I continued to kiss him, my body reacted to his every caress, just as it always had. I let my power up slowly, not wanting to alarm him. The minute it was all the way up, I ran it through him hard and fast, going instantly for any memory of me he ever had. Our mouths stayed locked and we continued to kiss, to moan, to express our love for one another as my power stripped him of his past with me. Carefully, I replaced it with good memories. Happier times and strong bonds with his cousin.

Pulling back, I yanked my magik out of him. Eion fell backwards as did I. Pain shot through me as I struck the pavement. "Oww."

"You can say that again. What happened?" Eion asked.

Sitting up, I smiled at him when every ounce of me wanted to cry. "I was running around that corner and I didn't see you there. Sorry."

Eion gave me one of his famous shit-ass grins that had always made me melt. "You, are the prettiest linebacker I've ever seen." He stood and extended his hand to me. "I'm Eion Mac Mason."

Taking his hand, I let him pull me to my feet and fought with all I had not to cry. "I'm Lindsay Willows. It was, umm, nice running into you, Eion."

"Lindsay Willows? The dancer?"

"You've heard of me?"

Shit, I missed a memory.

He nodded. "Yeah, a really close friend of mine, Tim Collins had a Lindsay Willows with him when his," he looked away a moment, "tour bus crashed."

"Yeah, I'm her. Tim was a great guy."

Eion nodded. "You weren't hurt, were you?"

His love for me was so strong it had managed to somehow survive, even if just a bit. It tore at my gut.

"No. I wasn't hurt. Thanks for asking."

Eion stared at me, as if he were trying to place how he knew me. "Your eyes are really red. Are you okay?"

I'd forgotten all about the sun and how bad my eyes hurt when I'd found Eion. "I'll be fine. I'm a little sensitive to the sun and I forgot my sunglasses."

"Come on, I'll take you in and have someone take a look at them."

Shaking my head, I offered him a warm smile. "I'm good. Thanks though."

Eion ran his hand through his hair and laughed. "Lindsay, you're probably going to run like hell but I don't think I can physically walk away knowing you're in pain. That makes no sense. I know, but it's the truth."

"There you are. I've got your glasses."

Exavier held a pair of black sunglasses in one hand and a glass of water in the other. He nodded towards Eion. "Patrick's going ape-shit in there."

Eion glanced between Exavier and I. "You two know each other?"

"Yep, she's the mate I mentioned but refused to give you details on."

I just stared at Exavier wondering how much of the conversation he'd heard. He closed the distance between us and handed me the glasses. The second I had them on, he pulled me to him and kissed my forehead. He let his power out and it ran over my eyes, taking the burning away instantly.

"Mmm, I hate to say it but I think we're going to need to head back in."

Eion gave Exavier a hard look. "That's one hell of a lady you got there. Treat her right or you'll answer to me, cousin."

Exavier smiled. "I know. She's amazing. And you have my word I'll love and protect her with all I am. I already promised her father, but now I'm telling you too."

Eion nodded. "Good. And Lindsay, should he get out of line, come to me. I'll kick the shit out him and see to it you're taken care of."

"Well, thanks. I appreciate that." I watched as Eion headed back into the building. The moment the door shut I gave in to the urge to cry.

"Shh, baby, you did what needed to be done."

"I'll head home when you're done today. I'm sorry I didn't tell you...I didn't know how."

Exavier held me tight with one arm and handed me the water he'd brought out. "I found you again a couple of days ago. I am so sorry, Linds. I didn't know. I would have told you. I would have protected you and the baby. I didn't know."

"You don't hate me?"

"I love you. I hate my mother for toying with us. It would have been me with you that summer. It would have been my child, my...umm... I love you

221

so much. I know I should be seething mad but all I want to do is comfort you, baby. I want you happy."

"I love you too."

His power ran up and over me. "Baby, let me lesson some of the pain from that night. Please."

"No," I said quickly. "Don't take my memories of her, Exavier."

"I won't, honey, but I can make it so you can move forward with life, like she would want you to." The minute I felt his power move through me, I knew he wasn't waiting for permission. The urge to fight him on it wasn't there. The urge to hold him was. I gave into it.

Chapter Thirteen

I took another sip of my bottled water and laughed at the guys as they lifted Exavier over their heads and held him there. They'd been up to their antics for several hours, drinking steadily and seeming to enjoy themselves.

Eion laughed hard. "He finally did it! The man finally worked up the nerve to find the girl of his dreams." He glanced at me. "The girl who is giving me a look like I better not drop him. I think he bounces. Should we see?"

"No," I said, moving forward fast. They'd been drinking since the director announced they would be pulling an all-nighter. When I questioned the drinking while working thing, Eion pointed out they weren't doctors so there was no threat of being intoxicated and needed in the operating room. He also pointed out half the shows they put on involved drinking at some point.

I would have argued but there really was no point. One was as stubborn as the other.

"Okay, gentlemen. I need Exavier to shoot the crypt scene," Pat called out.

They all groaned. "Don't make him lay on the bitch. We didn't know he found his mate...umm...matching socks, yeah," Karlon the keyboardist said, quickly covering for his slip.

"Sorry, set's built, label knows, it's happening."

Eion pointed at me and let go of Exavier. "Use her. She's Lindsay Willows."

I watched in horror as they dropped Exavier and he hit the ground. He groaned and then laughed as he lay there, clearly allowing the alcohol to take the edge off his pain. That or he was just insane. As of late, I wasn't sure.

He put his arm up and held it there a moment before pointing at the ceiling. "She's not only Lindsay Willows, she is my wife."

You could have heard a pin drop.

Smiling, I rushed towards him. "Umm, he's drunk. He means girlfriend."

Eion touched my shoulder and I wanted to wrap him in my arms and assure myself he'd really be okay. I held back. He snickered. "It's okay, Lindsay. We like to deny him too."

"Wait, Lindsay Willows the choreographer?" Pat asked.

"Yeah, care to eat your words now? I am no man's flavor of the week, director of the moment."

He reddened. I smiled. "Umm, sorry about that." He stared down at Exavier. "Can I get you to lay naked on a crypt with Lindsay under you instead of Hyde whom we have not gotten a single good shot of today?"

Eion stepped forward. "I'll lay naked any way you want me to if she's under me. That might piss Exavier off since she's his wife and all."

"I'm not his wife."

Karlon touched my shoulder and his power swept through me. It rolled around, banging into itself as it explored me. Heat rushed through me and I drew in a sharp breath. He pulled it away fast and chuckled. "Are you sure?"

Pravat, the bass player, pushed his chestnut brown hair back off his shoulder and grinned. "We owe the guy a bachelor party. Naked chicks, liquor and hopefully he gets licked by her. Sound good, Exavier?"

Karlon put his hand up. "It's got my vote."

"Nope, I don't think it's such a good idea," Eion said, sounding every bit as intoxicated as the rest of them looked.

I glanced at Pat and nodded. "I'll do it. Give us a bit and we'll meet you over there."

"Thank you."

"Aww, we want strippers." Pravat leaned over Exavier. "Get your lazy ass up. We want hot chicks, food and fucks. Don't you want to get as much ass in as you can before it's too late?"

I zapped him in the forehead with my magic. He spun in a circle looking for the source of the attack. "Oww, Exavier, I think this place is haunted."

"No, you're just an idiot." Exavier rolled onto his side and glanced up at me. "I love you, Lindsay. I love you with every fiber of my being. And I have loved you from the minute I laid eyes on you when we were just kids. That's a hell of long time to love someone but I have. I didn't think I could love you more. I was wrong. I do."

All the guys stared at him as if he were announcing he was becoming a monk.

"Did he just tell someone he loved them?" Pravat asked.

Eion nodded. "I think so. Though, I've never heard the man utter those words so I might be mistaken. He said it a lot so he's not giving me an out for him there."

"An out? I don't want one. I more than just love her, guys. She's my everything," Exavier said, grinning foolishly. "She is the only woman I've ever loved. Ever."

"Get up. You have a video to finish making." Using my power, I pulled him quickly to his feet and straightened his outfit, refreshed his hair and make-up.

"Whoa," he said, looking around with wide eyes.

"How the hell much did you guys drink? You metabolize things ten times as fast as humans." I glared at them all.

Karlon patted my arm. "That is exactly why we drank twenty times more than them."

"Exavier, are you ready?"

"Hurry up, man. You get to do her on a crypt," Pravat said, nodding.

Exavier's magik shot around us. The next thing I knew, we were standing on a completely different set. This one had a large crypt in the center of it. Fake graves were all around it. Fog covered the floor. Frantic, I looked around, terrified Exavier had magikally popped us onto a set full of humans.

"Relax, Linds. They're coming in now." He winked. "I love you in that outfit. We're keeping it."

"Huh?" Glancing down, I found myself in an off-white corset that laced up the front. Partway up, it was clearly too tight so it didn't meet in the middle. The majority of each breast showed, as did my stomach. The off-white floor-length skirt had tiny silk ribbons on it. Lifting it, I found layer upon layer of material. I shifted a bit and knew I wore nothing other than stockings and a garter belt beneath it. The cream, four-inch spiked, old-fashioned style boots left me feeling like I might tip over.

Reaching up, I found my hair was done in large ringlets hung loose to my waist. My eyes widened. "Exavier?"

"Wonderful! I see wardrobe found you. That is record time for them." Pat circled me slowly. "I didn't see this one when I was costume picking. I love it. An angel among demons. It's perfect." He smiled wide. "Exavier, untie her corset during the shoot. We'll pan around the two of you. Leave the skirt on. I think the idea you're in too big of a hurry to undress her fully is sexy as hell. They'll eat it up and it can only help keep it playable."

Everything happened so fast. One minute I was standing there staring at Exavier and the next I was under him on the hard, cold slab. He'd undressed in less than thirty seconds. No part of him seemed to care he was walking around a set naked. He just kept staring at me with hungry eyes. One of the assistants covered us in blood red satin sheets. Exavier had my legs spread wide and looked as though he wanted to devour me.

"Get ready with the music."

"Hey, Exavier, are you happy we forced them to add this scene? Playing guitar while you're screwing her would be really friggin' hard," Pravat said, sounding as if he was laughing more to himself than anyone else. "Bet he lip syncs now."

"Hey," Karlon called out. "Show some respect. He doesn't screw his wife. He makes *love* to her."

Pat cleared his throat. "Here's the deal. Sing when it feels right and kiss her when the mood hits you. Do your best to sing though. We'll have audio lay it all out to sound perfect in the end."

The lights dropped and the fog around us increased. The song started again, only this time Exavier sang the Fae chant right in front of me. Staring up at him, I felt myself slipping, losing sense of my person and giving in to him. Part of it was the chant that called to me. The rest of it was my need for him to be in me. Letting him pretend to make love to me was going to be pure and utter torture. I wanted the real thing.

Exavier moved his head down towards me. Our lips almost touched but he kept singing, making me want him even more. Closing my eyes, I gave myself over to him as I ran my hands over his back. I moaned softly in his ear when he kissed my neck and kept his place in the song.

Moving down my body, he caught the tie to the corset with his teeth and pulled it slowly. As it broke open, he licked the inner edges of my breast, carefully keeping my nipples from showing. Cream trickled from my sex. I wanted him there, filling me, taking me.

What's wrong with me?

As he sang, I listened carefully to the lyrics. It hit me then, why it was the sex on the crypt had been brought up by the band members. Exavier was singing about it. He talked about taking refuge in the womb of the one he loved. Giving her an offering she could not refuse. Laying her out before the gods, marking her forever with his power, his heir. Sanctifying the union with both the living and the dead. Keeping the daughter born from the tainted one for himself for eternity.

The tainted one.

The other Fae had often referred to my father as such. His father was a vampire and his mother Fae. I listened closer as Exavier continued.

He sang about how the Fae felt the tainted one's daughter wasn't good enough for the prince of darkness, the man who humans mistakenly labeled a devil when in truth, no such creature existed. He went into detail in regards to his duties of keeping order among the creatures of the night and how if he ever took the throne as King, he would do so with the woman he loved as his anchor or not at all. He was singing about us. About how it didn't matter that his parents and most of the Fae community thought I wasn't good enough for him. In his eyes, I was the world and without me, he was nothing.

Exavier's deep voice seemed to dictate my motions, my responsiveness to him. Not that it needed to. The desire to make us whole was overwhelming.

Exavier made his way back up my body, kissing and singing as he went. The minute he reached my mouth, I felt the head of his cock nudging at my wet entrance. My protest was lost the second his mouth captured mine. He drove himself into me. Plowing until completely buried. He absorbed my cries as he kissed me fast and furiously.

He locked himself deep in me, stopped thrusting and started rubbing, making a circular motion. The action left him pressing against my engorged clit, teasing it, pleasing me. Breaking our kiss, his eyes locked on mine as he picked right back up with singing.

The moment was more than I'd ever hoped for. Having the man I love in me, making love to me while he sang of the very same thing was too much. I gave in to it. My stomach tightened and my inner thighs followed fast. Instantly, my channel fisted his shaft as I hit my orgasm head on.

Exavier drilled hard into me, making my back arch and my body burn as pleasure flooded through me. In a flash, he was pumping, driving himself into me. I felt the sheet slipping as he took me to yet another peak. Grabbing hold of the sheet, I kept his ass covered and dug my nails into his skin to keep my mind on anything but screaming in ecstasy.

He rooted himself in me. Liquid hot fire filled me, collecting in my cervix as I held tight to him. Something was different. This was sex like no sex had ever been. It was then I felt the magik in each of us reach up and take hold of the other. Another rush of pleasure moved through me and Exavier came again, jetting his hot seed into me more.

I thought he'd stop. I thought he'd pull away. He didn't. No. Exavier kept going. Kept filling me, bringing me on a series of reoccurring zeniths. My head thrashed back and forth as I bit my lower lip to keep from crying out. Exavier was suddenly there, his lips taking mine. He swallowed my cries while he licked the blood from my lip.

Something pinched in my lower abdomen and I cringed at the sharp pain. Exavier broke our kiss quickly and stared down at me with worry etched on his face. The pain came again, this time stronger. Clutching on to him, I waited for it to pass as he stilled inside me.

229

Suddenly, I became very aware we were surrounded by people. Apparently, Exavier realized it as well. Looking at Pat, he wagged his brows. "So, how was that?"

Pat pulled at the collar of his shirt before wiping his brow. "That...err...will do. I think we can go with the one take. Everyone agree?"

"Holy shit, that was best acting job I've ever seen," Pravat said, sounding a bit winded.

"Acting?" Karlon made a garbled choking sound and just stared at us with wide eyes.

Exavier let a very manly smile move over his face. "Are you sure, Pat? I'd be more than happy to keep going until it's absolutely perfect."

Stroking Exavier's cheek lightly, I winked at him. "If your goal was perfection, then one take will do."

Pat clapped his hands. "Well then, I think we can wrap it up for the night."

Chapter Fourteen

I sat on the edge of the crypt where Exavier and I had made love, watching as he and his band mates played around with their instruments. I wasn't sure if it was Exavier using his power to persuade Pat and the crew to take off or if Pat just needed air after our little show on the crypt. Either way, we now seemed to have the place to ourselves.

There was something to be said for hanging in a fake graveyard in the middle of the night and watching hunky supernaturals playing with their big boy toys. They sat around on crates and stools, each one doing whatever it was they did. I shouldn't have been shocked seeing Eion slide up next to Exavier with a guitar on his lap. I knew he played multiple instruments. I also knew he sang too. Seeing them together did make my breath catch.

Exavier tapped his guitar and his foot followed. Eion nodded and began making the same sound. Exavier began to hum and Eion started to sing. The minute I heard the words, my face paled. It was a song he sang to me often about finding paradise in the arms of a woman who wasn't his own.

It talked about how the relationship defied all logic but controlled his every thought, his every action. The words cut through me as I realized for the first time in my life he'd written it about us. Part of me had known but didn't want to acknowledge it. It had always been easier for me to keep Eion at arm's length than let him into my heart.

I sat, silently watching them as they played. Exavier took over lead vocals and Eion went to humming in the background. Exavier's blue gaze locked on me and I saw nothing but love there. They drew it to a close and Eion patted Exavier on the back.

"Remember the night we wrote this? We were having some serious women trouble."

Exavier winked at me. "Yeah. So, you ever get over that girl?"

"It's weird but I can't even remember her name, so I guess so," Eion said, laughing as he took another drink from the bottle nearest him. "How about you? You ever get over that girl you've been writing songs about all your..." He glanced at me and his eyes widened. "Damn, I see why you've been obsessed over her all these years, Xavs."

Tipping his head slightly, Exavier cast a sexy smile my way. "She was worth every second of the wait, Eion. Every second."

Pravat snorted. "If you start going on about how much you love her again, I'm going to kick your ass and tape your mouth shut."

Exavier arched a dark brow. "Really?"

Karlon nodded and moved closer to Pravat. "I'll help him. We might even turn our heads the next time something comes a callin', wanting to challenge your sorry royal ass." He nudged Pravat. "As his head warriors we should really be permitted to hit him every time he does something stupid."

"You better turn your heads if something comes at me. Your attention better be on Lindsay. She is to be—"

"Protected with our lives," they said in unison, not one sounding upset with the idea.

"You do realize you're all going to have to cram into Exavier's SUV, right?"

They all nodded. Exavier held my hand firmly and pulled me around in a half-circle to face him. He was still in the black leather pants and mesh top and I was still thinking about him buried deep in me. "I love you."

"You've said that about a million times in the last hour. Now give me the keys. You four aren't driving anything, anywhere. I cannot believe you polished off another bottle after the shoot. Why?"

"Hey, I only had one more bottle. Pravat had three. Yell at him."

Pravat baulked. "We were celebrating the two of you being married. And since jackass doesn't want us to give him a proper bachelor party we had to settle for drinking in the fake graveyard."

"We are not married," I murmured under my breath.

"Then you should be. That baby needs the protection of a mated unit."

I rolled my eyes and shook my head. "Xavs, you have the weirdest friends."

"What did you say, Pravat?" Exavier asked, instantly sobering.

"Just that you're gonna be a daddy."

"This isn't funny." Anger bubbled just under the surface, waiting for a chance to strike out at Pravat for his sick sense of humor. "I can't have children."

"Well, you mean you couldn't have them. When I touched you to see if you were bonded to Exavier earlier, I sensed the struggle your body was going through to accept his seed so I fixed it. Consider it my wedding gift to the two of you."

"Exavier, tell him this isn't funny. I mean it. One, he can't heal a scarred uterus. No one can. And for anything to be in there we would have to have had sex before that. We did not."

"Linds, Pravat wouldn't lie about something as important as this. And if anyone could heal that, it's him. His father is a Fae god of fertility. If he's sure you're with child, then you are."

"But, no…we…" It hit me then. The dream. "It wasn't just a dream."

"No, Linds. It wasn't a dream." He watched me closely as I let it all sink in. "Please don't be upset with me. You seemed shocked after we mated and I couldn't stand the thought of you having no choice but to tie yourself to me because of your fear of them taking me. I couldn't. I love you too much. I cleaned up and waited to see how you would react. Don't be upset with me. Please, baby, I'll do anything. Please."

"Umm, is it me or is our prince groveling?" Karlon asked, laughing slightly.

Eion smacked him in the back of the head. "Shut-up. Let him finish his groveling. I'm enjoying it. Oh, and congrats on the baby. I want to be its godfather."

I locked gazes with him and couldn't stop the tears that came rushing at me. Eion's eyes widened. "Okay, I'll settle for being allowed to visit? Don't cry."

Exavier took me in his arms and held me tight. "Shh, it's okay, baby. This is meant to be and he will most certainly be our child's godfather. Don't do this to yourself, Linds. Don't."

"I'm not upset, Xavs. I'm happy. These are good tears. Really good tears."

He let out a deep breath. "You're not mad we're married and," he touched my stomach, "expecting?"

I slapped his cheek once for good measure and then kissed it. "I love you so much."

"Mmm, and I love you, even if you spend eternity kicking my ass."

"Aww, isn't that sweet," Eion said, laughing.

"Shut-up, just wait until you all find your mates. Lindsay and I will love picking on you all."

I hugged Exavier tight and he kissed the top of my head. "Mmm, I need to get my princess ballerina, mommy-to-be home and bed her again. Wait, I need to show her our house."

"Our house?" I asked, arching a brow. "I have a home."

"Yes, but you have a bathtub in the middle of your living room."

I smiled. "Bubbles."

He growled and rubbed himself against me. "I'd like to change my vote to getting her to our vacation home—formally known as Lindsay's place—so I can bed her while she's covered in bubbles." He wagged his brows. "I love you, Linds."

Epilogue

Exavier lifted me and set me on his lap in the center of the diner. Harly and Charles beamed as they watched the two of us, no doubt pleased to be future uncles. As Exavier's hands caressed my swollen belly, I couldn't help but smile. So far, everything in the pregnancy was as normal as being paranormal would allow. Pravat assured me the baby was fine and I believed him. So did Exavier and that helped tremendously. Pushing my sixth month, I felt as big as a house. Exavier seemed to love to stare at my stomach, rub it, put his head on it, anything to remind me I was carrying a watermelon around with me. I was so incredibly thankful for the opportunity to have another baby that I could do nothing more than tear up. I'm fairly sure he assumed my outbursts were hormonal. Wisely, he didn't comment.

"*Mmm*, I love you," he whispered, his mouth pressed to my ear.

Eion glanced in our direction from the counter and winked. "Know we can hear you?"

Myra moved up next to him and bear hugged him. He looked a little lost but hugged her all the same. When Gina moved in and joined, Karlon and Pravat wagged their brows. Exavier groaned. "I can't take them anywhere."

"Don't worry. I'm used to men like that. I know Jay." No sooner did I get Jay's name out of my mouth then he appeared, pulling Gina out of the mix.

"That will be just about enough of that," he said, catching almost all of us off guard.

Exavier chuckled and kissed my ear. "I told you. See."

He had been quick to point out, at our last get together, how focused Jay seemed to be on Gina. Exavier had given me a smug smile as he informed me how he had a little talk with the people in charge to work out a "glitch" in the mating process. I'd asked him to explain the "glitch" further but he offered up next to nothing—talking about how just because she was a slayer it didn't mean they had to keep trying to block Jay's instincts. All of it made my head hurt so I chose to ignore him.

As I watched Jay setting Gina on a stool, far from the prying eyes of the other men, I wondered if I should grill my husband about it when we got home.

"You could if you promise to do it while I'm buried in you," he whispered, obviously reading my thoughts again.

"Honey, be careful reading me or I'll block your ability to do it, just like I'm blocking you from reading what sex our baby is."

Exavier laughed and nipped playfully at my ear. "I would be blessed with a mate who can more than hold her own with me."

"Well, it's the least the Fates could do for me since my husband is the Prince of Darkness."

"Ah, so are you willing to acknowledge you're a princess ballerina again?"

Twisting a bit, I cupped his face. "Maybe. Kind of depends on what incentive you offer up."

He arched a brow and shifted a bit, allowing his rigid cock to dig into my ass. "Oh, the incentive is certainly up, Linds."

"Yes," I said, kissing his lips gently. "It is."

"We should probably stop now. They haven't even gotten to the cake yet and I already want to take you home and—"

"Exavier," my father said, entering the diner and holding a large present in his hands. My mother followed right behind him. He leveled his gaze on Exavier. "I trust you can refrain from talk of that nature until after we are gone."

"You'd think," Eion said, snorting as he took a sip of soft drink.

My father's gaze slid to Eion and then back to Exavier and I. "Everything happens for a reason. I believe we are here to celebrate a key example of that."

Exavier hugged me close. "I love you, Linds."

"I love you too, Xavs."

Mandy M. Roth

Mandy M. Roth grew up fascinated by creatures that go bump in the night. From the very beginning, she showed signs of creativity. At age five, she had her first piece of artwork published. Writing came into play early in her life as well. Over the years, the two mediums merged and led her to work in marketing. Combining her creativity with her passion for horror has left her banging on the keyboard into the wee hours of the night. Mandy lives with her husband and three children on the shores of Lake Erie, where she is currently starting work on her Master's Degree.

To learn more about Mandy, please visit www.mandyroth.com or send an email to mandy@mandyroth.com. For latest news about Mandy's newest releases subscribe to her announcement list in Yahoo! groups. http://groups.yahoo.com/subscribe/Mandy_M_Roth